Praise for *Wild Decembers*

"The novel is a dirge that keens and lulls by turns. The entrancing rhythms and refrains, the density and chant-like, drumming fragmentation work on the reader like music, right from the very first sentences . . . O'Brien combines this lyricism with a masterly storytelling instinct, so that *Wild Decembers* reads at once like an intricate poem and a taut, suspenseful page-turner."   —Molly Winans, *Commonweal*

"[O'Brien's] mastery of tone and register keeps *Wild Decembers* churning even when it's a foregone conclusion where all that anger will lead. Proof again that in the hands of an artist, no plot is hackneyed, no emotion too obvious."   —*Kirkus Reviews*

"A lush and melancholy tale about a mountain and the ancestral animosities of its inhabitants."   —*The Atlantic*

"Edna O'Brien is a force of nature, a wild Irish rose whose prose aches with the music and the passion of her native land . . . [*Wild Decembers*] is Irish to the quick, violent and sad and, in a strange way, beautiful."
—Jonathan Yardley, *The Washington Post*

"Ancient feuds, romantic passions and misguided ideas of fidelity blend together in this beautiful, though tragic, tale."
— Kate Flatley, *The Wall Street Journal*

Mundo MacLeod

A NOTE ABOUT THE AUTHOR

EDNA O'BRIEN has written more than twenty works of fiction, most recently *Girl*. She is the recipient of numerous awards, including the Prix Femina, the PEN/Nabokov Award for Achievement in International Literature, the Irish PEN Lifetime Achievement Award, the National Arts Club Medal of Honor, and the Ulysses Medal. Born and raised in the west of Ireland, she has lived in London for many years.

Also by Edna O'Brien

EDNA O'BRIEN

Wild Decembers

PICADOR

FARRAR, STRAUS AND GIROUX

NEW YORK

Picador
120 Broadway, New York 10271

Copyright © 1999 by Edna O'Brien
All rights reserved
Printed in the United States of America
First published in 1999 by Weidenfeld & Nicolson, Orion House, Great Britain
Published in the United States in 1999 by Houghton Mifflin Company, New York
First Picador paperback edition, 2020

The Library of Congress has cataloged the Houghton Mifflin
hardcover edition as follows:
O'Brien, Edna.
    Wild Decembers / Edna O'Brien.
    p. cm.
    ISBN 0-618-04567-8
    1. Brothers and sisters—Ireland—Fiction. 2. Landowners—
Ireland—Fiction. 3. Farm life—Ireland—Fiction.
I. Title.

PR6065.B7 W55 2000
823'.914—dc21   99-056110

Picador Paperback ISBN: 978-0-374-53875-0

Designed by Robert Overholtzer

Our books may be purchased in bulk for promotional, educational, or business use. Please
contact your local bookseller or the Macmillan Corporate and Premium Sales Department at
1-800-221-7945, extension 5442, or by e-mail at MacmillanSpecialMarkets@macmillan.com.

Picador® is a U.S. registered trademark and is used by Macmillan
Publishing Group, LLC, under license from Pan Books Limited.

For book club information, please visit facebook.com/picadorbookclub or
e-mail marketing@picadorusa.com.

picadorusa.com · instagram.com/picador
twitter.com/picadorusa · facebook.com/picadorusa

1 3 5 7 9 10 8 6 4 2

. . . fifteen wild Decembers
From those brown hills have melted into spring —
Faithful indeed is the spirit that remembers . . .

— Emily Brontë

Wild Decembers

PROLOGUE

CLOONTHA IT IS CALLED — a locality within the bending of an arm. A few scattered houses, the old fort, lime-dank and jabbery and from the great whooshing belly of the lake between grassland and callow land a road, sluicing the little fortresses of ash and elder, a crooked road to the mouth of the mountain. Fields that mean more than fields, more than life and more than death too. In the summer months calves going suck suck suck, blue dribble threading from their black lips, their white faces stark as clowns. Hawthorn and whitethorn, boundaries of dreaming pink. Byroad and bog road. The bronze gold grasses in a tacit but unremitting sway. Listen. Shiver of wild grass and cluck of wild fowl. Quickening.

Fathoms deep the frail and rusted shards, the relics of battles of the long ago, and in the basins of limestone, quiet in death, the bone babes and the bone mothers, the fathers too. The sires. The buttee men and the long-legged men who hacked and hacked and into the torn breathing soil planted a first potato crop, the diced tubers that would be the bread of life until the fungus came.

According to the annals it happened on Our Lady's Eve. The blight came in the night and wandered over the fields, so that by morning the upright stalks were black ribbons of rot. Slow death for man and beast. A putrid pall over the landscape, hungry marching people meek and mindless, believing it had not struck else-where. Except that it had. Death at every turn. The dead faces yellow as parchment, the lips a liquorice black from having gorged on the sweet poisonous stuff, the apples of death.

They say the enemy came in the night, but the enemy can come at any hour, be it dawn or twilight, because the enemy is always there and these people know it, locked in a tribal hunger that bubbles in the blood and hides out on the mountain, an old carcass waiting to rise again, waiting to roar again, to pit neighbour against neighbour and dog against dog in the crazed and phantom lust for a lip of land. Fields that mean more than fields, fields that translate into nuptials into blood; fields lost, regained, and lost again in that fickle and fractured sequence of things; the sons of Oisin, the sons of Conn and Connor, the sons of Abraham, the sons of Seth, the sons of Ruth, the sons of Delilah, the warring sons of warring sons cursed with that same irresistible thrall of madness which is the designate of living man, as though he had to walk back through time and place, back to the voiding emptiness to repossess ground gone for ever.

Heraldic and unflagging it chugged up the mountain road, the sound, a new sound jarring in on the profoundly pensive landscape. A new sound and a new machine, its squat front the colour of baked brick, the ridges of the big wheels scummed in muck, wet muck and dry muck, leaving their maggoty trails.

It was the first tractor on the mountain and its arrival would be remembered and relayed; the day, the hour of evening, and the way crows circled above it, blackening the sky, fringed, soundless, auguring. There were birds always; crows, magpies, thrushes, skylarks, but rarely like that, so many and so massed. It was early autumn, one of those still autumn days, several fields emptied of hay, the stubble a sullied gold, hips and haws on the briars and a wild dog rose which because of its purple hue had been named after the blood of Christ — *Sangria Jesu*.

At the top of the hill it slowed down, then swerved into a farmyard, stopping short of the cobbles and coming to rest on a grassy incline under a hawthorn tree. Bugler, the driver, ensconced inside his glass booth, waved to Breege, the young woman who, taken so by surprise, raised the tin can which she was holding in a kind of awkward salute. To her, the machine with smoke coming out of the metal chimney was like a picture of the Wild West. Already their yard was in a great commotion, their dog Goldie yelping, not knowing which part to bite first, hens and ducks converging on it, startled and curious, and coming from an out-house her brother, Joseph, with a knife in his hand, giving him a rakish look.

"I'm stuck," Bugler said, smiling. He could have been driving it for years so assured did he seem up there, his power and prowess seeming to precede him as he stepped down and lifted his soft felt hat courteously. Might he leave it for a day or two until he got the hang of the gears. He pointed to the manual that was on the dashboard, a thin booklet, tattered and with some pages folded where a previous owner had obviously consulted it often.

"Oh, no bother . . . No bother," Joseph said, overcordial. The two men stood in such extreme contrast to one another, Joseph in old clothes like a scarecrow and Bugler in a scarlet shirt, leather gaiters over his trousers, and a belt with studs that looked lethal. He was recently home, having inherited a farm from an uncle, and the rumour spread that he was loaded with money and in-tended to reclaim much of his marshland. Because of having worked on a sheep station he had been nicknamed the Shepherd. A loner, he had not gone into a single house and had not invited anyone to his. The Crock, the craftiest of all the neighbours, who went from house to house every night, gleaning and passing on bits of gossip, had indeed hobbled up there, but was not let past the tumbling-down front porch. He was proud to report that it was no better than a campsite, and in sarcasm, he referred to it as the Congo. Bugler was a dark horse. When he went to a dance it was always forty or fifty miles away, but the Crock had reason to know that women threw themselves at him, and now he was in their yard, the sun causing glints of red in his black beard and sideburns. It was Breege's first sensing of him. Up to then he had been a tall fleeting figure, apparition-like, so eager to mas-ter his surroundings that he rarely used a gate or a stile, simply leapt over them. Her brother and him had had words over cattle that broke out. The families, though distantly related, had feuds that went back hundreds of years and by now had hardened into a dour sullenness. The wrong Joseph most liked to relate was of a Bugler ancestor, a Henry, trying to grab a corner of a field which abutted onto theirs and their uncle Paddy impaling him on a road and putting a gun to his head. The upshot was that Paddy, like any common convict, had to emigrate to Australia, where he excelled himself as a boxer, got the red belts. Other feuds involved women, young wives from different provinces who could not agree and who screamed at each other like warring tinkers. Yet now both men were affable, that overaffability that seeks to hide any embarrassment. Joseph was the talkative one, expressing disbelief and wonder as each and every feature of the tractor was explained to him, the lever, the gears, the power shaft which, as Bugler said, could take the pants off a man or, worse, even an arm or a leg; then joyous whistles as Bugler recited its many uses — ploughing, rotating, foddering, making silage, and of course getting from A to B.

"It's some yoke," Joseph said, patting the side wing.

"If you ask me, she's a he," Bugler said, recalling the dangers, men in tractors to which they were unaccustomed having to be pulled out of bogholes in the dead of night, and a farmer in the Midlands driving over a travelling woman thinking he had caught a bough. Her tribespeople kept coming day after day strewing elder branches in wild lament.

They moved then to farming matters, each enquiring how many cattle the other had, although they knew well, and swapped opinions about the big new marts, the beef barons in their brown overalls and jobbers' boots.

"How times have changed," Joseph said overdramatically, and went on to quote from an article he had recently read, outlining the scientific way to breed pigs. The boar had to be kept well away from the sow so as to avoid small litters, but, nevertheless, had to be adjacent to her for the sake of smell, which of course was not the same as touch.

"Not a patch on touch . . . Nothing to beat touch," one said, and the other confirmed it.

"Would you like a go on it?" Bugler said then to each of them.

"I'll pass," Joseph said, but added that Breege would. She shrunk back from them, looked at the machine, and then climbed up on it because all she wanted was to have got up and down again and vanish. Through the back of her thin blouse one hook of her brassiere was broken and Bugler would see that. A red colour ran up and down her cheeks as if pigment were being poured on them. It was like being up on a throne, with the fields and the low walls very insignificant, and she felt foolish.

"You're okay . . . You're okay . . . It won't run away with you," Bugler said softly, and leaned in over her. Their breaths almost merged. She thought how different he seemed now, how conciliatory, how much less abrupt and commanding. His eyes, the colour of dark treacle, were as deep as lakes, brown eyes, wounded-looking, as if a safety pin had been dragged over them in infancy. He saw her agitation, saw that she was uneasy, and to save the moment he told her brother that the bloke he bought the tractor from was a right oddball.

"How come?" Joseph said.

"He said that if I couldn't start it, I was to find a child, get the child to put its foot on the clutch, but tell it to be ready to jump the moment the engine started."

"You won't find a child around here," Joseph said, and in the silence they looked as if they were expecting something to answer back. Nothing did. It was as if they were each suspended and staring out at the fields, brown and khaki, and nondescript in the gathering dusk; fields over which many had passed, soldiers, pilgrims, journeymen, children too; fields on which their lives would leave certain traces followed by some dismay, then forgetfulness.

"You'll come in for the tea," Joseph said to lighten things.

"I won't . . . I have jobs to do," Bugler said, and turning to Breege, thinking that in some way he owed her an apology, he said, "If ever you want supplies brought from the town, you know who to ask."

M Y BROTHER STAYED out there with it long after it
got dark. He was talking to it, touching it, and maybe
wishing, wishing. I had to call him in to his supper
three times, him that's so finicky about his food, him that likes
the Sunday roast and the crackling, custards put to set in a bain-
marie of lukewarm water for the right consistency.

"Your supper is going cold."

"Isn't Bugler a great man," he said, barely able to tear himself
away from it. You would think that it was a person and not a machine he was taking his leave of.

It began then. Or maybe it began long before. We don't know
what's in us, what demons are in us, love and hate, part of the
same soup. My brother, my highly strung brother, always on
about the sacred fetters of land and blood. Blood strains going
back to the flood. Our holding in the Domesday Book. Throwbacks. He's a great one for the throwbacks. In the winters he took
to going down to the Heritage Centre, to consult books and al-
manacs, him and Miss Carruthers, the keeper, very tart woman,
very learned, the pair of them tracing the genealogies, the radices
of life before Christ. And Helen of Troy — blue seas, blue seas
and a romping woman. He'd rave on about the men of Troy and
the men of Argos leaving their flocks and going down to the long
ships to wage a ten-year war, all over white-armed Helen, the
romping woman.

"Them times, them times," he'd say when he came up home

full of mythologies and with drink taken. I had to milk and fodder. Our forebears, he said, had trudged hundreds of miles to
plant themselves down in the wondrous infinity of Cloontha. According to the annals they had been evicted from the arable lands
of Kildare — a man, a woman, a horde of barefoot children setting out on a cart, scavenging, begging, or maybe even stealing,
and constantly being told to move on, move on, just like vermin.
The cart, he reckoned, would have been their lodgings at night, a
mass of bodies cleaved together like frogspawn. He always got
carried away when he came to the bit of their arriving down at
the low road, struck by the beauty of the lake and a big house
with its gardens and rhododendron bushes, grounds to bivouac
in, but that the father, the stern Moses, had the acumen to drive
his haggard family up the mountain where no one could find
them and hence no one could evict them. There would have been
no road then, as he said, only a track thick with rushes and wild
grasses, Moses having to hack his way ahead to lead his charges
to safety. Nothing up the mountain in the way of a cabin or shiel-
ing. Where would they have slept? What would they have found
to eat? Berries maybe or nettles. From his prognostications he
guessed that they had come on the spring well, the dark O of
it scummed with weeds and cresses, and sighting it, the father
would have knelt and drank from it and then ordered his family
to drink — the waters of life. It he termed the baptismal moment.

He got to like telling it, memorised it, mixed it in with the
Greeks, their hardships, their carnage, Ajax and Achilles and
our spearmen, one race all, one language before the Flood. He
practised it for the visitors who come in the summer, come —
"Yoo-hoo . . . Anybody home" — into our yard looking for rela-
tives or old sewing machines to convince themselves who they
are. Out there with them till all hours. They lap it up. He orders
me to bring them the tea and I put a folding table down in my little plantation, with its deep-red dahlias. I love my deep-red
dahlias and I love our Lord. My brother is at his most extreme
when he brings his listeners to the Field of Corpses. He asks them
to ponder on it. They become very quiet then, hushed at the

thought of the scattered remains, become as reverential as they might if placed before the buried emperors of the East with their wives and artefacts and bronze horses.

"So we seem to be on talking terms with the Shepherd," I said.

"We do," he said.

"Funny your asking him in for the tea," I said.

"Why wouldn't I . . . A handsome man like that," and as he rose I saw his hand reaching behind the plate for the solicitor's letter which had stung him so much the morning it came. We knew the words, the tough words, we knew them well —

Dear Mr. Brennan:

We have instructions from your neighbour, Mr. Michael Bugler, to write to you regarding the continued trespass of your cows on his field of four acres. Your cows have entirely depastured this field. They have also knocked down the fences, thus causing further damages. The cows were either delivered to you, or shown in the act of trespass. Nevertheless, you have made no effort to contain them.

We have therefore received instructions to collect from you, within five days of this letter, the sum of £55 for damages with our costs of £25. The damages are continuing, and unless there is compliance with this demand, proceedings will be issued.

Watching it burn made him gleeful, and he announced that he owed himself a drink.

"I'm in the high mood, Breege," he said, and so he was, and after a few slugs it was on to the parable about gentle furze bushes with their golden aureoles, Yellow Dick's Bog, our dead parents, the Book of Lecan, the ancient breast-pin, the voyage of Maol Duin, the bed of Diarmid and Grainne, Brodar the Dane that slew the aged Brian Boru in his tent. Lofty things.

"I thought you told the Crock that you would never talk to that man on principle."

"I was wrong," he said, chastised.

I scooped the stewed apples onto his plate, poured cream in zigzags over it, and waited for him to taste it. He ate without thinking, without tasting, his eyes glowing, full of a strange talk-ative excitement, as if the tractor had opened a friendly causeway between Bugler and ourselves.

It was a long time since I felt so lighthearted, so giddy — as if I were waltzing.

It began then.

B Y MORNING the tractor looked to have settled in, snug under the hawthorn, against the low wall, the garish red paint softened in the aftermath of rain and zillions of rain-drops on the bonnet. Three people had come to view it, the Crock and the saucy sisters, Reena and Rita.

"Ye came fast," the Crock said.

"And why wouldn't we?" Rita, the elder, said, and Reena concurred. A brand-new machine like that and a fine specimen of a man that owned it. Didn't they see him swimming down at the dock in his birthday suit. All hair. A caveman. Scapulars around his neck with the Agnus Dei relic, the little lamb of God.

"Mud and muscle," Reena said, and Rita giggled.

"Ye're the business," the Crock said. Their skills were legendary. Into a dance hall, study the form, a fellow coaxed out in two shakes of a duck's tail, so much for a kiss, so much more for a French kiss, so much for other favours, but never the full menu until they got him home in the house.

"You'd always be welcome to our little nest," Reena said.

"Would I now!" the Crock said, a touch of bitterness in his voice, because he knew that behind his back they called him the Iron Bedbug on account of his deformities.

They stand back from the tractor then, surpassing each other in praise of it, conjecture as to whether it is new or secondhand. The Crock reckons that it is secondhand. He hobbled across the previous night with his half-arsed flash lamp to have a deco at it, snooping around in case Joseph of Arimathea or Ivory Breege came out. He came to the conclusion then that it was secondhand and he would stand by that.

"It looks at you like a bull," Rita said, and then lifted her short skirt and mimicked charging at it. They had arrived on horseback, Rita holding the reins and Reena sitting side-saddle on the bay mare that was tethered a few feet away, snorting to get to a fresh patch of grass. In that flurry of taffeta was a hint of her bag of tricks. How well he could picture it without ever being there — their little abode, off down a bohreen, a drawn curtain, dried flowers, candlelight, some poor eejit carried away in a miasma of warmth and smarm, the Reena one taking her plait of hair out of its rubber band to thwack his chest. Sorcery. Witchcraft. So far, their witchcraft had yielded a farm of land at the other end of the province and several little fields inside other people's big fields. That was how they got their power, their game of Monopoly, as Rita called it.

"How many fields do ye own now?" he asked, letting out a bitter laugh that was his trademark, and why not, himself with a stump of a foot, a hump, one wet field with clumps of reeds swaying uselessly and a caravan that leaked.

"We're doing okay," Rita said. She was the brains and Reena the nymphet. She made the deals, bought and sold cattle, and harangued her friendly solicitor to write letters, to make hell for this person or that who got in her way. People feared her. Even those who did not know her feared her. At discos the men shied away from her, but that did not matter. Reena could coax them out, and soon after, Rita followed to ask if they would like to come for coffee later. The bachelors, especially the visiting ones, were the easiest prey. Rita had had her gearbox taken out a few years before. Boasted of having told the pup of a surgeon that it was no use to her and that he would be in court if he didn't do it. Reena had to be watched, not the full shilling. From time to time broached the matter of love or, worse, a baby. Feck love, feck a baby.

"Isn't it marvellous . . . It'll put Cloontha on the map," Rita said.

"Engage a gear," the Crock said.

"I'd love to . . . I'd love to get it going and go up there and congratulate the caveman," Reena said.

"I wouldn't do that . . . He might have a ladyfriend," the Crock said.

"Who . . . Not the Breege one?"

"He'd want something toffier."

"Like me," Reena said, and drew her skirt up to her belly. Never wore underclothes in any of the seasons.

"A child of nature," Rita says, and recalls a day at a horse fair miles away when a Kerry man asked them a simple question and within a week was ensconced in their kitchen, the pair of them dancing attendance on him and a map of his holding on their kitchen table. She thinks of the young guard who came about a dog licence and was foolish enough to let Reena cuddle him a bit, and then her jumping up on a chair with her bush showing, shouting rape, rape, and a young simpleton summoned to be a witness. They got a good few bob out of that.

Apparition-like Bugler appeared and was greeted effusively, compliments showered on him and on the new arrival.

"Your servant," the Crock called out, and lifted his good cap in deference.

The sisters surpassed each other in praise of it, standing back from it, then close up to it, tweaking it as they might a baby. Next, they excused themselves cravenly for being so excited, but confessed that it wasn't every day such a fandango appeared in the parish. At each and every opportunity they touch it, then touch Bugler as if both were interchangeable. Bemused and a little baffled he thanks them for their kindness. They have a teeny-weeny request. Has he christened it?

"Hadn't thought of that," Bugler said.

Names were trotted out, names of famous boxers, hurley players, and eventually, with some prompting, Reena came up with Dino the Dinosaur.

"Dino the Dinosaur," Bugler said, amused.

"You must excuse her impudence at christening your child," Rita said, and shook his hand very formally, introducing herself and her younger sister and assuring him that their father and his dear departed uncle were always on the best of terms.

"Is that so," Bugler said, tickled at their strategies, their touching the mudguard, then touching his arm, then asking if there was a name that he would have liked better, a saint's name perhaps. Reena then wondered if it might be an impudence to sit on it.

"Go ahead," he said, but did not take the little soft plump hand, with its deeking of silverish rings.

"Reet," she said in a babyish voice, and soon she was settled squarely on the seat, her strong pink thighs cleaved together, confessing that she might just burst with the excitement.

"Reen is the romantic type," Rita said.

"Oh really," from Bugler.

"Oh yeh . . . A rose on your breakfast tray."

"What colour rose?" His eyes meet Reena's as she parts her thighs a fraction and says "Guess." The invitation being quite blatant, he gives half a laugh. Then, to gloss things over, Rita says that if he has any bit of sewing or mending he knows where to come.

"A Mary and a Martha," the Crock says with a flourish.

"Which is Mary and which is Martha?" Bugler asks, looking down at a pair of legs of colossal girth from the ankle up to the knees.

"Are you going to lift me down?" Reena says. There is a strumpet gaze to her, her eyes yellow-brown, the dark tawny colour sullying the whites. They are more like half-sisters. She is asking again with little gasps for him to help her.

"I will not," Bugler says.

She jumps in effrontery, then walks across and leaps onto her mare while Rita follows, unties the reins, and leads them away, Reena staring back at them, at him.

"Who are they . . . Where do they live?"

"They are the notorious sisters, and they live three miles up from the graveyard."

"They got here fast."

"You said it — Sarsfield is the word and Sarsfield is the man."

The Crock is only too pleased to relate the stories which have accrued, some true, some not. He describes the time when Reena took a man to court, a poor mountainy yokel, for throwing stones at her. The fellow's defence was that stone-throwing in his part of the world, which was the backwoods, was a form of courtship. The judge was flummoxed and asked for two weeks' reprieve while he deliberated on this curious custom. When they resumed on the appointed date, it seems there had been more chance meetings and more stone-throwings.

"You can't have objected too much" was what the judge said to her, and placing her soft pink arms on the bench, she asked him to look at her flesh and imagine her bruises, et cetera. She ended up receiving a hundred pounds in damages.

"I get your drift," Bugler said.

"Jesus, she heard us," the Crock said as he sees Reena walking towards them, smiling, her eyes gold-flecked and brazen, a stalk of grass between her teeth. She strolls up to Bugler like she has forgotten something.

"I'll give you a ring sometime — will I?" she says.

"You'll give me a ring sometime — will you," Bugler says in reply. She stands there, the stalk of grass doing the circuit of her tongue effortlessly. She goes.

"Demons . . . Demonesses," the Crock says when she is out of hearing.

"Can I drop you anywhere?" Bugler said, lolling backwards onto his machine as if it were an armchair.

"No thanks . . . I'd sooner the fresh air," the Crock said. To mount a thing like that required a boulder or a mounting block. He stood watching it go down the narrow road, grazing the hedgerows, the sound a steady put-putting. A new sound in that place, new to the birds and the briars and new to the inhabitants. He saw the Breege one watching it, half waving, then hiding behind a wet sheet that she was pegging on the line.

Ivory Mary and Micky Dazzler. Girls and men all over the country clicking, all except the Crock, the exile boy. What sin had his strap of a mother committed to make him a freak? A stump for a leg, an iron prong for a hand, and a hump like a goblin's. His strap of a mother. Had she done it on purpose, caused it when he was supposed to be gestating inside her?

"Ugliest child ever born" was her chorus to visitors. A captain of the army home on holiday had come to see the newborn, the sixth child, and drawn back in disgust at the deformity. A captain of the army, no stranger to death and injury, was visibly revolted. The pairs of handmade shoes kept on the dresser down the years not in sentiment but proof of the inordinate expense.

The Breege one half-waving to Bugler, a slight but innuendoing wave. The signal before anything gets said at all. Girls and men in the same hoopla, all except the Crock. The only bit of satisfaction was from the book he kept under his mattress. Phoenician kings and queens. Desert tracks. Pomegranate fruit. Cedar and balsam and nard. At night he pored over it, choosing his sandalled queens at will, his cavort ending in a dying roar that shook the caravan. Sometimes his roars astonished him, but not too much and not for long. He had only to bring himself back, to the jibes, the insults, at home, at school, in the dances, in the discos; to that day on the train when he was twelve and learned what men and women are made of. He was going to see an orthopaedic doctor, his name and address pinned to his breast pocket, that and the bus fare to the hospital. Nothing extra, not even the price of a cup of tea. A couple got on, and minutes after they sat down they started in on it. The young man in a straw hat began to tend to the young girl. They both wore shorts and were very blond, nearly albino. She looked at her albino with a little utterance and then shut her eyes throughout. The young man's hands, nicely washed, went under the leg of the shorts, one hand to raise a buttock, the other to do its dallying.

He watched with a fierce and rapt concentration, gauging the refined hand, the momentum, the power in it that was more than hand, more than frigging; her ladyship with the eyes shut, dragging it on and on, the man saying things into her ear, it did not matter what, little cries then that were preparatory to the bigger cries, the hand moving with its sweet and knowing roughness, the cries being plucked out of her, louder, more, a thrill that she was mutely asking for, because they had played that little game before, many a time in private or in public, the hand squeezing that same fjord of flesh, the excitement as extreme for one as for the other, and then the honking of her, like geese going over the land, wild, ejaculant, the sound going up into a waiting sky, into an empty carriage with torn seats and two pieces of lizard luggage. Then he saw one eye open, one eye blue as a bead and calculant, then the second eye and her outrage at being watched, getting up, smoothing her shorts and hurrying along the corridor, muttering. The conductor returned with her, and he was hauled up to a little compartment beside the driver and told by a big fat man what a dirty boy he was and why did he stare at the nice girl and her nice boyfriend reading their book. She had brought a book to verify her story. Sonnets. He was told then that he could be sent to a correction school for a lifetime, and only out of the milk of human kindness would he be let go. He was made to kneel down and apologise to her, to say sorry. He did it.

"You ought to be ashamed of yourself," the big fat man said, and the girl agreed. He began then to laugh, laughing at something that was killing him inside, and his laugh was to be his weapon throughout his life, quite distinct from the thoughts he thought and the vengeances he hatched. The conductor told him to go to confession when he got home, and he pretended that he would, because what did it matter. They were rotten just as he was rotten.

"I will hurt them somehow . . . I will always find a way to hurt lovers" was what he vowed to himself. Mothers, fathers, liars, lovers.

"Breege," he says, as he comes up behind her, his arms longing to gird the waist, his fingers twitching. His chosen sandalled queen.

"Get out of here, Crock Hanrahan," she says sharply.

"A woman taken in adultery," he says, and laughs, then goes his way, hopping and bobbing across the fields, laughing his mirthless laugh. Breege watched him retreating at a pained and jerky pace, his body like a sack of potatoes inflating and deflating, depending on whether he was in hill or hollow. She dreaded him. She knew the rhyme that he had circulated about her —

> She's riddled in the tail
> And cockled in the skull
> And for twenty years of life
> She never saw the bull.

THE WOODS. The dusk. The hour for flighting. The dusk through which the small and secretive bird will fly for its evening feed. Joseph is describing it to Bugler as he has known it over the years, waiting for that single silhouette against the sky, that long beak, the signature mark, curved like a crochet hook. They stand at the edge of the heath, Goldie beside them, crouched but expectant, guessing the excitement that is to come, an excitement transcending blood, a thing of the nerves, the breed. Wind is rustling the evergreens, the sound like the sound of a massive sea, steady, unceasing. They speak in whispers, standing there at their posts, each with a loaded shotgun and a pocketful of cartridges. How proud Joseph is to be the squire, giving over his spare gun and his fire, showing Bugler how to carry it under his oxter, and when the time comes how to cock it and to aim.

"Are you cold?"

"Not a bit."

They are staring into the impenetrableness of the dark wood in which the birds have recently arrived on their long migration from Siberia or wherever, to winter in loamy crevices, in hiding all day and venturing out at twilight to feed in any bit of water or swamp that they can find. Joseph had feared that he would have to call it off because of a dense mist which had shrouded the mountain, obliterated it, and turned the woods into an endless swell of grey, an ugly surly mist not like the white vapour, the white lady, that sometimes ran and danced on parts of the mountain, a dancing lady which drunk men believed was the banshee.

The moon is up, the very moon that was nature's cue to their migration is now about to betray them, to show the passage of the feathers, so pale as to be almost colourless, the long beaks, their compasses into the sky before coming to land in the succulence of boghole or cowpat. She takes him by surprise, the very first of the season, not jigging and bobbing around as they sometimes do because of their poor eyesight, but a clear and radiant flight to which one of his round of shots calls a halt.

"The bull's-eye," Bugler says, amazed.

She drops murmurless, her wings flapping in consternation.

"I didn't kill it," Joseph says, and Goldie scurries off, and both men watch her return with it held gently in her mouth as if it is cloth; the wings still flapping, though not so rapidly.

"I don't like doing this," Joseph says, and taking the bird out of Goldie's mouth, he conks the neck on the stock of his gun as easily as he might crack a monkey nut.

Then he hands it to Bugler.

"Not a mark on her," Bugler says, feeling the feathers and the flesh.

"No . . . Goldie holds her with the gums, not the teeth . . . Ultra, ultra gentle, aren't you?" he says, touching her moist snout that is trembling. He rummages then among the feathers to find the one, the special feather, then snaps it off.

"There's a place over in England where I send them . . . They're trying to build up a picture of a vanishing species."

"And we're trying to kill them," Bugler says ruefully.

"Ssh . . . Sssh." Joseph runs as if levitating, and the shots ring out, eerily muffled in the mountain's silence, and once again the little parcel of near-invisibility comes teetering down, but this time the wings are mute.

"You're a great shot," Bugler says.

"It could be you that shot it."

"It wasn't."

"The ultimate goal is to get a left and a right . . . But you hardly ever do, because they fly alone."

"Why so?"

"No one knows . . . They are a solitary bird . . . They fly alone, they eat alone, they are alone, the only time you see a pair is when the mother has a chick under her breast."

"Under her breast!" Bugler said, touched.

Goldie laid the second bird down with a similar delicacy, and holding it up, Joseph explains that there is so little meat because the creatures have no stomach, all they do is suck. Joseph was happy to be out with Bugler, their earlier enmity seeming to have dissolved the way the mist did, friends now on account of a first moon in November and thousands upon thousands of birds coming from the salt climes to stick their beaks down as their parents had done in holes and bogholes in Cloontha.

"You don't draw them . . . You cook them entrails and all."

"Go on!"

"They're delicious," Joseph says, handing them both, assuring him that Breege will do the plucking, that she's a dab hand at it.

"I can't take the two."

"Yes, you can . . . We'll make a sharpshooter of you yet . . . We'll put bottles up along the gate and you'll be surprised how you pick it up."

They sit on a fallen bough, a faint singed smell from the shells, the two dead birds insignificant, and the few stars that have come out a milky colour and a great distance from one another.

"You're in the Field of the Corpses," Joseph says.

"That's a sad name."

"We have all kinds of names . . . the Calf Park, the Callows, Pony Hill . . . Yellow Dick's Bog . . . Pet names that have been passed down."

"You were reared here?"

"I was . . . It's God to me," Joseph said, and looking up at the few stars declared that God was not a bearded man in the sky but here . . . In Cloontha, especially at night, alone with nature.

"You never craved the bright lights?" Bugler asked.

"No way," Joseph said, and described how as a young fellow he'd creep out of bed at night to shoot pigeons, put a flash lamp at the foot of a tree, adjust the beam, and wait. His voice got high-pitched as he remembered the shower of them coming out of the trees, trees, leaves, and birds all jittery, all mad.

"Who taught you?"

"A man called Danno. He'd put a row of porter bottles along the top of the gate . . . My poor mother used to go mad. Assassins, she'd call us . . . My poor mother, she nearly died when she found out where I was going two nights a week after I got my first bicycle. I was going to a shooting gallery down in Limerick." Recalling the burly sergeant-major, he stood up and bellowed out the orders in a crisp voice:

> Fill your lungs with air —
> Have you got that —
> Release half of it —
> Squeeze the trigger —
> Exhale —
> Your heart won't stop —
> Close the disengaged eye —
> Fire —
> Fire —
> Fire —

He stopped then, deliberating on the crazy things a young man does.

"Would you like to have been a soldier?"

"I suppose I would, it's in the blood . . . An uncle was shot dead twenty miles from here. Him and a comrade . . . His dying words would wring your heart. I'll show them to you sometime . . . A priest copied them for my mother. A grand-uncle had to emigrate or face the firing squad, and a great-grandfather fought at Vinegar Hill . . . Wounded . . . He walked with a stick after that. They called him Da Stick. Brave men or foolish men," he said, and stopped shy. A lump had risen inside him, as it always did when he fell to remembering. He thought of his plans to go away and be someone and how they got thwarted, his mother finding the letter, begging him to stay, saying that if he left what would happen, their little farm would be chopped up, like in a butcher's shop, different people getting different cuts, strangers crossing in front of the kitchen window. So he stayed, and now there was him and Breege, the empty waiting woods when he went out at night, the suspense of it, each time like the very first time, humbled and excited, finding a reason for living, and a gleeful one at that.

"It's a lust . . . a lust," he said then, breaking open the gun barrels.

"You never married," Bugler said after a long interval.

"I nearly did . . . A girl called Catherine. Beautiful girl . . . She went off to be a nurse. She'd ring me every Saturday night . . . We hadn't a phone at home then. I'd wait down in the town outside the kiosk . . . Ah sure, she was in one place and I in another . . . Hundreds of miles," and then his voice trailed off as if he could not bear it.

"Marriage is a big thing," Bugler said.

"You can broil them or roast them, whichever you fancy."

"I don't deserve them . . . I missed."

"What's yours is mine . . . We're friends," Joseph said. He had never mentioned Catherine, not in the fifteen years, even though he had often relived it, the letter, the stamp with the picture of a stout hero, and the terse words: *I am moving to London. I will have better chances there. I'll write to you when things get less hectic. Best of luck, Catherine.*

They were almost home when Bugler volunteered it, quite flat, as if it was incidental: "I'm engaged to be married."

"Ah stop . . . From the New World?"

"From the New World."

"Good man. I hope she likes it, it'll be a change, it'll be a challenge."

"I like it. But will she?"

"Out there I suppose you were on your lonesome."

"Not really, blokes, sheep . . . You muster sheep. You shear sheep. You lamb sheep. You eat sheep. You dream sheep . . . Then the ladies come, and before you know where you are, you're engaged. Rosemary."

"We'll make her feel at home . . . Breege and herself can go to the city once a month."

"Breege," Bugler says, the mention of her somehow jolting

him, his remembering seeing her that Sunday, walking up and down the road in good shoes and good clothes, like a girl in a picture.

"She's very young, isn't she?"

"She is . . . a foundling. I'm like a father to her. You see, she came late . . . I often think it killed my mother those years later. My father died within the year. That's love for you."

They walk on, and then very stiffly Bugler says, "Oh, by the way, I'd rather the engagement was kept a secret."

"Mum is the word," Joseph said, and they parted as friends.

❖   ❖   ❖

Rain rushed down, its sound preceding it, not the usual rain; heavy with hail, and a wind from the four corners of the world gathering force, gusts of wind storming the treetops, branches wayward, Goldie's plate spinning and whirling down the yard, and the two dead birds that were laid on the bonnet, for plucking, coming alive, their breast feathers unfolding as they lifted off and did a small circuit that simulated freedom, simulated life. When she caught them they felt soft and furry, like cold gloves that had been left outside.

The place had been empty for storm, for things to be stirred up, uprooted, and put down somewhere else, the way she had been empty for something and now it was there. Her brother and Mick Bugler were friends.

"My brother and Mick Bugler are best friends." She wrote it with a bit of white flour on the top of the range after she had made bread. She often wrote things in that manner, to make them lasting.

Dear Bugler,

You asked me to tell you of some of the old customs, things our folks did and that I saw and did as a youngster. Well, my grammar isn't always correct, nor my turn of phrase, but you will be able to cope with that. I will start with stones, because they were the bane of our lives. They sprung up in the fields like mushrooms, hosts of them, big stones, medium stones, and scutty little stones that refused to budge out of the earth. It was a menial job, but it had to be done. To put it into perspective I will go back a little and explain its place in the crop rotation. The green field was ploughed in November, so that the frost would make the soil friable and easy to till. The oat crop was sown in March and harvested in August and September. The stubble was ploughed so that potatoes or turnips could be sown the following spring. When they were harvested, wheat or barley was put in, and before the next crop, which would be hayseed, was the time to pick the stones. Once the hay grew, the stones would be disguised and break the blades of a mowing machine. The bigger stones would have been removed two years before, turned up by the plough and taken away in a horse and cart to mend a wall, to keep cattle in and other people's cattle out. Now, some stones were too big and could not be moved, so they had to be blasted with gelignite. That was the dangerous bit and naturally the most exciting bit, so I will save that for the end. As for the smaller stones, you had to pick them up and put them in a bucket. The bucket could only be half full because of the weight of it. You couldn't use a horse and cart, because the horse wouldn't stand still in the freezing cold. So the stones were put in little piles and carried away in the buckets. It was torture. In frosty weather the coldest time was one hour before dark. They would stick to your fingers, the very same as putting your hand inside a freezer for a minute or longer. That was the time of year when the woodcock came, and just at nightfall my friends and myself would wait for them, then maybe go down to the village and fool around, and then back up to the woods with flash lamps to shoot pigeons. I said I would tell you about blasting the rocks. It was a tricky business. It called for great skill and great concentration. The procedure consisted of a stick of gelignite the size of a candle, a detonator which is a little brass cylinder full of fulminate of mercury, and, finally, a length of fuse cord about five or six feet long. The fuse cord was at one end inserted into the detonator, it was closed — sometimes with the teeth — and stuck into the stick of gelignite which had already been inserted into a hole in the rock. It was packed with clay to make it airtight, the cord hanging out from it, then the fuse was lit and you got behind a stone wall or some safe cover, and with luck the rock would shatter to pieces and blow all over the field. That kind of work is history. People just hire a mechanical digger or a bulldozer, but let me be the one to say that there was something exciting about that wait behind the wall, the first sound of the blast and bits of stone flying up like birds, solid birds that could kill you with one blow.

As for the present, our way of life is changing, but some things remain the same. Take the bogs, the blanket bogs, as they are called; they are sacred places and the storehouse of our past. To dig deep into a blanket bog is to cut through time to unearth history. There is layer after layer of living vegetation. The peat is a haven for wildlife of every kind. Were you to explore it you would find more birds and beasts and insects than there were in Noah's Ark. No one cuts turf now, as they say we do not have the summers anymore to allow it to dry. Laziness. Yet in one sense we are preserving our past. We may not be the richest county, but we have more memories and more mystery by far.

Joseph

EVENING IN THE TOWN. Strains of music pulsing out. Husky notes. Pounding notes. Thu-thump. Thu-thump. Thu-thump. Near. Far. The dinner dance. Love on the cusp. The sweets of sin. Hotel doors wide open for casks of porter to be wheeled in.

"You'd think it was Christmas," Noreen says.

"It won't be long now," Eamonn replies.

In the street levity, expectation. In the lanes, kids with old curtains and straw hats, in hiding, to scare the grown-ups. New blouses hauled out of carrier bags. Satin with little pearl buttons that come undone. Platform soles to kick out the beat. Mothers ironing white shirts for their wild colonial boys. Streamers, pale primrose, pale pink, flung up to the rafters. Noreen on a ladder tacking their scalloped ends to the cornices, a stout arm, her full breast heaving.

"What about your man?" It is Eamonn talking to the monk, a frocked figure in a stained-glass window, shades of a time when the premises were a convent.

"Put a frill around him," from Noreen. Eamonn goads her to give the poor sod a little birdie. She stretches higher, thighs bare, braced.

"I bet he'd like a one-to-one."

"Wouldn't we all." Noreen says.

Comfort in that. A dance is for a one-to-one.

By nine o'clock the place will be packed, a cave of colours,

blues, magentas, heads of hair still wet with a mermaid's wet-
ness, men in white shirts, fledgelings in the doorway, eyeing the
form. Mick Bugler too, in a red bandit-style shirt. Cries and
hollers. Howya Dessie, Howya Gussie, Howya Pat. Howyas.
Fields forgotten. Cattle forgotten. The price of cattle forgotten.
The pits of slurry, the gassy issue of ammonia quite quite forgotten. Diversion. The sweets of sin. You only live once.

"The nuns used to be starving . . . They could ring a bell for
alms, but they were too proud."

"The creatures."

"I wonder if McQueen had to have it desanctified when he
bought it . . . Got it for a song."

"Desanctified . . . With the things I see here. Five and six on
that banquette . . . Wife-swapping," Eamonn tells her.

From her a shriek of laughter, with a tinge of indignation and
modesty.

Black frost all day, the ground, the fields, rock solid, and the
roads treacherous, but nevertheless there will be a crowd on account of the dance being for a good cause. The cause of charity.
The sweets of sin. Out the back road from the town two young-
sters are assaulting the hedges and terrified of the dark, marauders scrambling for holly.

"Noreen said it has to be with berries, otherwise it's not
festive."

"Her and her berries."

They snap a few sprigs off a young rowan tree.

Breege won't know until six o'clock whether or not they are
going . . . Joseph won't say. She has clothes airing by a paraffin
heater upstairs. White blouse, black pleated skirt, black stockings.

❖   ❖   ❖

Bugler stands in the doorway saluting with the warm smoulder
of his eyes. Taller than all the rest. Thu-thump. Thu-thump. Thu-
thump. Breege sees him. Shivers. All of her agog at being there —
the excitement, the hollers, cigarette smoke, bare arms, bare
shoulders, precious wineglasses gilded in the back mirrors and
music flooding out. Mrs. Flannery keeps jabbing her to empha-

sise her fury with Patrick J. Flannery gazing at that American girl and talking God knows what bull.

"Watch. He'll light her cigarette now." And so he does. She predicts how the match will be kept alight to roam over the girl's gloating face, and so it does until it burns down to his grimy fingernails. Sue-Anne, a cousin from Boston, having to have her beauty sleep until six in the evening. Patrick, as promised, went up to waken his guest. Asked what kept him so long, he simply said he was learning about life in the fast lane.

Joseph and the Crock are at the bar, with spare pints of porter, each pressing hospitality on the other to make up for the recent imbroglio. Joseph had caught the Crock stealing timber and ordered him and his wheelbarrow off their lands for *saecula saeculorum*.

"I can't take much more of it," Mrs. Flannery says, searches in one pocket, then another for a handkerchief, and blows her nose repeatedly.

"She'll be gone back soon."

"You don't know the agony of love."

Breege feels colour starting up and down her neck, zigzags behind the sheath of her white blouse. Bugler is smiling across at her. The smile has made up for those times when he passed her so abruptly, jumped over a wall to search for an animal because some dolt had left a gate open. As if she was the dolt who had left the gate open. She must not be seen to be overhappy, Joseph would suspect.

"Tickets, ladies," Eamonn says, pointing to the prizes with the rim of his straw boater — a big television, a set of Waterford glasses, and a vegetarian cookbook. Mrs. Flannery asks tartly if she could win a husband along with a television set.

"Thought you had one."

"Him," she says. Patrick is standing over them boyish and bashful. He is made to pay for the tickets. The Crock has arrived with two vodka-and-lemonades for the ladies. Bugler crosses, his smile preparatory to asking her up.

"Later," she says to the barely audible invitation. The floor is empty except for two old men dancing ceilidh in defiance of the boppy music that is being played, shouting to one another. "One, two, three, one, two, three," to keep the beat.

"Please yourself," he says, and moves off as if a little daunted, tapping the tables that he passes in some kind of pique. The Crock lisps a low whistle.

"Bet you're the first lady ever to say no to him."

"Oh, he'll siphon off all the talent till he gets to the last dance." That from Josephine, standing above them, her body like a blancmange in her off-white crocheted dress.

"Oh, Jesus, look," from the Crock. They look. They see. Bugler is dancing with Lady Harkness, steering her solemnly, as if she were an ocean liner in her peppermint green; her smile seems to be saying that there is nothing in the whole world more beautiful than an old-time waltz.

Gradually, the floor fills up. Young men with young girls in bold improvisations. Breege thinks that by the time he asks her again she will be prepared. She will have gone down to the ladies' and dabbed herself with Mrs. Flannery's powder. It is in a floppy pink swansdown powder puff that is stitched onto a georgette handkerchief. The lady visitor from Boston brought it. It smells like the chemist shop in the city, the counter away from the dispensary, with toiletries and perfume bottles on a tray. The four corners of georgette are knotted to keep the powder from spilling. Mrs. Flannery mashes her hands. The atmosphere is hectic now. Howya. Howya Gussie. Howya Dessie.

Sy, the compère, is calling out the revels in store. First half, anything goes; around the house and mind the dresser. Interval for supper, with entertainment from the one and only Magdalene. Second half, rock, smooch. The one and only Magdalene is sitting on the stage, her ankle by way of a joke yoked to the leg of the piano with red crepe bunting. A gaudy stump. She smiles, tremulous. Sequins stitched to her black dress are likewise twinkling away. Sy says what an honour it is to have her in their midst. Yippees from the crowd. Barmaids, smiling, kerchiefed, weave through the mêlée with laden trays. Heads of hair mop the floor.

Young men, ardent, bold, throw their partners up in the air as if they were puffballs.

"I'll kill him . . . I'll kill that man." Mrs. Flannery is seeing her husband's ringed hand move slowly along the velveteen buttocks. Calls to him, simply calls his name, but peremptory. Standing on a chair, taunting — does he think he is a teenager and he the wrong side of fifty. Vixen-like, she is on the dance floor hitting him, aggrieved.

"Oh, a shit attack." Eamonn saunters across to rescue matters with a "Now now." Couples pause in their capers to look. A lull in the esprit. Music comes to a halt. One of the old men who had been dancing says a recitation to the kneeling monk in his aspic of stained glass:

> My back it is deal
> My belly's the same
> And my sides are well bound with good leather.
> My nose it is brass
> There's a hole in my ass
> And I'm very much used in cold weather.

❖   ❖   ❖

As supper is announced, folding chairs are slung down and there is a crush to a desired table. No use being with a bunch of dopes. Piping-hot stew in big urns, one for each table, and twelve earthenware plates. Noreen shouting out the orders: "Who'll be mother, who'll be mother?" No one wants to be mother.

At their table it falls to Bugler to be mother. Sleeves raised, he ladles the stew onto the upheld plates. Says he can't be too particular as to who does or does not like onions. Give them to your neighbour. Old Bill Muggavin with no teeth walks around looking for a place and tells the floating streamers that he lost his clock fifteen years ago. Words of praise for Bugler's expertise. Comes from being on a sheep station. Fifty men in the mess. Half an hour at the most for lunch or dinner. Lambs and sheep in their thousands, waiting. Funny that you never got hitched up, Mick. From Josephine. Doesn't answer. Rosemary's face becoming fainter with the passing days. Not able to summon her up the way he used to, lying in his quarters at night, her photograph falling out of the last letter. Rebuke.

Voices bassooning. Rifled crackers. Excitable whistles. Lady Harkness with fingers in both ears. The holly pickers ogling people to buy a last book of tickets. Get lost, Brud. Get lost, Ned. Sy promising that very special moment. So close to Breege does Bugler sit that she wonders, Is it accidental because of the tight squeeze, fourteen at a table meant for twelve? Joseph two tables away with his back to her. Bugler being quizzed about life in the outback. "Ah now" is all he will say. On his other side a cripple. Paralysed from the chest down. Road accident. Fella coming out a side road at a hundred miles an hour. Big settlement. Lucky not to be in a six foot by three foot. Words of sympathy. Never know the hour or the minute. Thankful for small mercies. Bugler offers a hand. Cuts the mutton in chunks with the short scissors which the cripple carries in his blazer pocket. Then a cry. An outcry. Where's the wine. Where's the bloody vino. Bottles slammed down, bottles with pictures of neat, ordered vineyards, and a view of a castle. Castle Gondolfo. Isn't that a summer residence of His Holiness the Pope? Some gulping the food, others complaining of it being rough and ready. Assumpta, just back from Sun and Sea, thinks they could at least have been given a starter at that price — twenty-seven fifty. A melon fan or soup. How was the holiday, Assumpta? Brilliant, absolutely brilliant, nothing to beat the South of France. From Lady Harkness a yodel. Vacationed there in the hills above Nice. What a clientele. Sir Winston Churchill in one villa, Lord Beaverbrook in the next. The Aga Khan sending an emissary to her table. His Highness thought her the most beautiful woman in the dining room. Sir Clifford going mad, quite mad. Bought a pistol. Josephine galled at the cheek of Assumpta and her South of France when it was Lourdes with a group from the diocese, invalids. Dipping them in the holy baths and wheeling them around the grounds at Rosary time. Seconds for some, but not all. Lady Harkness averring that the best way to cook game is to do it while they're still warm.

Forget that rubbish about letting birds hang for a week. Game should be cooked straightaway before they toughen. Husband and wife, a wealthy couple who had been thought to have separated, at a table, cooing. The hypocrisy of it. Brian, an off-duty guard who was called to the scene, admitted that it got quite nasty. A certain person, the husband in question, meeting another person in his factory and growing attracted to her. What started out as a cup of coffee and a cheesecake ending in a full-blown affair in a hotel on the coast. Shocking altogether — wife having to go to casualty that Saturday night and husband wrote off two cars. Brian is begged to enlarge but won't. Professional ethics. Says then that attraction is just addiction, nothing more. Is shouted down. Whoever heard such bollocks. Attraction is attraction, eh, Breege? She doesn't answer. That gal is deep water from Lady Harkness. Lady Harkness with choker of black seed pearls, polite to all, but haughty. Shameless about the use of the only telex that is supposed to be for emergencies, for accidents, deaths, power cuts, yet receiving such trifles as:

> Good morning, Lady Harkness,
> A beautiful frosty morning.
> Your account from Bunting and Knowles for a memorial stone — overdue.
> A Christmas card from Daphne and John in the Seychelles.
> The minutes of the meeting for the Royal Foundation for the Blind.
> At last the estimate for the garden wall opposite the library window which collapsed. A bit steep.

Magdalene sings while they eat. A light, sweet, tinkly voice. All about love. Waiting for love or just seeing it passing by like thistledown. She has donned black satin gloves, her arms reaching out to her audience, wooing them. Bugler is asked if he thinks she has It. He looks and listens. Seems a very nice girl. He is next to Breege. She can feel his wandering touch. They talk to everyone else at the table except each other. Two months passing on the tractor and now this, this. Baked apple and ice cream topped with lit sparklers are being passed around. A feverish feeling.

Sudden darkness. Screaming. Jesus Christ. Is it a bomb? Sy an-
nouncing, "Yous are all to kiss the person next to you, and if
there's no one next to you kiss the wall." "I have no wall." "Kiss
my arse." Bugler turning to Breege, her blouse so cold and
starched, her lips full and violet colour from the down spotlight.
Drinks her in. Slow count to five. "Wakey wakey" from Sy. The
moment has passed. Lights come brazenly on. "You dirty things.
Was that nice?" Yes. No. No. Yes. Sy swears to God he read in a
book that an apple a day keeps the doctor away and a birdie a
day keeps divorce away. Bugler slowly detaches himself with Are
you okay to her. She daren't answer. Had no idea she would be
so. So. The lips slightly parted, disclosure in the parting. Deep
water.

Rita, with cabbage crown and a frilled cabbage miniskirt,
comes across, throws her arms around him, and says feck. She
was next to a fella with no teeth. Elbows the cripple to hoof off in
his wheelchair, sits herself next to Bugler, inclining onto his lap.
Hey ho . . . Here we go. Has a request. Her kid sister, Reena,
would like the next dance. Okay? And wouldn't mind being
brought home. We'll ask you in for coffee and peppermints. A
rose on the breakfast tray and a fresh egg in the morning. Ever
put your hand in under her after she lays, going bloody berserk
and then klook-klook-klook. Does he keep hens? No. Pity that.
Great comfort. Klook. Klook. Klook. An egg flip for the constitu-
tion. She pulls him onto the floor. Chalices of Irish coffee, foam-
crested. Elderly people asking for pots of tea.

Blotched from crying, Mrs. Flannery asks Breege to stay with
her, not to go back up. They are in the ladies' room. Someone has
draped the pale blue lavatory paper around the mirrors. Mrs.
Flannery bemoans how much she loves that man. Would cut her
wrists if he went with another. Asks in God's name why she
flipped. Why she made such a show of herself. Entreated to be
told what exactly she did, then begs not to be told. Says then how
kind Patrick was, how affectionate when they went into the garden to patch things up. She weeps afresh at that hot bitch sleeping
only a wall away from them for two more nights. Loud cheering

as obviously the winners of the raffle are announced. Breege longs to be back there, on the verge of the skaty dance floor.

"Come on . . . We might be winning something," she says, and coaxes the woman up.

Bugler, with his jacket off, is onstage singing and holding the cookbook, which he must have won. It is a song about a town in the North devastated by war, his voice almost breaking as he laments a community divided. Magdalene watches enrapt. Buttons of his bandit shirt have come undone, his torso dark and bony. The crowd show their approval by joining in. Good on you. Well sung. Encore. When he comes off the stage, various girls touch him and he touches them back. Magdalene is helped down and walks beside him, her long velvet glove nestled to his bare arm.

"Micky Dazzler," the Crock says as Bugler on impulse hands his winning trophy to an old woman who has jumped up to kiss him.

"Micky Dazzler." Joseph is beside Breege now. Soon time to go. She sees her own hand twining and retwining a bit of her own hair in the gilded mirror. Crestfallen.

❖　　❖　　❖

The tractor was back. In its old familiar place under the hawthorn tree. In the moonlight, veiled in frost, it seemed like a glass coach. Joseph crosses to it, scolding it at first for being so presumptuous as to come back without an invite. Bugler usually brought it up home, up to the Congo, but must have been in one big hurry to get on that dance floor. Having scolded it, he mellows somewhat and begins to talk to it in a maudlin way.

"Oh, dear Dino, charmed to see you, how do you do, we thought you had gone up yonder for good and now it seems you're back — do you prefer us, Breege and me . . . Go on, say it, you'd sooner us than the Shepherd. Micky Dazzler he has just been christened, in case you don't know . . . Oh, what a swell, an all-round man, can cut a dash on the dance floor, level a field, shoot game, and click the girls. Three cheers for Micky Dazzler, hip hip hooray."

When he touches a knob on the dashboard, music starts to pour out, and he draws back from it alarmed.

"Jesus. He's got a stereo in you . . . Well, I'll be damned," he says, searching for the place he had accidentally touched.

"For God's sake, Joseph."

"Listen, Breege . . . Listen . . ." She is dragging him away.

"What's the hurry? What I say is true . . . The Shepherd is number one, and very soon he will be growing rye . . . Rye fields in Cloontha and cranberries on his marshy land. I have it this evening from his very own lips. But a word in your ear, Breege . . . Tricky Micky means to take us over. Treasons, stratagems, and spoils."

"What's wrong with rye . . . What's wrong with cranberries?"

"Everything!"

Turning to face the carved bowl of the mountain, glassy in the moonlight, he delivered his ode —

"Who came first, Bugler or Brennan? The Brennans came first, the Brennans of the moor. The Buglers played bugles and came hence from Wales with the soldiers . . . Welsh men . . . And on the last day the Brennans will be first, for many are called but Brennans are chosen."

❖   ❖   ❖

The dance hall was deserted, spare tables and folding chairs stacked in a corner, with Eamonn and two girls sweeping up the debris, sweeping it into the middle of the floor. There were cans, cigarette packets, a pair of red braces, and several odd earrings that sparkled untowardly in the dust. Rita is looking for Reena. Reena is looking for Rita. They miss because of going in two different directions, one to the ladies' room, one to the car park. They meet back in the hall in a hail of risen dust.

"Where's Bugler?" from Rita.

"He's gone."

"He's gone! Where to?"

"He went with Magdalene . . . And the harp."

"Jesus Christ, in holy feck's name, you mean to tell me that you let him go?"

"I couldn't stop him."

"You half-baked, big-arsed pollop, you let him go . . . You didn't even try . . . All you had to do was hold your bush up against him."

"He wasn't interested in me."

"Plan A — tell me what was Plan A."

"We were going to bring Bugler home and get our hooks in him."

"Plan A, we were going to bring Bugler home, and Plan B we were going to bring Bugler home and every fecking plan in the alphabet . . . Now he's with that bitch with her lands in Tipperary . . . She's loaded."

"Oh, Reet." Reena starts to cry, the tears dropping onto the posy of chrysanthemums which she took from the table. Everyone grabbed something, but all she managed was this small bouquet and half a red candle. Eamonn sweeps around them while they outscream each other, tells them the party is over. Soon they are screaming at him, saying they are not fecking leaving, they want reimbursement. With shooing arms and the broom handle he herds them towards the exit, saying very quietly, and very gently, "Girls, girls," then gets them to the front door, pushes them out, shuts the door, bolts it, and whistles a sweet Jesus of relief. The last thing he wants is to be up in court for assaulting them.

Once out of the town they hit a fog so thick that it is impossible to see twenty yards ahead. The car is like a sled on the icy road, not a glimpse of a house or a light of any kind, only Rita cursing and plotting her revenge on one and all. She is driving recklessly, her cabbage crown askew, the little bubble car like a cauldron because of her invective.

"I'm sorry, Reet," Reena said, picking off shreds of the chrysanthemums as if they were coconut, then spitting them out.

"Sorry, feck . . . Two times twenty-seven pounds fifty, the price of a load of hay."

When they passed their turning, at the top of the town, Rita tore down the hill, through the fog, knocking some tar barrels put there because of roadworks.

"Where are we going, Reet?"

"See if that tin of turpentine is in the back."

"Why?"

"His fecking tractor is in for a surprise."

"How so?"

"Teach that bastard Bugler a lesson while he's getting laid in the luscious Golden Vale."

T HREE MEN ARE around the tractor, clutching it as though in a fervent embrace. Their hands and clothes already muddied and their faces taut with effort. They have been there the best part of an hour and tempers are fraying. At first it was quite jocular, Bugler giving the orders and the others complying, Joseph and the Crock at the back wheels and the salesman, a stranger, at the side, Bugler on the driver's seat with the open manual shouting out the several orders, the men pushing and sweating, trying to rock it out of its inertia.

At dawn he had got back and slept a couple of hours on a chair and then to work. He feels cranky. A mistake to have tarried in horse country. Daddy's girl, the lady crooner, acting the helpless maiden in the foyer of the dance hall, with no one to bring her home. Her cousin hadn't shown. Jonathan hadn't shown. Nearly in tears. Silent in the car. A drive of thirty-odd miles, little towns fast asleep except for the neon glare of the petrol stations, then a country road, a big front gate, a cattle grid, a stately home, but ending up in the saddle room with all the gear, the rods and the brushes and a rocky horse, things to turn a bloke on. The gee-gees. Where did a nice girl like her learn the tricks? "Oh, I started when I was twelve."

"You're sure it's not the diesel?" the Crock calls out.

"Dead sure."

It was the first thing he had tried, had put a rod into the tank thinking that maybe some hooligan came in the night and siphoned it off. Eventually, he ran up home to get the manual, and like a pupil calling instructions out to an adult he checked and rechecked every single thing — pistons, crankshaft, gasket, nozzles, clutch, stabiliser, bar and brackets, everything.

"You should never have put it under a tree . . . The ground is always loamy," Joseph says.

"Fuck your loamy," Bugler hisses between his teeth. If only they would push, if only they would put some brute strength into it.

"Rock, lads, just rock," he says. He is by turn coaxing and then abrupt. Once again he turns the ignition on, waits for the fuel to heat, and yells at them to push. As it moves a fraction, mud flies from the back wheels, flicking onto their faces, almost blinding them.

"Push . . . Feck . . . Push," Bugler shouts.

"We are pushing," Joseph shouts back, but already it has stopped and sunk with a deadliness. Bugler jumps out, tightens the axles, and says he thinks he knows what to do. It needs more pressure on the one side, it needs tilting to set it off.

"It could swing around and do for us," the Crock says.

"It won't . . . It's rock solid."

"I have to go in a minute," the salesman says. An hour of his day is wasted, and so few houses in sight, no one to sell cattle feed to.

Bugler has slunk in under it, his legs as long again as the top half of his body, jutting out, his leather gaiters not nearly so swanky as in the dance hall, mud on them.

"Tom-catting . . . You can tell." The Crock whispers it. From underneath Bugler is ordering Joseph to do this, do that.

"Hold on . . . Hold on," Joseph says.

"Use your eyes . . . Use your brain," he shouts back, telling Joseph to turn the key, to turn the blasted key. Suddenly it starts to move, and as Bugler crawls out, they give a huzzah of victory. Within seconds it has stalled again, an ugly look to it, the brick-red bonnet mutely saying, "I am not moving out of this spot."

"We'll tie it to the car and tow it," Bugler says, pointing to the stranger's very new Fiesta.

"That's not my own car, that's a company car," the man says, apologetic.

"The company won't know," and turning to Joseph, he asks for a rope.

"It's in the shed," Joseph says sullenly. Calves and cattle are lowing to be fed, milk has to be brought to the creamery and Breege fetched to Lady Harkness's house with the laundry. It is something she does privately, for a bit of pin money. He thinks of the care she takes with those garments, the washing, the rinsing, the starching, and when they are ironed they look so regal on the big table in the front room.

Bugler uncoils the rope quickly, knots the one end twice around the seat, and positions each of them so that they draw on it now like a team, like four oarsmen together in a race, their cheer restored, their eyes anxious, giving a show of strength almost superhuman. They get it almost to the gate when the rope breaks, and united in their frustration they each say "Feck" at the exact same instant, as if they had rehearsed it.

"She'll have to go to emergency," the Crock says, and touches the mudguard almost fondly.

"Come on . . . Come on, Dino," Bugler said imploringly, and strove to lift it between his knees, hugging it, remonstrating with it as if the fault was a mere moodiness, not wanting, not yet able to admit that he had been sold a pup.

"I'm afraid I have to be off . . . I have appointments," the salesman said.

"Wait . . . Wait," Bugler said, and picking up a hen's trough he wedged it under the back wheels.

"What good will that do?"

"The juice isn't getting through . . . There's a blockage."

"Aren't you working arse-wise . . . It's the back wheels you should be jacking up," the Crock says.

Tempers have risen again, and he thinks of that yard of tractors, useless ones, piled on top of one another and the rotten luck of picking a goner. Rosemary's money, or rather Rosemary's daddy's money, who prided himself on his wealth and his agnosticism.

"Maybe someone wanted it banjaxed," the Crock says with a wink.

"Or maybe witchcraft . . . I was told of a famous witch in these parts, she had a blue bottle for cures," the salesman says.

"She had the power," the Crock answers back.

"Did you or your sister notice anything fishy?" Bugler asks.

"We're not your caretakers," Joseph says, nettled.

Conceding at last that he will have to get help, Bugler asks where the telephone is.

"Where do you think it is?" Joseph says, irked at the thought of him going into the house where Breege is, taking her unawares.

"It's a dead Dino," the Crock says once he has gone.

"Do you have anywhere I could wash?" the salesman asks.

"That's clean grass," Joseph says, and to prove his point he bends down and wipes his hands in it and the salesman does likewise, flinching. They commiserate with each other on how they have been exploited.

"He's not bloody up," Bugler says, hurrying back and flinging the various tools into his bag.

"It's early," the Crock says.

"If he was in any other country he'd be up."

"What's that supposed to mean?" Joseph says, resenting the gall of a man new to the place coming to conclusions.

"They're not on the ball . . . None of you are," Bugler says tauntingly.

"The sooner you take that machine out of here, the better for all concerned."

"It will be out of here."

The look that passed between them so vicious then it might have been their two dogs, Goldie and Gypsy, in one of their sparring matches.

❖ ❖ ❖

It was dark when the tractor was to be heard chugging out of the yard.

"Good riddance," Joseph said. All day he had been grumbling about this and that, a heifer that had got sick, a bill from the opticians that was astronomical, and his own yard a public convenience for Bugler. Earlier, when he saw her bringing out tea and sandwiches, he asked sarcastically why she had forgotten the lace tray cloth to go with it.

"They must be frozen stiff," she had said.

Mattie, the mechanic, hadn't come until after work, and they were out there working with torches, the engine stopping and stalling as it had in the morning, and then quite suddenly the sound of it no longer sluggish, strong, repetitive, chafing, ready to go again.

When she came back in, Joseph asked if by any chance she had been inveigled to push the yoke.

"You drank too much last night," she said.

"A showman . . . nothing but a showman . . . the way he hogged the limelight . . . up on the stage with the crooner . . . singing a song he only just learned. What does he know about the North or the South either?"

"Someone put turpentine into the diesel tank . . . that's why it wouldn't go."

Bugler had showed it to her out there, pointed to the black-green spew of oil, the higher blades of grass leaky with it, and for some reason she had felt ashamed, as if it was their doing.

"He makes waves and he makes enemies," Joseph said, then drew his watch up close to his face to confirm the time the squatter had left.

Much later she stood in the place where the tractor had stood. There was only the patch of trampled grass, the spew of spilt diesel, and a pullover which he had forgotten. She would miss it. It had been company. She would hear him at all hours doing things to it, making improvements to the inside. Once she was in her plantation, she'd gone out there to think, and when he passed by, it gave him a start to find her in the leafed darkness, on a bench. He asked her what the hushed border of flowers were and she told him that they were dahlias, deep-red dahlias.

Dear Rosemary,

I know you're cross. The thing is, I work from dawn till midnight and after. You'd be surprised with the amount that there is to be done. Everywhere I look there's another job, another problem, another. No time off. Today for instance was a drama. The tractor wouldn't go. Someone poured turpentine into the diesel, one of those dear friends and gentle people who live on this mountain. It's ten o'clock and I'm sitting down to my supper of leftovers. Don't be cross. We will have a wonderful house yet, but everything takes time. I intend to go into farming in a big way so we will be rich. I miss my little ducky, especially at night! But it is better that my little ducky does not come until the spring, the daffodils and all that. Don't ask about the weather. Rain rain rain. It's dropping onto this letter. Your fiancé is builder, builder's mate, carpenter, plumber, and farmer, but he is still your Shepherd.

He signed it, read it over, and for some reason added, "Don't expect miracles."

Where in Paris can you see a glass pyramid?
What is the Swahili word for journey?
Which county in Northern Ireland is known as the Orchard County?
What nut is used in the manufacture of dynamite?
Patrick H. Pearse led the 1916 Rebellion — what does H stand for?
According to the Ordnance Survey, at what point does a hill become a mountain?
Where did Michelangelo depict God's creation of Adam?
What chemical element is the sun partly made from?

By the time they had got to round eight of the final quiz night, the tension and excitement had escalated, as those who supported Joseph's team and those who supported the schoolteacher's were at loggerheads, shouting each other down, some accusing Dunny, the quizmaster, of rigging, of favouritism, even nepotism. "What the hell is nepotism" came from the back of the room. It was because there had been a question as to which Greek god was conceived through a shower of gold, and with Joseph being something of a Greek scholar, he would know the answer easily.

"Jesus Christ," shouted one of the hecklers, but he was hushed. For nine weeks they had assembled every Tuesday, sat themselves at their appointed tables, joked, sparred, bit on their pencils, smote themselves for not knowing such and such an answer, and vociferously objected to questions such as how many windows in the vocational school or which classroom had a picture of Granuaile the pirate queen. Those who had dropped out along the way had been given consolation prizes of pottery mugs which they banged on the table to confirm or withdraw their support. Speculation abounded as to what the prize would be, the biggie, as it was touted. Some thought a cut-glass bowl, others in the know said it was massive.

During the lull after the first batch of questions, Derek the barman passed around plates of sandwiches as a surprise gift. It was neck and neck. Joseph and Alfie, the schoolteacher, fighting it out alone because they were so erudite, those on their teams merely sitting there to lend moral support. Every chair, every stool was taken, and latecomers including Bugler had to be content to stand in the hall.

Joseph was in his best suit and white shirt, with Miss Carruthers, the Crock, and Eily, the new bank clerk, beside him. The side of his cheek next to the fire was scalding, and he drank tumblers of water. His opponent, Alfie, had taken off his jacket and sat in his shirtsleeves, studious, ponderous, like a young cleric discussing some article of theology with his own group.

"I went wrong over the emeralds," Joseph said, embarrassed. The question had been which country exported the most, and mistakenly he had said Peru.

"I tried telepathy," Miss Carruthers said, her voice high, hysterical, and scolding. Despite the heat, she wore her fox-fur collar, and the little buttony amber eyes seemed to glare across at Alfie and the burly man with him, whispering in his ear. They were unpopular because they always came first in quizzes and at the debating societies. Always when they won they looked very smug and shook hands with each other several times, proud of how knowledgeable they were.

"It's neck and neck."

"Keep the cool."

"Deep breaths," Eily said. She liked Joseph; she knew that he had come to the bank one morning to ask for a loan and had seen the bank manager privately.

"I'll be all right if the questions are classic or mythological."

"You'll be all right . . . period."

They might have been in an examination room with the locked boxes being opened, so solemn did it all become. Dunny stood in front of the bar, arms folded, while Derek shouted for quiet — lads, ladies, lads.

What is the biggest-selling brand of spirits in the U.S.A.?

Joseph looked from one to the other of his group, every least muscle in his face tightened as he searched for an answer. Himself and his opponent caught each other's eye and looked away.

Give the name and age of the newest star in the firmament.

When the last question was given, the crowd sat back, relieved, as if they had weathered some great hazard, and the two pieces of folded paper were handed over to Dunny, who withdrew to do his sums. Drinks were called for, with Derek trying to appear impartial and serving everyone in their right turn.

When Dunny returned waving the sheets of paper in either hand, it was thought that the result must be a draw. He valued this moment, basked in his importance, thinking of the homework he had done, week after week endeavouring to find questions that had not been asked before. He looked from one contender to the other. The celebrants now were restless, what with the room very warm, the glaring neon strips, and his scouting the faces, daring them to guess. Then, opening the home-made calendar in which he printed all the scores, he shouted out in a formal voice, "Table 4 scores 10.94. Table 5 scores 9.72." There was clapping and cheering, people rushing across to hug Joseph, to share in his victory, drinks being sloshed from overfull tumblers, and suddenly the burly man getting himself up onto a tiny round table, calling "Objection . . . Objection." The result, he assured them, was null and void due to a foul in the rules.

"Name it," Dunny said, piqued.

"The last question contained two questions in one . . . That's an irregularity."

"I make the rules . . . And I break the rules," Dunny said, triumphant.

"We want a recount."

"You can have it . . . He got both right and you only got one.

He got Bacardi as the most popular drink and Protostar as the name of the new arrival."

"Jesus . . . Was it Bacardi?" Eily said, and lolled back, asking Derek to kindly bring her a Bacardi and Coke so that she could celebrate.

"I chanced my arm on the Bacardi," Joseph said.

"Don't be a crybaby," Dunny said as the burly man refused to come down off the table. There were shouts and boos then, people asking for Maxie, the hotelier, to come forward with the bloody prize.

"It hasn't come yet," Derek said, and was shouted down, all agreeing that Maxie was too bloody mean and so was Maxie's missus, and why wouldn't they be, being foreigners.

When a car pulled up at a hectic speed, Derek jumped over the counter in answer to the horn being hooted repeatedly. The crowd waited, then Maxie in his chef's hat and Mrs. Maxie beside him came in carrying something in a blanket. Mrs. Maxie turned out the lights as she always did when carrying a birthday cake or even a slice of birthday cake, while her husband followed slowly, singing some song from his own country. At first people speculated that it was a little piglet as Maxie found his way between the tables, opening the blanket a fraction, and then he stood before Joseph and the lights were turned on. It was a fawn greyhound with black spots like inkspots all over its body, its snout moist.

"Cripes," Joseph said, abashed.

"The compliments of Heidi and myself."

"Oh, Breege," Joseph shouted to Breege in the corner as if calamity had occurred to them.

Then slowly Maxie pulled the blanket aside like a blazoned toga and stood the little hound on the counter for everyone to see. It looked so pristine, the fawn of its body fading into a paler fawn and the smudged ink markings the very same as if they were dripping, its eyes looking out at its new world and the column of people.

"It's too much altogether," Joseph said then.

"You mean Heidi and I can keep it?" Maxie said, and made as if to present it to Heidi. Derek, unable to hide his feeling for it, crumbled a few salt nuts from the end of a packet and set them down on the counter along with a saucer of water. The hound looked, sniffed, then decided on the water, and drank daintily, spilling out the last few drops. Its eyes were a pale green from which the darker pigment had been drained and they were shaped like almonds.

"Boy or girl?" someone called.

"Girl," Cahill, the old man, said swiftly. He had known grey-hounds all his life and he had bred greyhounds until they broke him, but he loved them still.

"What will you call her?" someone shouted.

Names were suggested, names that were usual for dogs, then fancy names, names of tennis players and film stars, and even one of a saint, which was booed out.

"I'll call her Cecilia," Joseph said, turning to Miss Carruthers, who had been such a stalwart on his team.

"Oh no," she said, stricken with embarrassment and rising with tears in her eyes.

"Why not call her Violet Hill . . . Where she's come from," Maxie said.

"Is that okay, Breege?" Joseph said, then running his hand down the foreleg of the hound, he lifted one of her paws and brought his face close to it and christened her Violet Hill. The crowd applauded. Stroking the delicate bone of her back, he thought he had not felt so happy or so popular in years, maybe never. Looking at him Breege thought, He's happy now . . . He's proud, and looking towards Bugler in the doorway, she thought that he was thinking that too.

"You'll course her first," Cahill said, and everyone waited and deferred to him, because he always kept silent until he had something to say.

"You'll help me, Cahill?"

"I will so . . . We have to blood her . . . Let her taste blood, be-cause that's what she wants. That's what they want."

"Is that what you want, Violet Hill?" Joseph said, and snug-gled her to himself as if she were an infant, and felt her trembling within.

IT WAS RUGGED TERRAIN, the tractor bouncing and hacking its way through a wilderness of briars and bushes, all tangled together, fighting for life, fighting for light, the branches scraping the bonnet, scraping her face, wisps of old man's beard clinging to her hair, the wheels slurping in the mud, then spitting it off and ploughing forward.

She sat in the back, swaying from side to side, a devil-may-care feeling reminiscent of being in the bumper cars at a carnival. Bugler had given her a rug, which kept slipping off her knees. She could have sat beside him, but she declined and instead chose the wooden trailer fixed to the back, and lay there bumping and dipping as the tractor either lurched in mossy ground or reared up when the wheels snagged in another freakish growth. The place smelt of dank, of leaf mould, of fungus, a place where none had ventured in years. He drove slowly and with a tremendous concentration. She could tell by his rigid back, the set of his shoulders, and the way his head kept swivelling from side to side to be prepared. Now and then he turned to look at her with the broad sweep of a smile, but she could not hear what he had said.

It had come about by chance, her painting a gate, painting it silver because she was sick of how rusted it looked, and his going by and asking if she was having a party.

"I wish I was" was what she had said and what prompted him to say, "Get in . . . We'll go for a spin."

As they climbed higher, they could hear the sound of a river. It came as if from afar, wild and vigorous and whizzing, then the sight of it so thrilling up there in the emptiness, a deep amethyst-coloured, plashing river, clean and icy cold.

They had got out and stood on the humped bridge to watch it, to marvel at the way it rushed along, so carefree.

"I always thought rivers were green or brown," he said.

Through a lattice of trees there was the remains of a house, a cabin, weeds and grass sprouting from the roof, fruit trees and rose trees gone wild, entwined, disfigured, everything mutated, mutating, except for one little birch tree so spindly it looked like a lonesome ballerina.

"My mother used to tell me about this place," he said, amazement in his voice at having come on it. He went on to tell her how his mother used to walk up on a Sunday, all by herself, to get a biscuit, and one day when she went the woman was washing her hair in a basin and when she lifted her head up the long black stream of hair gave her a witchlike look. His mother thought the woman was going to a dance, but it was to the asylum she was sent.

"What was her name?"

"I'm ashamed to say I forget."

They looked at the little ruin, absorbed into and dwarfed by the brooding wilderness, and at the wild garden, the only testament to a woman whose name nobody remembered.

In the river below, a salmon rose up out of the water, bowed like a bright sword thrust up into the air, then down in the water again and up again, glinting, playful.

"That salmon has been all around the world," he said.

"Like you," she said.

The summit had the emptiness of desert, no trees, no birds, no shelter, a vista of dun brown, the two of them standing so close as if they had coalesced and his voice quiet, ruminative, telling her how he had always wanted to come back because his mother had kept the memory of it alive for them and had instilled in him the certainty that one day he must go home.

"Some of this was her dowry," he said, and wished that he could have brought her back before she died.

"What was she like?"

"Lovely . . . She had a beautiful voice. There was a song she used to sing about a young girl in the grounds of a castle . . . 'The Castle of Dromore.' Maybe you know it."

"I don't."

"I'll try and find it for you," he said.

"Do you feel you have come home?"

"I do now, here . . . With you . . . But not otherwise. I'm not liked . . . They say I'm bad news. I don't know why."

Without asking, he took off his jacket and draped it around her. "You're freezing," he said. A quick shiver passed between them, lonesome in its wake. Bending, he broke off a stalk of tough grass, ocherish in colour, and gave it to her. A braided keepsake.

REENA IS IRONING HER HAIR, her cheek almost resting on the ironing board, ironing strip after strip of it as if it is a long garment, then smelling the clean soapy smell and envisaging the thought of him tossing it. The fire is on, the flames cracking and playing on the whitewashed walls, making funny-bunny shadows. They have opened a bottle of the tonic wine and put it in the hearth to warm, loot got from Desi the publican for a kiss in the back passage of the hall. Mad to see her garters. She has the Sunday ones on for Bugler, black lace with red rosebuds.

Here in their little abode he will stand, in the middle of the floor probably, look around, screw up his eyes, and stroke his beard, surprised at how cushy it all is. They will have candlelight for that extra romantic touch. Her hair completely ironed, without even a crinkle, she starts to pin the organza bows and stands before the long mirror puffing out her pink cheeks as if she is blowing bubbles or balloons. She can't stop kissing him in her mind, good kissing, wild kissing, not like the peck she gave Desi, with his stained teeth and his stained tongue, trying to make a dinner out of it.

"Will you stop that moping and get some clothes on you," Rita says, hurrying in and flinging down the groceries — sliced bread, butter, chicken and ham paste, and a home-made apple pie with the design of a cross on the browned pastry.

"I think I'm in love," Reena says, fixing the last little bow onto her temple for that cutie look.

"Don't talk shit."

"Suppose, Reet, suppose he fell in love with me and me with him and we had a baby."

"You listen to me, this is business . . . Do you hear . . . Business."

"I hear you."

"Hay . . . And grass. Then grazing . . . Then a weeny little bit of a field . . . Then a field."

"You're the brains, Reet."

"And you're the brawn . . . Wait till he sees your bubs."

"Wouldn't you like a dip of his wick?"

"If I want a dip of his wick, I'll have it."

"Suppose! Suppose I fell in love with him and you did too . . . We'd be clawing each other and scratching each other's eyes out."

"Get dressed," Rita said for the second time.

"I'm all itch. I'm roasting."

"Go out and douche yourself in the river."

"You were the one that first spotted him down at the docks . . . You said he had limbs on him that would crack a woman's thighs. Tell me, Reet, will I wear a petticoat?" she says, affecting flounder.

"Of course you'll wear a petticoat . . . You'll wear the camisole, bloomers and petticoat combined . . . Our dear dead grandmother's."

"With the little buttons!"

"With the little buttons."

"Reet . . . Suppose he doesn't come after all this."

"He'll come . . . He'll come . . . I know when a man is hungry or thirsty."

"Jesus . . . I'm upside-downy . . . I'm all goosepimples."

"Douche yourself and be quick about it."

❖   ❖   ❖

It was by the light of a lantern that Bugler threw out the bales of hay and watched them jump, jostling each other, like tough opponents jumping for a ball.

"Ye're as good as men."

"We're better," Rita said. The talk then got on to men and women, the difference between the sexes, and soon it was to the married men who were back on the game and a new masseuse, who insisted that her clients completely undress since she undressed herself.

"We saw her through the window . . . Guard Cuddity was there for his bad back," Reena said.

"Ye're terrible women altogether."

"We're terrible women altogether," Rita said, taking the pitchfork from him as the work was done.

He brushed the hay off himself and kicked the dust from the toes of his shoes while he waited for his money, a half smile on his lips.

"You'll come in for the tea?" They both said it.

"I won't . . . I'm rushed off my feet."

They began goading him then, asking him was it so that he couldn't trust himself with any woman, and especially not with gorgeous specimens like themselves.

"I'll come some Sunday when I have time."

"You'll come now . . . We can't let you go without a bit of supper," Rita said, ignoring his excuses and telling the world at large that men who live alone are right fools, don't even know how to fend for themselves.

"Friends . . . Friends," he said, raising his arms in some sort of appeal.

"We'll unchain the dog," Rita said, pointing to a gaunt mongrel at the opposite end of the yard, whining with hunger.

"Is he vicious?"

"He'd eat you," she said, and laughed, and linked him across to the house.

Low-lit candles in little clumps and a blazing fire were what met him. As he looked around they pointed to some heirlooms, jugs and vases along the dresser, a sausagey cushion of velvet to keep the draught out, and then with coquetry Rita pulled a cloth away to show him the apple pie, made with her own humble hand.

"Well?" Reena said, her eyes on him, dancing, shining, two shades of yellow in the iris, like a cat's.

"Oh, very nice," he said, and watched her take a knitting needle, warm it in the fire, and then dunk it into the wine. She whirled it a few times, took it out, the red liquid dripping off it, and held it to his nostrils.

"It mulls it," she said, winking.

Soon they had him sitting down, drinking, talking of store cattle, the risks, the way the prices changed in the marts from one week to another so that a person never knew, and milking itself going out of fashion.

"I love milking . . . It's my therapy," Rita said.

"It's your therapy," he said. He knew he should get out.

"I'm all itch, Reet."

"Why don't you change, love . . . It's the fecking hay. It gets into the pores."

In the candlelight amid bursts of laughter he saw garments being pulled off and pelted across the kitchen, a jumper, a vest, a flowered cotton skirt, which she had to peel down, nothing left but a garment that was knickers and slip. She walked across and stood before him, her breasts in the candle flame pink, pink shelled, yet with the sturdiness of gourds when she held them.

"Can you open the wee buttons?"

"What's this . . . the Black Arts?" he said, half-blasé.

"Are you afraid of us?" Rita said in his ear.

"Ah, no, he's shy . . . I love a shy man," Reena said, taking his hand in hers to undo the eight tiny mother-of-pearl buttons from the navel down.

Naked now, she begins to dance, her hair, then her head, then her torso working themselves into a frenzy, the various organza bows dropping of their own accord and the kitchen now like some den of malarkey and wantonness. Jumping onto his chair to reach for the melodeon that was above the mantelpiece, Rita has one foot on the seat of the chair and the other locked into his groin. She paused. Then his hand of its own accord went under the skirt to where she was stark naked.

"Is this an invite?" he said, the hand just resting there, feeling the cool of the flesh in contrast with the warm bush, his blood starting to pump.

"Was that nice?" she said as she took down the melodeon and sat on a wooden barrel, her legs wide apart, and began to play a rousing medley. Reena danced with abandon, using her hair as if it was some fetish, and splaying open her fingers to show vivid hennaed crevices. Almost twice she fell, then staggered, regained her balance, and eventually she threw herself upon him, her arms coming around his neck, her legs girdling his middle as she kissed him repeatedly with a repertoire of lewd and coaxing words.

He felt the other one undoing his laces, then his shoes being taken off and his socks as he dug his buttocks into the back of the chair to stop her from removing his trousers.

"What's all this?" he said.

"Two for the price of one," Rita said, and began to fumble, saying where in hell's name was that codpiece, and finding it, she measured it in her mind, then from under a vase got the ruler and measured him for fun, telling her sister not to forget it, to make a note of it for her little table of measurements in years to come.

"Give a poor man a break," he said then.

"Draw the shades, Reena dear," she said, and crossing she dragged a folded mattress from under the milk stool, unrolled it, and flung it down.

"I'm an engaged man," Bugler said, reaching for his shoes and socks.

"Bollocks . . . You rode the songstress in her father's saddle room, we heard."

Caught like that and with Rosemary coming before the summer, he feels trapped.

"Look," he began, getting earnest. "Why don't we sit and talk and have a glass of wine like good friends."

"Strut your stuff, Reen," Rita said. It was the cue for Reena to lie out on the mattress, lift her hair above her head, and then, with each and every articulation of arms, legs, and limbs, try to entice him over, the movements reflected on the wall as limbs of flame, inflammatory.

"For God's sake," he says, rising. Rita, having divested him of his trousers, is now hanging them on the kitchen clothesline next to the broderie anglaise garment. She stands back from it then with a little song.

> As I was going to the fair of Athy
> I saw an aul petticoat hanging to dry.
> I took off my drawers and hung them thereby
> To keep that aul petticoat wa-rm.

Reena is now propped with cushions and stroking a georgette scarf to add to her enticements, moving and arching, serpentine, a corpus of different pinks, all of her in a quiver and the mouth emitting little gasping sighs. He stares with a prolonged and mesmerised stare.

"Better than the lakes of Killarney," Rita says from behind his back, and pushes him forward as Reena's arms come up to lessen the thud of his fall on the thin mattress.

"Sweetheart," and she holds him a fraction above her so that she can see him seeing the gluttony that is in her eyes.

"The business," Rita says, settling herself on the barrel with her melodeon.

"His coconut's shrunk," Reena says from the floor.

"Nurture it."

"Will you clip back my hair . . . It's in my mouth."

"Good girl . . . The Resurrection and the Life."

From time to time Reena lifts her face to breathe or to arch her neck, Rita watching with a rapt attention, the accordion on her lap, half opened, with now and then random notes of stray music coming from it until the moment she feels drawn to crouch down, her voice now a repetition of urgencies — "Give it to him, Reen . . . Give it to him . . . The rich reluctant bastard. Show him who wears the trousers in this hideaway house."

❖   ❖   ❖

When he wakened it was almost light; a slit of it came through the crack in the shutters which she had drawn. He saw himself up and dressed and off out, gone, and Jesus, the mess. He would have to knock a few quid off the hay to keep them from spilling. They were sound asleep, two bodies clasped together in a mimicry of galling innocence, a strand of Rita's long hair under his elbow as he eased his way out. On the barrel the half-open melodeon, strangely obscene, the fawn semi-parted pleats as if about to start up again and jinx his getaway. He saw her eyes, narrowing, scheming, darting from his face down the length of his body and up again. It was Rita wide awake.

"What time is it?" he said as nonchalantly as he could manage.

"It's morning," she said.

"Morning," he said, and crawled out to pick his own clothes from the jumble of garments in the corner. His trousers were still hanging up.

"There's an outside tap," she said as he went towards the door, and as an afterthought she threw him a bit of torn towel.

After he'd washed, he looked up at the sky and tried to figure out what time it might be in western Australia.

"Well," he said, coming back in, his shirt sticking to his wet back.

"Well," she said in an unceasing blink.

"We'd better settle up," he said.

"Settle what! Love," she said, her voice oversmarmy.

"For the hay."

"Ah, go on with you."

"I had to buy that hay myself . . . I had none of my own. I paid dear for it."

"You'll have hay this year. Plenty of it. The fine fields you've reclaimed . . . Or stolen."

"A deal is a deal," he said, angry.

"After what we've done for you . . . Buttering your bread on both sides . . . We're not whores, mister. We're ladies."

"Ladies pay their way."

"We can give you an IOU if you want to frame it . . ." and

she turned and lifted her rear end to him, muttering, *"Pog mo hón."*

"Is that Dutch?"

"It's the local Dutch . . . Kiss my arse."

"Where's your purse, missus?"

At that she began to shout, and Reena wakens, her sleepy green eyes like mashed gooseberries as she is told to sit up and witness Mr. Mick Bugler trying to ravish her sister.

"Rape . . . Rape." She keeps repeating it as he opens the door and goes out.

Standing in the hayshed he whistles to control his temper. The bales were already cut and forked in amongst their existing little pile of hay. She had done it while he slept and had not even bothered to sweep away the scraps of coloured binding twine.

"Bitch . . . Bitches," he shouts out, going back to find the door being closed in his face.

"Give me my trousers." He hammers on the door, only to find that they have put music on to drown out his voice.

As he drove away, Rita stood in the yard, barefooted, a grey blanket over her, like some venging effigy carved out of a living clay.

"You'll be back . . . You'll be back," she kept shouting.

The morning had a jubilance, the dew melting and lifting off the hedges like a torn gauze, small birds no bigger than thimbles daft and doughty, chirping their first uneven notes, and a fruit tree in flower, the soft pink tassels tapering back and forth, forth and back, and not a stitch on his lower quarters. He drove fast to avoid the Noonan twins, who would be going to prepare the altar for first Mass, and he was out of the town and up the mountain road congratulating himself when lo, he is ambushed by the Crock, rushing forward with a leaflet in his hand.

"I cut this out for you. It's on how to make silage."

"Creep . . . Creep."

Laying the newspaper cutting on his lap, the Crock commiserated: "And the eyes of them were both opened and they knew they were naked and they sewed fig leaves to make themselves aprons."

His cackling laugh reached a bed of hot young nettles and an oak tree, where a colony of brown birds had assembled, some grooming themselves, others piping their lusts out joyously.

THE ANIMALS SLIPPED and slithered over the wet cobbles in the makeshift pen where Boscoe, the part-time helper, and Joseph had driven them. As each one was pushed forward for its injection, Joseph caught the face and wedged it between the rungs of the gate, then held it down for the vet to inject twice. Sinead, the assistant, wrote down the particulars of each animal, the tag number, the age, the breed, the sex, and the measurement of the injection. Some jumped at the prod, others took it differently, whisking their tails violently on their clotted rumps, and some relieved themselves repeatedly. Goldie tried in vain to climb over the pen, which had been constructed from old bits of wooden creel and cart ends.

"That's a lovely dog," the vet said.

"She's a no-good dog," Joseph said, and swiped at her.

As the Crock came up the road, his singing preceding him, Sinead said he had some bit of news to report. They had met him down in the village when they stopped to get petrol.

"He has something juicy."

"What?"

"He'll tell you."

"The Shepherd spent the night with the sisters." The Crock shouted it as he came around the corner of the entrance wall.

"How do you know?"

"I saw him . . . He rode up home after six . . . and the gas thing . . . he was in his birthday suit."

"Holy smoke!"

"The sisters kept his trousers as proof."

"They're demons," the vet said, and reminded Sinead of the night he was called for a sick yearling and the way they didn't want to let him go.

"I'm disappointed in him," Joseph said, looking from Breege to them and back to Breege again.

"I'm not . . . He'd go with anything in a skirt," Sinead said.

"Ah yes . . . But he's engaged to be married," Joseph said.

"Go on."

"To who?"

"A lady in Australia . . . a Rosemary."

"And you never let on," the Crock said, irked.

"He asked me not to . . . He asked me to keep it to myself."

Breege hears it and gives a little involuntary jump like some of the animals after the prod. She went quite peculiar. She felt empty. What is empty. What is full. Full is when she couldn't wait for night, when she lay down, piecing together moments, seconds, his wave from the tractor, the "Howya, Breege" and the can of mushrooms that he left on the step, small mushrooms, the pink insides, so evenly, so daintily, serrated as if a razor had slit each one, and that other time down at the pier when a lady politician in a maroon suit unveiled a plaque for the victims of the famine and Bugler had turned to her and said, "You're better looking than she is." Things. Things she had made too much of and would have to let go.

"We'll see how they take," the vet said, peeling off his plastic gloves, which Sinead refolded for him.

"We don't want any sick ones. We don't want any lumps . . . It would break me," Joseph said.

"Sure you have piles of money," the vet said, and jumped the wall, and then hoisted Sinead over to cries and giggles as to what would his wife say.

"What's wrong with you?" Joseph said scoldingly to Breege. "You're miles away, you always give these people coffee and cake."

"We'll have it when we come back," Sinead said.

"You always give them coffee and cake," Joseph repeated, even more stern.

"Ah now . . . She's probably thinking what prezzie to give Bugler . . . whether it should be an eiderdown or bed linen. Aren't you, ducks?" from the Crock.

The day would have to be got through. Then the night. Emptying. Emptiness.

B Y NOT ASKING HIM IN, Lady Harkness showed her hand. Each year Joseph had sat in her little study with its red lacquered walls, two heaters, a rug over her knees, the opened ledger, and the pen and ink ready to mark the date of the renewal. She would even pour a glass of sherry. For well on ten years he had rented the grazing of her field down by the lake, he had kept half of his herd there. It was a good field, better than mountain grass, sweeter. He used to love going down there, he used to joke to Breege about having two kingdoms, one on the mountain and one in the valley. Sometimes of a summer's evening he would sit and look out at the water, dotted with islands, reflecting and thinking that God had set him down in one of the loveliest places on earth. No more. She broke it to him snappily, said that sadly she had had a better offer for the field and had gone ahead with it.

"I'll top it," he said.

"I gave the other party my word."

"May I ask who the other party might be?"

"Mr. Bugler," she said, irked at being questioned so.

"You could at least have discussed it with me."

"This Bugler chap was so insistent, called, telephoned, so friendly."

"But you and I are friends for a long time . . . Breege comes to help you out."

"I know. I know . . . I'm just a silly old woman. All I could think of was — the roof's rotted, the greenhouse has fallen down, the tennis court is all nettles."

"You could still cancel it."

"Oh no . . . It wouldn't look good," she said, and she rose then and with a sharpness showed him out.

He was on the step when she mentioned that she would like his herd removed in the next seventy-two hours, as Mr. Bugler was anxious to take possession.

He stood in the dark grounds, made gloomier by the encircling maze of rhododendron bushes, feeling not yet the hot anger that he would feel, just a kind of wretchedness, like a child being shut out, and all of it done so skilfully, with such aplomb. He would lose on those cattle on which he had hoped to make a pile.

He passed Nelly's Bar vowing not to go in, because if he went in he would blabber. At the end of the street he met the Crock coming up with two dead hares which he was hoping to flog to the Dutch couple who ran the hotel. Soon they were in the bar, him telling it, the Crock goading him on, interjections from one or another about Lady Harkness with jewellery hanging off her, man-mad, always was. There were those who had seen Bugler go there more than once, and always at night.

"He's a thief . . . That's what he is," Joseph said.

"What will you do, Joe?"

"I'll have to sell them."

"You'll be giving them away at this time of year."

"I know. But I can't get grass. There is no grass to let and there is no hay."

"And you and he, weren't ye friends?"

"Friends! He could park the tractor whenever he wanted. He could take timber for his fire. My sister leaving eggs and cakes for him . . ."

"Ah, she's in with him . . . That's why he gave her the ride."

"What ride?"

"She went on the tractor with him. Off up the mountain."

He was still hearing them as he stood at the counter, on which two complimentary drinks awaited him; listening, feeling with a shocking calm the turbulence which had started up in him, digesting the enormity of it, her silence more telling, more significant than the venom with which they were trying to unsettle him.

He tasted one of the drinks, passed the second one back, and after a couple of mouthfuls he said, in an anxious voice, "I'll be off."

They watched him go.

"Hark, hark, the dogs do bark," the Crock said, and added, "Poor Joe, poor cuckold."

❖   ❖   ❖

Finding her out-of-doors angered Joseph even more. She was in the disused dairy sorting out a pile of shallots, their pink skins in the light of the lamp giving off a pearled glow. She looked the picture of contentment, sitting on an upturned box, the wireless on, talking to Goldie. Everything that had been insinuated became true, became fact. Blind of him not to have noticed the change in her appearance, the glow, bits of her hair held up with a tortoiseshell comb and other bits straggling down, come-hitherish.

"What's wrong?" she said, seeing his face so white, that shocked sere white of a burnt-out fuse, consternation over something and a rage with her.

"The bastard."

"Who?"

"Who! Your Shepherd went down to Lady Harkness two nights ago and rented the lake field behind my back . . . the field I have rented for fourteen years."

"Who told you?"

"She told me . . . She sent for me. I have three days to move my cattle so that his pedigree herd can be driven in . . . three days, seventy-two hours. You'll never wash her linen again."

"Calm down, Joseph."

"Is it true that you drove up the mountain with him . . . to the wild?"

"So!"

"Sat in the creel on the back of his tractor . . . like Cleopatra on her barge . . . You forgot to tell me. It slipped your memory."

"I don't have to tell you everything," she says overcalmly.

Then, as if it was to her stomach: "Was he a gentleman?"

"More of a gentleman than some."

"I expect you pointed out to him the boundaries between his lands and ours."

"I don't even know them . . . no more than you do," she said, and the sarcasm of it was too much for him.

He flew into a passion then, and he hit her once across the face, a hard, chastising stroke, like a schoolmaster's stroke, but when he saw her bare arm go up helplessly to defend herself, he drew back and looked down at his palm, constrained. It was ruddy from the stroke, the colour in his hand and his face that of two Josephs, the infuriated one and the one who felt ashamed.

"Think down the road . . . How unhappy you would be with a man like that," he said as he went out. She could hear the outside tap running as he splashed his hair and face to cool off, then she heard the van tearing out of the yard, lurching over the worn cobbles and grazing the buff pier that wobbled from so many of these hurried comings and goings.

"He hit me . . . He hit me," she said stroppily to Goldie as she began gathering up shallots that had got overturned.

But she was not stroppy inside. She was afraid. They would hunt her down, and with a bloodthirst they would take from her that lit taper of hope.

"I'll have to hide what I think, what I feel . . . the way you bury the nuts in the autumn," she said to Goldie.

I WANTED TO GO outside and let Gypsy loose and chase it up home, but I daren't. It barked and barked all night, and I could picture it on its haunches barking its guts out. It was a sparry dog, it sparred with everyone. No one knew exactly where Bugler got him, it was just there one morning in the front of the tractor, like a mascot, yapping, a mongrel, lean and with spots, so that by right he should have been called Spot, but instead Bugler christened him Gypsy. My brother hated him from the start, said he was not like a dog at all but like a hare with the ears pointed, or a little piglet ready to be roasted. The grudge my brother bore Bugler was all visited on Gypsy. He went on about how it corrupted our Goldie, made her reckless, brought her off at night. He forgot that for hours on end the two dogs lay side by side under one wall or another, depending on the sun, lay there quiet, moving only as the other moved, to bark at a car in the distance or jump up when I came out with their dinners. He said it was to teach the dog a lesson. He always referred to it as "it," not giving it the benefit of being a man or a woman. It was a he-dog, Gypsy, and it used to come at night, luring our Goldie away. They went miles off and would come back in the mornings sleepy, sated, and with blood on their mouths. Gypsy knew where to go, where to find foxes or the lambs or sheep that were wounded. Joseph put it in an empty cow stall with a sack over it to muffle the roars, holes in the sacking to keep it from expiring altogether.

All night it cried, and Goldie from the warmth in the kitchen cried back. It was the first time she had been let sleep inside, so she must have been satisfied with herself. The cries from outside got more lonely, more eerie as the night went on; they ate into me.

In the morning the tractor tore into the yard at a terrible speed, mud flying off the big wheels and Bugler already up in his seat, ready to get out.

"I want to talk to your brother."

"He's asleep," I said, calling out from the landing window.

"Get him."

"Can I talk to you?" I said.

"No, you can't," he said, savagery in the voice.

From inside I watched them argue. Joseph kept taking off his cap to scratch his head and putting it back on again. A bad sign. By mistake he put it back at a rakish angle. Then he stood up close to the tractor as if he were trying to mount it, to unseat his opponent. I could guess the language, the wrongs of years and the recent wrongs all lumped in together. All of a sudden Bugler began laughing, no doubt mocking the puniness of a man pitting himself against a machine, the half-baked idiocy of thinking that a foot in a torn felt slipper could kick in a mudguard. When Bugler got down I knew that they were squaring up to each other and that it could lead to blows. My brother turned away, went to the shed, and came back with Gypsy, whom he gripped by the forelock and flung across the yard in a vicious motion.

Coming back into the house, he ordered me to get a notebook and tot up any journeys, any errands that Bugler had done on my behalf. We would refund him. Picking up a jug of milk off the table, he went to drink from it, but put it down in disgust.

"This milk is sour . . . it's putrid," he said.

"I can't help it if the refrigerator is broken and no one will come to fix it. I can't help it."

"What did people do long ago . . . What did our mother and father do before they had refrigerators?"

"Look, I know you're cross and I know why."

"You don't know the half of it."

"We can't send him money . . . it's an insult."

"You're still soft on him," he said, glaring.

"I am not soft on him," I said in a burst of defiance, but the blushing gave me away.

When I scooped the milk out of the jug, it felt peculiar, it felt alive, like a plasma in my hand.

Hello, Breege.

THE CASTLE OF DROMORE

October winds lament around the Castle of Dromore,
Yet peace is in its lofty halls,
My loving treasure stored.
Though autumn leaves may droop and die,
A bud of spring are you.
Sing hush-a-bye, lul, lul, lo, lo, lau,
Sing hush-a-bye, lul, lul, loo.

Bring no ill wind to hinder us, my helpless babe and me —
Dread spirit of Blackwater banks, Clan Eoin's wild banshee,
And Holy Mary pitying me, in Heaven for grace doth sue,
Sing hush-a-bye, lul, lul, lo, lo, lau,
Sing hush-a-bye, lul, lul, loo.

Take time to thrive, my Rose of hope, in the garden of
    Dromore;
Take heed, young Eagle — till your wings are weathered fit
    to soar.
A little time and then our land is full of things to do.
Sing hush-a-bye, lul, lul, lo, lo, lau,
Sing hush-a-bye, lul, lul, loo.

It was left in the little plantation in an envelope.

JOSEPHINE'S HAIR SALON remains open all the year, and she prides herself on the fact that she does not just pander to summer visitors who breeze in, sit outside the hotel eating their toasted sandwiches and taking photographs.

The salon is half a terraced cottage with a concrete back yard for a coal shed and in the front window a placard of a brunette and a sample folder of nylon hairs, little switches, ranging in colour from ash blond to jet black. In that small linoleumed room with its smell of ammonia and hairspray everything gets told. Josephine is the first to know who is pregnant or who has miscarried, the first to ferret out secrets too terrible to tell. Lovers are her speciality, clandestine lovers meeting in their cars. Of Josephine, people say, "She would go down in your stomach for news." Yet they confide in her because they cannot help it. Something in her invites it, her motherly way, her soft stout arms with the healthy growth of black under the armpits, and her thin lips permanently open, as if she is drinking her listeners in. Her particular forte is that she always agrees, never contradicts, always says, "That's right . . . That's right," regardless of what she is thinking inside.

"I love when it's just us," Lady Harkness says. She says it faithfully each week as she rubs her hands to show off her bracelets, the envy of all, even Josephine, who jokes and says, "You'll leave me them in your will." Sometimes she even gives them a little kiss. Lady Harkness comes only on Thursdays to avoid the Bol-shies, and usually there is that nice girl Fiona, who has just got engaged and has wedding jitters.

As Josephine looks up and sees Breege peering through the window, she winks and says, "I'd love to get my hands on that head of hair."

Lady Harkness, although set and ready to bake under the drier, is reluctant to go because of the wonderful tips Josephine is relat-ing about weddings. They are from a special issue of a magazine for brides — Bridal Clothing, the Bridal Beauty Box, the Bridal Secrets, and the Bridal Wedding Stationery. She reads excitedly: "The latest trend is not to insist on a June wedding at all, as ho-tels, not to mention friends, will be already chock-a-block. Move from the traditional June date and the traditional white dress to something more eccentric. Become a trend-setter."

"No white dress," Lady Harkness says, aghast, and shrieks as Josephine spells out the alternative: "ice-blue satin hot pants."

"Say again."

"Ice-blue satin hot pants."

"That's diabolical," Fiona says. She has been paying £10 every Friday to a designer in Limerick and does not want to hear this hot-pants rubbish.

"There's more," Josephine says, propping the magazine as she mixes the colour for Fiona's highlights.

"There is also a definite move away from the traditional gold ring."

"Heresy," Lady Harkness says, her left ear and her left jaw poked out so as to miss nothing. One half of her face is a scalding red, the other half less so, and her scalp pained-looking from the sharp teeth of the rollers.

"What else?" Fiona asks, soured.

"Break in that new bikini afore ye go."

"How do you break in a bikini?"

"It doesn't say . . . It just says to be very careful on the honey-moon of the nasty sun glare headache, as it will spoil the fun, and also to make sure the sun gets to those two dangerous spots at the bra strap and the bikini band in order to achieve an even tan."

"Donal and I are going camping in the west . . . Hill-walking . . . We hate that sun glare," Fiona says, and closes the magazine. Breege has been standing there taking it all in.

"You're very quiet, Breege," Josephine says in her soft, over-friendly voice. She has noticed the blushes. Breege's blushes are something of a feature, being of a very rare and flaring shade of pink and seeming to wander over her cheeks in an intemperate way.

"What would you choose for your wedding day?" she asks her then.

"I haven't thought about it."

"That's because she has no interest in men," Fiona says.

It is too much for Lady Harkness, too sad altogether, and defying Josephine's strictures, she has to come out from under the drier to give Breege a little talking-to: "No interest in men . . . My darling, at your age I was never off my back. The day it happens, Breege, you'll know . . . And you must ring me up. Promise . . . Nothing in the world can stop nature. When we lived in the north of England, a local farmer had this pair of peacocks, and the male would come across to our barn because we left food and water for our own birds. He would help himself and often stay for a week at a time . . . We mentioned it to the farmer and he said, 'M'lady, come the spring the hen will want him and he'll come home,' and we said, 'How will he know that the hen wants him,' and the farmer winked. 'He'll know . . . he'll know.' It will be just like that, Breege. You'll meet the man that you have met in your dreams and you'll go all gooey. You'll melt in his arms . . . It was like that with my American lover, the other two were friendship. Pooh for friendship. You want to go all gooey . . . He was a bounder, of course, but it was worth it. A summer of absolute bliss. I always connect it with the smell of sweet pea. My bedroom windows open after lunch . . . He'd slip away from the other guests and climb up. My plumber, he called himself, my emergency plumber, and my poor Clifford downstairs playing backgammon . . . And he knew, but he loved me, he loved me so much, he always said, 'If you buy a canary you've got to let it sing.' Naughty really, but lovely."

"Lady H., I'll be needing that drier for Breege anon."

"Sorry, Jo . . . Sorry." Lady Harkness mimics the fright of a little girl and shrinks back under the glass dome, blinking ceaselessly in a feigned apology.

"So you're for the chop," Josephine says.

"I just want it washed and set."

"These ends are all broken. I can't let you out like that, no hairdresser would." Ignoring Breege's protestations, she takes the scissors and nips rapidly, the pieces like little question marks on the floor with coils of hair from early on.

"I don't want short hair," Breege says, standing up. She is almost in tears.

"Okay. Okay. So who's the lucky man?"

"There isn't."

"There is . . . I've just had one of my hunches," and skimming some of the tears onto her forefinger she walks around the salon, triumphant.

"Teardrops," she says.

"Josephine, you're beastly," Lady Harkness says.

"I'm only joking," she says, but once she has Breege captive at the backwash she pursues her quest. She hopes against hope that it is not the new technical teacher with his sloppy cardigan and his macrobiotic diet. She has come to the definite conclusion that it is someone who has recently arrived. She thinks down one side of the street, then up the other, out the two roads, the lake road, the chapel road, then her guesswork takes her up the mountain and she suddenly realises who it is, recalls all that blushing and mopiness the night of the dance and hiding in the cloakroom with Ma Flannery.

"It's the Shepherd . . . It's the Shepherd," she says to herself. She can hardly wait for lunchtime, to have her ladies combed and primped so that she can shut the shop, go into the kitchen, make herself a cup of coffee, and then sit down to ring the Crock.

Dynamite. She is not going to tell him in one swoop. He will have to guess. She will tease it out. She will give him one or two clues, then put him off his scent. It will kill him that she detected it first. It will kill him anyhow. Him always gawping after Breege and sending her that valentine and hiding behind the laurels to see her getting it from the postman, then opening it up.

"I WILL LAY a trap for her." From the moment Josephine told him, the Crock was berserk. Could it be. Ivory Mary and Micky Dazzler. Could it be. And she so modest and her long chaste white nightgown on the clothesline that he often went to and touched, imagining her wearing it at night with a candle beside her bed, and him getting in the window and scaring the bejesus out of her, lifting the gown to see her white legs and her white thighs and her furry Mary. It could be. He should have smelt a rat at Christmas time. She bought three pairs of socks in the drapery and Joseph only received two. Bugler and herself meeting at all hours, anywhere, everywhere, a spider getting into her web, hi diddle diddle, their springtime rite. The boathouse, he reckoned, would be one of their couches. Easy as pie. Bugler had reason to go down to see his pedigree herd, and she went twice monthly to the graves to cut the grass and tidy them. In the boathouse, pillowed, heave-ho; whispering levitation, a water lily stuffed into her mouth and Bugler brandlebuttocking her. Ivory Mary no more. Mary Magdalene now. "I will lay a trap for her."

IT WAS ABOUT a month in all that she lived this heightened
state, this vertigo, finding messages here, there, and everywhere to unsettle and stun her. She had a secret, a purse of
secrets.

> Peace O Queen
> I will hie me to the myrrh mountain
> To the Frankincense Hill
> You are all fair my darling
> No blemish is you
> My love is a light illuminating the shadows
> By night I thought of thee
> The utterance of thy mouth.

Her energy was prodigal. She painted windows and wainscoting,
and the hall, which had been a weeping shade of blue, was now a
silted gold.

"You have gold on the brain," Joseph said to her.

Before he wakened she was out in her little plantation, searching, reading, rereading, memorising, then tucking them into an
old purse that she hid under the laurels. The first communication
had been puzzling — "I beheld thee and." It was in capital letters
and had been left in the milk parlour beside the old churn where
she kept eggs and vegetables to keep cool. The second was on a
large sheet of paper, folded into a tight pert square. She had

found it when she went out one night to get wood and read it in the back kitchen by a faint light:

> Oh you Queen Sabbath
> Oh anointed bride.

The page was daubed from having been in a dirty pocket. She took it upstairs, read it again, thought to leave it under her pillow, but was so smitten with it that she brought it down to the kitchen where Joseph was having his supper.

"You look wild," he said, and fearing that he might see it tucked inside her blouse, she rushed over and threw it into the range. She could picture the shape and the curve of each letter, vowels and consonants, and the way the two lines ran on from one another, the only disappointment being the ink, which was faint. "Oh anointed bride." Curling now into a crescent of pale ash.

In bed she allowed herself to dwell on them. It must be Bugler. It had to be. After all, he had left the words of the song secretly like that and another morning a can of fresh mushrooms. On Saturday night when she got back from Mass she went to the dairy knowing that there would be something waiting. She had felt it when she prayed. What met her first was the smell, the pungent smell of wild thyme, something about it so suggestive, a dark green spray of it laid along the letter, perfuming the words:

> Tell me my true love
> Where do you pasture
> Where do you fold at noon
> Follow the sheep's tracks
> And graze your kids
> Close to the shepherd's huts.

That he had dared use the word shepherd was a further proof, and she walked up and down the yard to control her nerves.

That night in a dream a bird lay next to her on her pillow, its beak soft, not needly, and from its soft beak drops were squished into her ear. They were gold drops. Within the dream she heard Joseph say, "You have gold on the brain, Breege." In the morning the bird was gone. Monday she went to the village to enquire about the dress. She had seen it all summer on a hanger outside Mrs. Bolan's drapery, locals and visitors stopping to admire it. It was a black crêpe de Chine with cloth roses appliquéd throughout that from a distance looked like real roses in bloom. Only close up could one see the fine needlework, the scarlet threading shot with gold.

"You remember the black dress," she said. Mrs. Bolan remembered, raised her hands in an exclamation, and said, "Do I not."

"Is it gone?"

"Well, it was gone, and then one morning it was back on the doorstep," and shuffling off into the back, still grousing, she returned with it on its hanger, a ruff of white tissue around the collar to keep it from getting dirty.

"Wasn't it waiting for you?" she said to Breege, and holding it up estimated that two and a half inches would have to come off the bottom. Yet in the tiny fitting room she changed her mind, said it was the perfect length, as it came just to the calves of the leg, a flattering thing on a young woman. In there, both of them sneezed uncontrollably because of the bales of cretonne curtain material that were stacked against the wall.

"It's made for you," Mrs. Bolan said, adding the proverb about there being no need to gild the lily. Unlike other older people she did not begrudge young ones their style and the fancies that they got into their heads. She put her open-mindedness down to the fact that she read novels and was always pestering the librarian for another book by Tolstoy. He was her favourite because the book lasted an entire winter and she loved reading about balls and hunts and Natasha eloping in the dead of night. Seeing Breege, the face so cream-coloured with the eyes an inky black, reminded her of Natasha and of being young herself once and her husband proposing to her as they cycled down the lake road.

"What's the big occasion?" she said then.

"Oh, nothing," Breege said evasively.

"Ah, go on . . . a twenty-first or something?"

"Could I pay in instalments?" Breege said.

"Of course you can pay in instalments . . . that's what friends are for," Mrs. Bolan said, then unzipped it, helped her out of it, and in the shop folded it carefully and put it in a cardboard box, like a sleeping doll being put there to sleep. It looked so beautiful, so poised.

"And sure if you don't pay up, I know where to find you," she said, winking, as she copied in her cash-book the first deposit of five pounds, then drew a rudimentary calendar for the amounts owed for the next seven weeks.

Breege hid it in the very back of the wardrobe with coats and a bolster to keep him from seeing it. Joseph had his own wardrobe, but for some reason he kept his best suit and his overcoat in hers. After he had gone to sleep she would get out of bed and try it on. Even the roses seemed to breathe in the panel across her stomach. When Bugler saw it he would guess it was new; it smelt new.

To keep them from getting damp she changed the hiding place of the letters. She brought a biscuit tin from the house and put them in the dairy, adding each one as it came.

> To a mare among Pharaoh's cavalry.
> I compare you my darling
> Your cheeks adorned with bangles
> Your neck with beads
> Your groove a pomegranate grove.

She looked it up in Joseph's dictionary: "The pomegranate has been known to man since time immemorial; largely regarded as a symbol of fertility, possibly because of the large number of seeds contained in the fruit. The Phoenicians took it from Western Asia to Carthage." He had requested a meeting for the Sunday at two.

She chose the corner of the field that was farthest from the road. There being no wall to sit on, she piled a few stones together and made a perch of them. It was stifling. The dress was hot and so were her black stockings. She was really dressed for indoors and for nighttime. No matter where she moved to, the sun bore down. There was no shade to be found anywhere. One half of the field had been ploughed and the earth looked cross and disgruntled at being overturned. By contrast the young grass seemed to drink in the sun and gave back rays of greenish golden light. She listened, not knowing whether he would come on the tractor or on foot. What would they talk of? Not Carthage and pomegranates, not the myrrh mountain, and yet not their own mountain with its rock face and morsels of earth in the crevices. A black cat came sneaking through the grass to look at her, a miscuriosity. Black cats that were supposed to be for good luck.

After a little while she realised that he was not coming and that those letters were not in his hand at all. She felt helpless, helpless to get up though the sun beat down on one side of her neck.

❖   ❖   ❖

Joseph was dozing on the outside step when the telephone rang. He decided to let it ring, assuming it was Lady Harkness trying to coax Breege to make pies and scones for her. It stopped but then started almost at once, and he went into the house in an exasperation. There was no hesitation, simply a voice, a woman's voice overloud, overenthusiastic, saying, "You ought to know where your sister is . . . look in the dairy and you'll find out." Then there was laughter at the other end as the phone was slammed down.

Out in the dairy he knew even as he lifted the lid of the biscuit tin, knew it by the smell of the thyme, smelling its way into the letters, knew their poison. When he read the first few words, he put them down, mortified by the lewdness, the vileness, the ravishment.

He met her out on the road, but heard her footsteps before he saw her, the brazen high heels on the hot dust-baked surface. Then he saw her as he had never seen her before, a Jezebel in a clinging dress with a gash of sunburn shaped like a fish down one side of her neck. She smiled at him to brave it out, but there was no braving, as she saw by his eyes.

"You tramp."

"For God's sake, Joseph," she said, and walked past him. He walked behind her, studying the glints in her brown hair, trying to read her body by the suppleness of it and by the seam of one black stocking, which was crooked where she had redonned it in a hurry. It was like a spider crawling up her leg until it disappeared under the flounced hem of her Jezebel dress.

"**N**o better than a streetwalker," Joseph said as he backed her against the kitchen wall. She didn't answer, as there was no time.

She saw what was coming and that she was helpless to prevent it. In the sockets of his eyes rage, that mad rage that is the inverse of love. He struck her first with his hands, struck wildly and sometimes in his fury missed altogether. He laughed, bitter mirthless laughter, and challenged her to admit it, that yes, yes, she would have thrown herself at Mick Bugler, craven. His temper grew all the greater because she refused to answer. He struck her now viciously. Her confession was essential to him. If she did not admit it, it would lurk inside her, like a child, like Bugler's bastard seed to contaminate her. When she refused to answer, he picked up the nearest thing — it was a clothes brush — and with the wooden back he hit her on the face, the face which had signalled its debauch. Hearing her teeth champing off one another, she thought they were cracking, and swerving to avoid him, she fell and struck her temple on the edge of the kitchen table. In some gasp of sanity he pulled back at the sight of blood.

"Holy Jesus," he said, covering up his eyes, and she got past him and up the stairs and along the landing to her bedroom.

There was no key to the door and she stood with her back to it, feeling with her hand the blood wetting her hair and running down the side of her temple, feeling no pain at all, only the enormity of what had happened. In one hour on a sultry Sunday, a lifetime of hope and battered hope and discovery.

When she heard the car starting up, she went across to the bathroom, wrapped a towel around her head, wedged it down with an old straw hat, not once daring to look in the mirror. In the room she dragged a chair and a chest of drawers to secure the door, but knew he could break it down if he so wished. She was still sitting there when darkness came on and the cows of their own accord came into the yard waiting to be milked. There was no one to milk them, because she would not go down. Phrases of the letters came to goad her:

> Look up to the barren heights
> Is there any place where you have not been ravaged?

How could she have not suspected? How could she have believed that Bugler, so taciturn, would ever have expressed himself in that way? She cringed as she recalled the waiting, fanning herself uselessly with her own hot hand, rehearsing the first shy words, then that cat slinking through the grass, a black cat with a white paw, and her hissing at it and it staying there with a knowing, spiteful look, then running away, urgent like a messenger. A black cat that was supposed to be for good luck.

She now saw through it completely. There was the Crock who would have conspired with Josephine and others waiting to catch her out so that they could nudge one another at Mass, then rush up to her afterwards and invite her for a coffee to the hotel. Bugler would soon be told of it and they would all have a good laugh.

When he came home late, she shouted out the window that cows were waiting to be milked. Later he turned the knob of her door several times and then went off to bed, desperate. He was up early, earlier than usual, and he left the first mug of tea outside the door, then another and still another, telling her that they were going cold. She knew by his abject voice that he was sorry. Never once in all their childhood or youth had he touched her. The opposite. When she cut her fingers once on a razor blade that was wedged into the top shelf of the dresser, he put them in his mouth to spare her the terror of the lively spurting blood. So many little memories came to her, the pair of them swinging on a gate on a summer's evening, hoping for visitors, going down to the river-bank to find sorrel, talking to each other from their twin beds at night, his telling her how he was her knight and would defend her against all. When each of her parents died, it was he who broke it to her, said they were gone up to heaven and looking down. She was ten and eleven then.

By evening she felt strong enough to go down. The stove was piping hot and the table laid: signs of clemency. Taking one look at her bruises, like the purple of pansies, he flinched and idioti-cally began to hum. Fear had come into the house and with fear comes falsity.

"Do you need a doctor?" he said, mortified.

"For what?!" she replied, and by her intimation he did not have to ask any further. He searched in the drawer then for painkillers and put them beside her plate. They ate in silence. It was cooked ham and pickles that were oversour.

Even before she went to the dairy she knew that the letters would be gone. The biscuit tin was gapingly empty, the lid thrown to one side, the bunch of thyme on the floor dirty and trodden upon. It was as if bandits had been. She sat, then, for a long time among the cobwebbed mantles and talked to herself. She was telling herself that if she could live through it, allowing each and every second of it to go inside, the expectancy, the lu-nacy, the bitter fall, that then she would feel it to the marrow of her being and she would be able to bear it and the hurt of it would be hers and hers alone. It was like staring at the rock face of the mountain, its greyness, its sheerness, its cold despair going behind the eyelids, behind the eyes, into self so that self and rock face were one, hope and stone, stone hopes to kill any lingering memories of Bugler.

❖　　❖　　❖

A week later his hired hand, Boscoe, and himself went to the City Mart and he came home with a gift. It was a leather handbag, the clasp a thick knob of amber with streaks of light running inside it like sun rays. There were pockets for her keys, her comb, her money, and her flapjack, as he said.

"Miss Carruthers chose it," he said, and because it was made in Genoa he looked up the name in the encyclopaedia and read out its characteristics, the population, the climate, and the special attractions for a visitor to that city.

She was standing in the middle of the kitchen floor, the long corded strap dangling from her wrist.

"You can go to him if you want," he said bashfully.

"I'm not going anywhere," she said, quite crisp. She had missed Mass for two Sundays, and when she heard the tractor coming or going she bolted and hid behind a wall.

I T WAS IN Nelly's Bar that Joseph and Bugler finally came face to face. They had exchanged heated words up by a dumper and again at the garage when Bugler tried to return a cheque which Joseph had sent him. But it was in Nelly's Bar, with its artefacts, its old stone crocks, and its three china sleeping dolls, that Bugler would confront him and make a mockery of him. Nelly watched it all, half smiling, presiding as she did behind the counter in her cardigan and her knitted cap skewered with a big hatpin.

"Is this your dirty work, Brennan?" Bugler asked, and tossed the newspaper cutting down the length of the bar. He merely cited the odd word from it. He did not read it in full, as there was no need. People had already read it when it appeared in the parish journal and was signed "Anonymous." Everyone knew it was Bugler because of the references to the bearded one who came like a thief in the night. There were guffaws as Bugler read out the fancy quotations — "the arrow that flieth by day or the plague that walketh in the dark" — and joking objections about the eagle with divers feathers.

"Were you trying to say something to me?" Bugler said, strolling down the bar to where Joseph sat.

"If the cap fits, wear it," Joseph said, refusing to look up.

"Afraid to fight me?" Bugler said.

"Easy now, Mick . . . easy. He has a short fuse," someone said.

"You call me a scorpion . . . so what does that make you?" Bugler asked, then added jocularly, "A snake. We are talking biblical, aren't we?"

"Hit him, Joe . . . hit him."

"He hasn't the guts . . . Joe Chicken," Bugler said, and then standing above him, he swore at him. "Get off my back, Brennan."

"Get off my mountain," Joseph said.

"It's my mountain too . . . it's halved."

"Your half is only yours because your people worked for the landlords. They were bailiffs. They were hated. That's why most of them emigrated . . ."

"Well, one of them is back," Bugler said, taking him by the lapel and jerking him up. He struck him then, not a hard blow, more a gesture of vindication and disdain, and taken so by surprise, Joseph stumbled and hit blindly, aiming at the torso, and soon they were pegging into one another, chairs kicked back, people standing to one side, calling for it to stop, yet no one intervening, because that would mean thwarting the pride of one or the other. It didn't seem very dangerous, just a skirmish between two men who were born enemies and no worse than any brawl in the street in the small hours of a Saturday night. When Joseph fell backwards there was alarm. Grabbing hold of the counter to get up, he touched on a tray of glasses which came crashing to the floor, broken pieces of glass scattered everywhere. As he stood up they saw that he was holding a thick shard and all was commotion then as a few of the men ringed around him appealing to him to put it down and Nelly telling Caimin, the young barman, to fly up the street to get a guard. Coming outside the counter she crossed and spoke to Bugler, who deferred to her and, picking up his hat, went out.

The aftermath became as rowdy as the brawl itself, with people reconstructing it, saying how quick it had been, how sudden and how close it got to becoming nasty. Joseph was brought to the fire, shaken, a thin rivulet of blood running down his neck, and women asking him if he was all right. Caimin, who was disappointed at the fact that it had ended so abruptly, began to describe it to the guard: the two types of punches, one an amateur and one a pro, with Bugler having the upper hand from the start, the macho, the know-how.

"Joe gave as good as he got," one of the men said.

"Don't be daft . . . He was nowhere near," Caimin said, and taking the clipping from the floor, he asked Nelly if they could frame it and hang it as a souvenir of the night middleweight Brennan lost to the champion Bugler.

"Don't mind him, Joseph . . . he raves," Miss Carruthers kept saying. As new people came into the bar they were told different versions as to who started the fight, whose fault it was, who lost and who won. Nelly sat furious, ruing the stone jar that got knocked from a shelf and her dried flowers that were like hen meal over the floor. People pressed drinks on each other. Glasses of porter, three-quarters filled, stood like trophies on the counter, the fawn gouts of foam dimpling softly and subsiding into the yeasty brew. Joseph sat silently but with an expression of furious dismay in his eyes at the way he was being belittled.

"Bugler is a rat . . . An out-and-out rat," one said to console him.

"I won't allow that," Nelly said sharply.

"That's because he got you a gander for your goose."

"So he did," she said, reddening.

"And where did he get it . . . He stole it out of someone's farmyard."

"He's a bad neighbour. He's lethal," Joseph said, for all to hear.

"So are you . . . After what you did to his dog . . . It was a lethal thing to lock him up," Caimin said.

"His dog kept coming every night to bring our Goldie off to the woods . . . corrupting her."

"Like his master," Caimin said, egging him on now.

"What's that supposed to mean?"

"Your sister . . . She meets him in the woods. Their love nest . . ."

Joseph rose then and with a ludicrous sense of his own powers began to hit at Caimin, who egged him along, repeating the taunt, mentioning the part of the wood, the rug flung down beside the tractor, and presently they were locked in a fresh fight, with Caimin easily scoring, and for the second time in the one evening Joseph was seen tumbling backwards, except this time the trapdoor down to the cellar had been opened as crates of beer were carted up. He vanished before their eyes, down into a well, a darkness from which came the thud of his fall and then a dreadful silence.

"Sweet Jesus," Miss Carruthers said as Caimin, pleased at his heroics, shinned down the thin rope, and after what seemed an age he shouted back up, "He'll live."

There was laughter then and jokes about so much diversion in one night, enough to fill ten columns, the gallant story of swash and buckle in Nelly's Bar on an otherwise lacklustre winter night.

IT WAS AZIZ'S night to be with Breege. Once a fortnight his father or a neighbour dropped him off and he came racing down the steps with his satchel and his tin box, which contained his medicines in case he got his little convulsions. She had found him some years before at the gymkhana, separated from all the other children, hiding behind a barrel because he was scared of runaway horses. As always, he stood in the middle of the kitchen, too shy to run to her and hug her skirt, the way he had when he was younger.

"I was expecting you two Fridays ago." To that he hung his head, which indicated that mother and father were quarrelling again and he had to stay at home to keep them from getting a divorce.

"I have a new trick," he said, taking out his prized pack of cards and flicking them with great dexterity. She was to pick a card while he closed his eyes, then return it to the pack, where he would magically find it. When he picked the wrong card he laughed, his laughter feeding in on itself, a husky laugh which she loved and which for no reason at all she sometimes heard in the empty kitchen like a bell or a chime starting up of its own accord.

"And now, ladies and gentlemen," he said, bowing and launching into his aria. It was in Italian, his tongue too thin for the cumbersome words and his making up for it with exaggerated gesture and an anguished swoon over a maiden long in dying. Then it was permission to lift the muslin cloth, to see what dainties she had made for him. They were iced buns with glacé cherries, and with his forefinger he touched the soft icing, bruised a few grains, and put them delicately to his lips.

"I know what I'm going to get you when I'm big," he said.

"What?"

"An emerald."

"An emerald!"

"Fionnula has emerald hair."

"Who's Fionnula?"

From his bag he took out a schoolbook which he had neatly covered with brown paper and began to read from it.

> Our stepmother has changed us into four swans, Fionnula continued, and she put a spell on us so that we would remain in the shape of birds for nine hundred years. We had to spend the first three hundred years on a lake at Derravaragh, the second three hundred years in the icy waters of the straits of Moyle, and the third three hundred years on the island of Innisglora off the West Coast. However, though Aiofe, our stepmother, could rob us of our human form she could not take our voices away. We learned many things but most of all we learned to sing and soon our music and songs became known the length and breadth of Bamba. Those who came to see us would say that we were not ordinary birds because we could speak and because we could sing.

Closing the book he waited for the applause and joined in with it himself.

"And guess what?"

"What?"

"The stepmother was found out because the king asked for the mirror of truth and she couldn't lie to that, and guess what else: our arithmetic teacher is having an affair with our arts teacher, they kissed in the toilets."

"An affair," Breege says.

"I'm a chatterbox."

"Chatterbox," she says, and squeezes his cheek. She loves his visits, she loves him, his skin the red brown of polished apples and his eyes identical to his mother's eyes: big, sad, brown eyes with the yearn of Damascus in them. His mother sometimes pined for home, her sisters, musk and amber, cooking spices and silken shawls, threatening to leave and bring him with her. That was when he got his fits, because he wanted his mother and father to stay together for ever.

They had had their supper when Joseph came in, his coat sleeve pulled way down over his hand.

"What's up?"

"Nothing's up . . . Why do women always think there's something up?" he said vexedly to Aziz.

"Uncle Joe . . . Uncle Joe." Aziz ran to him, but was pushed aside as he crossed to the stove and took out his handkerchief, which was bunched up.

"God Almighty . . . There's blood on it," Breege said, crossing over to make sure.

"He wanted to fight, your friend Bugler . . . He drew at me in Nelly's Bar. Ask anyone. How could I not fight him . . . I couldn't look myself in the eye again. Or you."

"How did it end?"

"Bad," he said, and he stuffed the handkerchief into the fire. Then he switched out the light and they sat in the dark kitchen, the shadow of the flames leaping on the kitchen wall, Aziz on her lap, scared, his stockinged toes curling and uncurling, the handkerchief burning, Bugler's blood burning, a scorching smell and then a gasp from each as they heard a car stop outside.

"I'm denying everything . . . and so are you," Joseph said, afraid.

They waited and then heard the car go on, and thinking it was Bugler, Breege said, "That must be him now . . . Going on up home."

"Thanks be to God," Joseph said, and then he fell to his knees and in the dark began to pray aloud: "I beseech thee, most sweet Lord Jesus Christ, grant that thy passion may be to me a power by which I may be strengthened, protected, and defended. May thy wounds be to me food and drink, by which I may be nourished, inebriated, and overjoyed."

"What's wrong with Uncle Joe?" Aziz whispered, and began to shake the way he did prior to his fits.

GUARD SLATTERY PACED as he read out part of the statement which he had typed for the third time. He was proud of how smart he had been, smart and cute, getting Joe Brennan to talk, to rave, stitching himself up until there was no retreat. He was proud of how he pounced on him while he waited in line at the creamery for his tankard of milk to be taken in, walking up to him quite casual, saying, "We have a complaint that you assaulted a man," Brennan denying it at first, saying, "You have the wrong man," and then conceding and saying, "It was to teach him a lesson." It was a breeze from then on, just a question of convincing him that he was better off coming down to the barracks and making a statement because denying it was absurd, too many people knew. Going in the barrack door he recalled how Brennan stalled and tried to back out of it and how he had to push him in, telling him he was more likely to get off if he pleaded guilty. They had chatted about this and that to get him in a relatively relaxed mood, and eventually he babbled.

"On the night of the eleventh instant I was in Nelly's Bar, where I had two hot whiskies for a cold. Mick Bugler came in and goaded me. Earlier he tried and failed to return a cheque to me which I had sent him in the post for work he did. He removed stones from the pasture, but I didn't want any charity from him, which is why I had sent him a cheque. He threw it back at me. In the pub one word led to another and we had a scuffle, where I incurred a cut down my neck. People stopped the fight and Bugler left. I left soon after and got into my van to drive home. I had no intention of seeking him out. All I wanted was to be up home and in bed. At Lyon's Cross there was a car in front of me letting somebody out. I knew this car to be Bugler's. It was a girl, a woman, he was letting out and he took his time over it. She climbed the gate and up the hill towards the Glebe House, where there are squatters. I'd given him plenty of time. I then blew the horn a good few times and still he didn't move. He opened the door and shouted back at me and told me to 'fuck off.' He then closed the door and stayed where he was on the road. I blew the horn a few more times. I then got out and went over to his car. I opened the driver's door and started punching him with my right fist. I suppose I was mad at the time. I then went and took a stone off the wall . . ."

❈   ❈   ❈

He put it aside then until he had some lunch to tickle the brain cells. He was imagining himself standing up in the court for the first time in his life giving such professional evidence. On the table beside him were the various exhibits which he had taken from the scene — a bottle of Lourdes water, dirty swabs of cotton wool with which he had soaked up the bloodstains on the ground, loose money that had fallen out of Bugler's pocket, various stones, and the one big stone, the big fella, covered in bits of vegetation and dried blood. In a neat hand he began to label each one.

❈   ❈   ❈

The morning the summons came Joseph decided to hide it for the time being.

THE CIRCUIT COURT

Michael Bugler
Plaintiff

and

Joseph Brennan
Defendant

You are hereby required, within ten days after the service of this Civil Bill upon you, to enter, or cause to be entered with the County Registrar at his Office at the Court House, an appearance to answer the claim of Michael Bugler.

And take notice that unless you do enter an appearance you will be held to have admitted the said claim and that Plaintiff may proceed therein and judgement may be given against you in your absence without further notice.

THERE WERE TWO solicitors in the village, O'Dea, a local, and a Mr. Leveau, who came from the city and took his lunch in the hotel before going to his rooms. As soon as Joseph sat with him he realised his mistake. The long, uninterrupted flow of speech was addling him.

"Now, we could be dealing here with a known symptom, the inferiority of the returned exile . . . not a native son . . . a bit of an outsider. It may not be visible to a lay person, but dealing as I do with human nature in all its vacillations, I pride myself on recognising the symptoms of your Mr. Bugler. Estrangement I call it. It is not the diaspora as such. Diaspora has more of a global connotation, a mass feeling prevalent among those who, though they have never met, know themselves to be aliens in an alien land. Estrangement occurs in the mind. Are you with me? This Mr. Bugler might have had some hard knocks, snubs, hardships, call it what you will. A sheep farm in Australia, or for that matter in Timbuktu, is a dive, a rough place, totally uncivilised. A bachelor life into the bargain. Slights, insults, other races calling him a Paddy or a Mick. Poles, Swedes, Germans, somehow, they all see themselves as being that little bit superior to Paddy and to Mick. Couple these sneers, these taunts, with a bachelor existence and you arrive at a bit of a complex. Add to it the lonely sheep station, a few dogs for friends, some boozing on a Saturday night, and you arrive at a displacement, by which I mean the longing for home. Are you with me? The irony is that this mythic home means more than it might to you or to me. We know who we are. To a man like him, faraway hills look green. There would be no actual memories in his childhood. It would be a question of stories around a fire, recitations, Mother Macree *ad nauseam.* Voyeuristic if you will, but memories all the same. No roots. The need for the root becomes the grail. And of course, of course, he never dreamed that it would become real, that he would actually inherit a farm and a shack. His fantasy converted into fact." He thought for a moment, removed his spectacles, wiped them with a chamois, and said it was not the first time he had had to deal with such a case, the overweening ambition of the returned exile, and then he felt it his duty to spare a word for Bugler's uncle, who had died so tragically, said no farmer with any sense would go into a field with a bull, even his own bull.

"What do you think will happen to me . . . what's the worst that will happen to me?" Joseph asked.

"My dear man . . . not so fast. I'm trying to paint you a picture of the psychology. Bugler is summoned home because of a tragedy . . . He gets a letter off over in Australia. He's told about his inheritance and he has to make a choice whether to engage an auctioneer to sell it or to come home and make a fist of things. I have to say that I do have a sneaking admiration for the way he has set about it single-handed . . . reclaiming whole areas of marsh, I understand."

"He'd like to take me over."

"But you did hit him . . . that is a plain and incontrovertible fact."

"I did."

"And you've given your statement to the Garda."

"I had to . . . They wrung it out of me . . . that young guard."

"So my task is how to play it to the judge."

"Will he fine me . . . or will I go to gaol, which?"

"That reminds me of a little story. In the district court a few mornings ago two motorists are down for speeding, a lady and a gent. The gent, who had only been doing ninety miles per hour, is fined two hundred pounds, and the lady, who had been doing one hundred and ten miles per hour but had flashing eyes, gets off with a caution, because she flattered His Honour."

"I'll think it over," Joseph said, rising, perspiring.

"I know what you're thinking, Mr. Brennan . . . You're think-ing that you would be better off with Mr. O'Dea up the street. Mr. O'Dea, who trebles as undertaker, cattle jobber, and man at the Bar . . . he's more your cup of tea."

"I'll think it over."

"That will be twenty-five guineas," Mr. Leveau said, and he stood by the oil heater, warming his hands, a frigid smile on his face as he watched Joseph take out the notes, eventually having to search in his pocket for shillings and sixpences, to make up the required sum.

H OSTS OF SEAGULLS circled at different altitudes, their long-drawn-out wails spiteful, as if one batch cried back to outdo another. Their shrillness coming down out of the whey-green cavity of sky onto the court building and onto the groups bunched up in coats and anoraks, summoned from their fields and their holdings, into a kingdom of judgement. The cries of the seagulls more raucous far than the crows at Cloontha.

"Dominus illuminatio," Joseph said as he stood in the path and looked at the sprawling stone building with small blind panes of glass in the several windows, its vestibule pillars flaking.

To one side was a grotto made of thick knobbled stones, the white plaster Virgin, with both arms outstretched, giving audience to a kneeling girl. Breege thought that maybe it was erected there to encourage people to put aside their enmity and quash their cases. O'Dea confided to her that often cases were quashed just prior to being heard, people sobered up once they saw the gravity of things. O'Dea was her ally now, imploring her to talk sense to her cracked brother with his Greeks and Red Branch knights.

In there in those stale rooms, in the biding dust, lay all the wrongs and all the rights, worn ledgers with the backs scarred, their edges frail and frayed, yellowing page following yellowing page, histories long forgotten.

From the branches of a big tree soft damp blobs of ice fell on their heads, and she knotted her scarf tight, then pulled it tight down over her face so as not to be seen. The scarf was of georgette and smelt of camphor. It had been her mother's. From the corner of her eye she searched for Bugler's frame, Bugler's shadow, her heart in jeopardy.

"You shouldn't have drunk," she said.

"Two Sandemans," Joseph said, and challenged her to make him walk a straight line on the edge of the steps.

"Three Sandemans," she said. The knot of the scarf hurt her swallow.

There was much commotion around the entrance door, people running this way and that, beckoning to each other, the barristers with a sort of suave ascendancy, strands of their wigs flying, giddily, like a young girl's.

"There's still time, Joseph," she said, squeezing his arm.

"I'm no Joe Chicken," he said, separating himself from her.

Inside it was quite dark and dingy, a tiled floor of oxblood red, with some tiles missing and windows grimed with dust and cobweb. People huddled in groups, most of them smoking and talking to each other in very low voices with expressions of doom. All of the wigs cried out for washing and combing. Two men in almost identical pullovers looked as if they were bracing for a fight as they paced and muttered oaths to each other.

"He trains lions," O'Dea said, pointing to one and then pointing to the other, "He also trains lions, for a different circus," then turning to Joseph remarked on his being like a boiled egg in a pot, hopping up and down. The moment the doors were opened people filed in.

It was cold as an outhouse. Green walls oozing a darker green damp and the wooden benches full of marks and scrawls like the counter of a public house. A young man in handcuffs with two guards on either side of him, already seated, kept staring at nothing, his eyes like hot coals.

At that instant Bugler came in and sat directly across from them. He had had a haircut, and his beard and his sideburns were trimmed. He sat looking down at his hands as if he was reading something on his lap, and as often with him, his real life seemed to be running on inside him and outside things seemed of no consequence at all. Breege thought he had never looked so handsome or so lean. Behind him eight or nine guards sat very close together with an air of stiffness, the brass buckles of their belts brazen as weapons in the sere light that dropped down from a skylight window.

The judge seemed in a very irritable mood, tapping his fingers at the inanities that were being said to him. From time to time he lifted his wig, scratched his head vigorously, then glancing down at the witness in the box, he wagged his finger and spoke rebukingly: "Moving cattle when you shouldn't and where you shouldn't is an offence . . . The Brehon laws are out, finished."

"Yes, your honour."

"Adjacent lands, even on a godforsaken mountain, are not your own lands."

"Yes, your honour."

"Is that your defence?"

"I won't do it again . . . It was just a prank."

"If you do it again you'll be in gaol for your prank."

"And no one in the whole wide world wants to be in one of those places. Dungeons."

"My dear man, cut out your philosophics and corral your cattle."

"Your honour . . . I know you're a family man, as I am myself . . . To leave wife and child would be a bitter blow."

"Family man," Judge Dalton said, unable to repress a smile.

True they had a large house, a garden with azaleas, cups on the mantelpiece from his hunting days, but he saw as little of wife and boy as possible. Boy, mammy's boy, already twenty-one and still considering a career. Mammy topped his eggs in the morning and asked if he had a nice sleep and nice dreams. Although retired from the chase, he was still welcome at the several dos, and life could be said to be tolerable except for the gout. Each day after sitting listening to these drones, he drove to the hotel and stayed there until he was sure that mammy and mammy's boy were habu in their beds. The conjugal duties, frozen in an era that seemed as distant as the Flood, had left him a disenchanted man.

Either his virginity or Agatha's intercession to saints and blessed martyrs marked that night in that hotel room as a complete fiasco. That and the damage to Agatha's insides when mammy's boy was born. Whiskey doubled as wife and rarely did he lose his grip on the wheel. The few times that he was caught out and pulled in off the road ended happily. Ergo, a guard recognised him and either apologised or offered to drive him home. Scientifically speaking, he would describe his heart as resembling a bit of gizzard and his lower region as pickled in a similar solution in which onions and gherkins are pickled. A successful man, oh yes, a Rotarian, their first house replaced with a bigger house and still a bigger one as he progressed and buttressed his income with livestock and show horses. They were asked to lunches and dinners, met other judges, high commissioners, diplomats, receptions where Agatha was extravagant in the praise of the dresses and jewels of the other ladies, tugging at their sleeves and bemoaning her own humble wardrobe. She reckoned that these strange women had lovely houses with big clocks and antiques and bone china on their breakfast trays.

"You're talking tosh," he shouts to the farmer who has now resorted to the time-honoured subject of moiety.

"Moiety . . . What does it mean?"

"I'm not fully able to answer that, your honour, except to say that the mountain where I drove my cattle is mine as much as his. It's commonage."

"I'm fining you one hundred pounds, and I don't want to see you back in this court again."

"God bless your honour."

There was a sudden moment of consternation as the man in the handcuffs decided to free himself and dragged his captors down some steps, followed by two of the three reporters.

Scanning his list the chief clerk decided to change the order of things. Breege hears Joseph's name and Bugler's name being called out and sees Bugler walk up to the witness box, calmly. Having sworn on the Bible, he spoke of a friendship which turned sour after he rented the grazing of some lands which the defendant used to rent. Prior to that, they were, as he said, friends and neighbours, they shot woodcock together, helped each other on the farm, he being available to do things with his tractor, cutting timber and removing stones from a field, something the defendant had welcomed. What he minded most was not the assault but the hurt to his dog Gypsy, who had been locked in a shed for three days while he was away in the city on business.

"He's a no-good dog . . . He was driving our Goldie astray," Joseph was heard to shout as local guards glared across at him to shut up and the clerk called for order. When Bugler had finished, the judge thanked him for being such a reliable witness who did not waste his words.

Next it was the turn of the guards and the witnesses. The court heard of bruising, lacerations, abrasions, fractures, and stitches. The woman who had taken Bugler in surpassed herself with a detailed description of the night in question.

"I am the wife of Malachi O'Byrne. We came to this parish less than a year ago to breed ponies for pony trekking in the summer. Our clients are mostly foreign and we don't mix much. On the evening of the eleventh instant it was late and I was trying to get my daughter Patricia to go up to bed. My husband was off on a job. Next thing the dog began to bark like mad, and I opened the door to see what was wrong. The fright I got. Patricia began to scream, she thought it was the pookah man. He was covered in blood, soaking wet, and I thought he was going to have a heart attack. I had no choice but to bring him into the house and sit him down. I called the barracks. Guard Slattery came in very good time. I learned then who the injured man was. I had never seen him before. He was very shook."

Having given her evidence, she looked, waited, was told she could go back to her seat, and before doing it took the opportunity to bow to the three sides of the court.

The attention quickened once Guard Slattery began to speak. At last they were going to hear Joseph's side of things. The guard read very slowly, allowing them to imagine he was Joseph; even his accent had thickened that little bit.

"I remember the night of the eleventh instant. Mick Bugler and myself were in Nelly's Bar, though not drinking together. We had words and a scuffle broke out which was quickly quashed. I left Nelly's at about ten o'clock and got into my van, which was parked nearby. Just after Lyon's Cross there was a car stopped letting somebody out. I knew this car to be Mick Bugler's. I gave him plenty of time to let the person out, it was a woman, a ladyfriend. I then blew the horn a good few times, and still he did not move. He opened the door and shouted back at me and told me to eff off. He then closed the car door and stayed where he was on the road. I blew the horn several more times. I then got out and went over to his car. I opened the driver's door and started punching him with my right fist. That is how I got the bruise and the mark on my knuckles. I was going to leave him alone, but he got nasty and started calling me things. I then went over to the wall and picked up a stone. I went back to the car and hit him with the stone across the face as he was sitting in the car. There was blood on my hand at this stage. When he got out I punched him under the jaw until he fell back. I kept hitting him with the stone as hard as I could on the face and on the head. While he was on the ground I gave him a good few kicks, anywhere and everywhere."

It was too much for Joseph, hearing this exaggerated, trumped-up version of what he had said in his statement, and though he had sworn to Breege and to O'Dea that he would not go in the box, he had sprung up now, full of vindication. All of a sudden there was excitement, people craning to hear and to see, the sisters on the edges of their seats, Rita saying to Reena that the acoustics were fecking deadly. From the sway of Joseph's back Breege knew that he was going to disgrace himself.

"It's concocted evidence."

"You mean you did not assault that unfortunate man on the night of the eleventh instant at about 10:35?"

"He asked for it . . . Handing me back a cheque in front of everyone . . . 'I return your cheque uncashed.' "

"Apparently it was not enough . . . He lifted stones with his machine, he harrowed and seeded your field to grow turnips . . ."

"The seeds were mine, they were my seeds. All he did was lift the stones and spread manure on the field."

"That was a lot of work."

"He owed it to me . . . He parked his tractor in our yard. He could take timber whenever he wanted. My sister spoilt him with cakes and things."

"Let us keep to the point . . . He harrowed your field."

"He dragged a bush over it."

"Mr. Brennan, do you deny that all was palsy-walsy between you until he rented the grazing of certain lands?"

"He stole them."

"You seem to have a grudge against this man."

"His tractor is driving us mad . . . At all hours. Droning . . . Droning. It's destroying the hedges. It's stopping the birds singing. They don't sing so sweetly any more . . . As for the roads . . . they were not made for a machine like that. He's wearing them down."

"You speak as though the roads were yours."

"They're more mine than his . . . My family were the first in Cloontha. We've been there for ever . . . His were Buglers from Wales. They followed the soldiers playing bugles . . . That's why people call them buglers, in case you didn't know."

Breege turned to this one and that, her face full of apprehension, fear in her eyes. O'Dea had been called out, and the only one to meet her gaze was Guard Slattery, who looked at her, peeved. Bugler sat stiffly with his head down.

"Is his dog Welsh?" the judge asked, with a note of mockery which was lost on Joseph.

"He's a nothing dog . . . A mongrel. I would never pick a male dog. I always pick bitches . . . They're more intelligent. They have a protrusion on the crown of the head that proves it."

"My, my, you are a scholar."

"I try, your honour."

"You could have settled this row, you could have gone up to your neighbour or met him somewhere and said, 'Let's shake on it,' you could have atoned."

"Not if you paid me. Not for all the wealth that freighted into Orchomenus even into Thebes, Egyptian Thebes."

"A scholar?"

"The Greeks, your honour," and feeling now that the judge was partial to this erudition, he began to spout, regardless of the laughter that was beginning to splutter out from the visitors' seats.

"Zeus, King, give me revenge . . ."

"You have lost me."

"The husband of Helen getting his own back on Paris . . ."

"Why are you wasting my time. What is a small farmer like you doing spouting this rubbish. You're a bog-trotter."

"You're an ignorant man, if I may say so."

"Do I hear correctly?" the judge asked, and his colour was beginning to change.

"Making little of me just because you're up there . . . A jumped-up grocer's son . . . I've looked you up in the records."

The judge's face reddened, purpled as he half rose from his seat. At that moment, O'Dea ran from the doorway towards the bench waving his hand with a pen in it. "Your honour, I wish to apologise."

"I have rarely seen a more reckless witness."

"Correct. But, your honour, imagine having to defend a man like that . . . Just put yourself in my shoes."

"Your client is drunk."

"Not really drunk, your honour. Maybe he had one or two."

"Do you expect me to fall for that?"

"I am begging you to hold your fire . . . I mean, take the chastised Picasso."

"Picasso," the judge said, and looked around as if he was in the company of raving inmates.

"Yes, Picasso. He painted a lot of doves in the last year of his life, but because he was a Communist the public would not buy his doves. Even the Kremlin refused."

"Mr. O'Dea, I am not getting your drift."

"Your honour, people can change . . . Picasso changed. My client could, as you put it, atone for what he did."

"He's a head case."

"He didn't mean it . . . It's in the genes. The family were all the same. A kink . . . The mother used to walk the roads in the moonlight . . . Up and down."

It was too much for Joseph. He rose now, kicked and stomped with his new boots, shouting out that his mother was a lady to whom present company could not hold a candle.

The judge rose, his voice quaking with anger, his jaw bull-like and booming out the sentence as his fist hit the bench with the force of a gavel: "I am sending you for fourteen days to Limerick County Gaol."

"Your honour," O'Dea begged.

"Contempt of court and contempt of person."

"It's Christmas, your honour . . . It'll break hearts."

"Court adjourned," the judge said, and hurried behind a folding screen with the clerk following and picking up documents which were strewn in his wake. The bit of floor which his gown had swept clean emphasised the biding dust on either side.

"In Jesus' name, Joseph," O'Dea said, making a gross and violent swipe at the reporters who had converged around them.

"He rubbed me the wrong way," Joseph said.

"You blew it . . . Zeus, Thebes. Feck."

Bugler was standing and looking across at them as if he might come over. Breege, still sitting, kept her head down.

"Will he go to gaol?" she asked, like someone coming awake from anaesthesia.

"I'll go down to the hotel and see if I can get a word with the judge."

"I don't want his blasted pity," Joseph said.

"Muzzle him," O'Dea said, hurrying off, biting his pen as if it were a liquorice stick.

By the time they came out, everyone had gone, including Bugler. The grounds were deserted, only the seagulls stormed the sky, which was now packed with thick muttony cloud. It was a busy town, people hurrying to lunch and blowing their hooters, either in friendly or vindictive fashion. They began to walk. They were together and not together. She knew that if she spoke a single word he would explode right there in front of people. When he stopped to look at something she walked on, and when she stopped he did the same. From the cake shops there was a smell of warm bread and the meringues in the window were spewing apart, their insides a frail pink. In the butcher's shop window prices of the different cuts of beef and mutton were chalked up and a little row of toy lambs was placed along the sill. From a loudspeaker a man kept urging people to give blood and gave the location of the caravan beside the monument at the top of the town. A shop window full of new shirts had ties done up around them.

In the chapel he stood beside her and she could feel his agitation. Behind the sconce of lit candles and spluttery flame there was a prayer printed in red and gold ornamental lettering:

> May this candle be a light for you to enlighten me in my difficulties and decisions.
> May it be a fire for you to burn out of me all pride, selfishness, and impurity.
> May it be a flame to bring warmth into my heart towards my family, my neighbours, and all those in need.
> I cannot stay for long, but I wish to give you something of myself.
> Help me to continue my prayer.

They walked through side streets, then a tiny alley that led them down to the river. On the solid stone bridge there were hanging baskets with moss and flowers, their metal braziers thudding back and forth. The water was a dark brown, and just beneath it, lifelike torsos of seaweed that moved and slithered like belly dancers. A woman with two small children was also studying the water, telling her children how it was full of bugs and worms for the fish to feed on.

"We better not be late," Breege says.

"If I go to gaol, who'll mind you?"

"We better not be late," she says again.

He looks at her, his face chastened, his blue eyes watery behind his fogged lenses, and she realises that he has been crying.

O'Dea was waiting for them on the steps. By the way he waved and his satisfied smile they knew something had changed.

"You're a lucky man . . . Bugler has decided to drop the case."

"Now why would he do a thing like that?"

"Jesus wept . . . You should be down on your knees," O'Dea said; then, taking Breege's arm, linked her jauntily down the steep, imposing flight of steps.

THROUGH THE LONG drizzling afternoon and evening they sat, light rain on the courtyard outside dropping onto the tubs of ivy with floodlights stuck in among them, and as it grew darker neon strips came on in the office windows across the way. Joseph and O'Dea drinking quietly, happily. O'Dea teasing his client now, saying how he nearly hung himself, getting the judge's gander up like that.

"I wouldn't have minded going to gaol."

"In with city gurriers . . . you wouldn't have stuck it," O'Dea said, and laughed, urging Breege to have a little drop of port wine and to take her coat off or she'd bake in the heat of the fire.

Bugler is a few tables away with two strangers, but she has not looked in his direction, she is too ashamed to.

"Faith, you were maladroit in the box," O'Dea said, still laughing. He is in his element, what with the warmth of the room, the drawn velvet curtains, a red plush like theatre curtains, the smell of turf smoke, and the faint sound of sods shifting themselves in the heat. He has launched into the stories that he tells so often, relaying them now again for Breege and Joseph because he can see how nervous, how strangled they look in that grand room and the antagonist only a few feet away. The drink makes him expansive, reminiscences flowing from him as, turning from time to time to compliment Breege, he says, "You are excessively sensitive and excessively petite."

"You've seen a lot of life, a lot of human nature," Joseph says sagely.

"I've seen a lot of folly," O'Dea says, sits back in the chair, stares into the fire, and then it is the parable of Brady versus Bonner, two unhappy families on either side of the stream.

"It was thus," he said, his voice pitched higher for others to hear. "There was the Bradys and the Bonners with a river between them but no bridge, Brady having to carry his women and his children when the floods came. So it was a question of trying to get Bonner to agree to a bridge, but he wouldn't budge. The case going to a first court, a second court, a third court, an all-day sitting ending in the upstairs room of the local hotel; teams of solicitors, teams of barristers, warring engineers, and in the middle of the sitting the high court judge having to be wined and dined because of his status. Messages going to and fro, agreement almost, maps, opes, red lines, blue lines, the seal about to be stamped on it when old Mrs. Bonner stands up and says they are being rooked, ground is being taken from them on their side of the river. She storms out, the Bradys follow, cars tearing up a country road, and at midnight a settlement reached under the stars. Handshakes all around, until the next day or the next week when neither party would pay costs, each considering themselves to be the winner and not the loser. Litigation starting up all over again."

He ceased and laughed, bemused, into his tumbler of whiskey, declared there was a mischief in it from day one; that they were never meant to be friends.

"That could be us," Breege said nervously.

"You are excessively sensitive and excessively petite," he said for the second time.

Looking at Breege then, he helped her out of her coat and warned her, "My good girl, never marry . . . Whatever you do, don't, don't marry."

"You married young," Joseph says.

"Too young . . . met her on a balcony."

Turning to Breege, he said he would make her laugh. He didn't like to see such a melancholy expression, he would amuse her with the story of Flanagan, the horse who was able to pick locks with his pronged teeth.

"A judge beyond in Tipperary got promoted to a court not far from here. In due course he sent for his favourite Flanagan so that he could ride him. Flanagan and a mare were put on a train, arrived at his gateway, and were put in a field next to the road. Well, Flanagan doesn't care for the new surroundings, so he gets his teeth to work all night, and the following morning it's down to the railway station whence he had come the night before; clogs into the ticket office, terrifies the stationmaster's wife, who is putting in her teeth, takes a counter with him, floats over two filing cabinets to a back passage, and with the Flanagan nose for a level crossing leaps to the place where he had dismounted the previous evening. No oncoming train. So it's over a half-door into a waiting room, chairs and benches keeled over, a glass window broken, Flanagan now going berserk on account of being trapped in an enclosed room, and men too frightened to go near him manage only to quell his assaults by feeding him and his missus buckets of oats. Next night same scenario. Flanagan and the mare are turned back and a rope put on the gate. Flanagan in the fullness of time masters how to undo knots. Nothing for it but a padlock. Well, the padlock is put on the gate and our judge sleeps sound until he is alerted to the fact that Flanagan and the mare are out on the main road again causing pandemonium. Down to the gate. He mooches around to find the lock and the key flung into the grass. He had the bad luck to share an avenue, a causeway, with a Mrs. Boyce, a returned Yank whose vernacular principally included the words 'Oh gee' or 'I'm thinking of making a killing.' Over he goes to her, but oh gee, the subject of the lock is not interesting to her, all she wishes to know is the price of steer so that she can make a killing. He asks how the lock got there. Oh gee, it's a mystery. Moreover, he did not have the right to put a lock on the gate. It belongs to her. She had it made, she had the piers put down, and she has the receipts for same. He tries to reason with her, says if the Lord Himself built a gate, the purpose of it is to keep animals in check. Oh gee, she agrees, but a lock-eating horse belongs in a circus and not in a field. He says it was not Flanagan who threw the lock and key away, that much is certain. Oh gee, another thing is certain. She is not in favour of a lock. It will slow things up for Paud going in and out. Could Paud be persuaded to suffer the nuisance of opening a little lock? Oh gee, she doubted that. A lock was not going to bite him, and if an animal got out on the road and killed someone, it could be manslaughter, it could be trouble for everyone. She would think it over. Same scenario. A new lock thrown into the high grass. The judge decides on a fence to keep his Flanagan in. Oh gee, a fence is no good. A fence is cutting a slice out of their side of the avenue. Paud sits on the gate and stops the workmen coming in. More letters. An injunction. Circuit court, district court, high court, and Flanagan having to be sent away, and on her deathbed, Oh gee, Ma Boyce proud of one thing, that they beat the judge."

He mused for a moment and said admonishingly, "It's in the genes . . . I have a lot of time for DNA, but the English fucked up our genes."

"That's a great story," Joseph said, relaxed now, the shame of the morning dissolving in a muddle of drink and warmth and laughter as O'Dea's story was applauded by several listeners.

"I'll tell you what we'll do . . . we'll send a drink over to your man," O'Dea said, pointing in Bugler's direction.

"Oh God, no."

"Oh God, yes . . . we're gallants." He had only to look at Joseph to see by that abject and thawing expression in his eyes that he was glad of it, glad to make the peace. They watched the waitress go across, saw Bugler and the two men hesitate, then nod, and on her way back the waitress gave them a little wink because the outburst in the court had been relayed by one and all.

"Yes . . . it's in the genes," O'Dea said solemnly, asking Breege if she knew her history.

"Some," she said clumsily.

"Well, my dear girl, you should know it, because it all happened on account of a woman," and deciding now that his listeners were as merry and as carefree as himself, he settled into his history lesson.

"O'Rourke was King of Brefni and Dermot McMurrough was King of Leinster. O'Rourke ran off with McMurrough's wife and brought her to his keep in Brefni. McMurrough charged after her with his private army, but he was beaten off, so he shot over to England to explain his case to Henry II, to ask for cavalry to get his wife back. Henry was reluctant until McMurrough persuaded him that the French or the Spanish could land in Ireland and get to England by the back door. Henry sent his Norman knight, Strongbow, and when the Red Coats in their chain-mail landed in Wexford and marched through Leinster they frightened the life out of our lads in their bearskins, hiding in the hills. Nine hundred years of turbulence to follow, and all because of a woman."

Turning to Breege he said that it was his bounden duty to qualify that — "I love women, don't get me wrong, but whatever you do, don't marry," and determined now that everyone should hear, he recalls again the famous meeting — "I met her on a balcony . . . sixteen golden years back . . . that fucking balcony . . . the young Brunhilde . . . so vivacious . . . charming plaits . . . youth . . . the lot . . . a lifetime of salads and soya milk." He was reflective then, musing, talking into his drink, the water of life, lucky to be away from his freezing office and Miss P. with her ejaculations, away from Brunhilde and the little Huns who were strangers to him. He paused, said he would like to ask a question of the distinguished company. "Where," he asked, "where lieth the seat of the affections, in the body or in the soul?"

They were silent, constrained, knowing that he had been overheard.

On his way out Bugler stood by the table looking from one to the other.

"Thanks for the drink," he said.

"I'm a bridge over troubled waters," O'Dea said, and laughed. They each laughed, and then Bugler smiled at Breege; it was a shy smile, but it came from deep within and went beyond the confines of the place, back out to the far reaches of the mountain, the ballerina birch, and the fugitive amethyst river.

"THEY'RE OFF . . . they're off." The words so heady and affirmative, carrying up the course, where the hare of the same dun green as the grass is running for its life, ears pointed, and packed into the little furry frenzied volume of flight is the knowledge that this might be its last one. The two hounds waiting down below to be let slip are sending out sounds both bloodthirsty and despairing.

Joseph stood apart from the crowd, the better to be able to see the race, to live it, silently telling Violet Hill to remember everything he told her, instilled into her when he rubbed the liniment into her muscles, into her being.

They are slipped — the Red and the White, etiolated creatures, faint as smoke, bodiless almost, charging forward as if their lungs were carrying them, so close at first they might be merged, then just barely separating, creatures unsubstanced, their bluish breaths preceding them through their plaited muzzles, the crowd cheering, impossible to tell who is leading, then the hare turning and Violet Hill turning with it, the hare scrambling to escape, both hounds circling it in a crazed whirligig as the crowd shout at the hare to "Get in . . . get in."

Joseph is halfway up the field towards the post, not knowing whether the red or white handkerchief will be raised, and all the while the crowd yelling, yelling, then the hare vanishing into its hole and an instant of unspeakable suspense as the white handkerchief, Violet Hill's colour, is raised by a man on horseback.

The cheer that burst from the crowd had in it that barbaric and resonating timbre which exults in victory.

Afterwards when he held her she was like a nerve, the wet tongue thin as a willow leaf flapping from her lower jaw, her whey eyes drinking in the praise. Coquette-like she lifts one leg for it to be shaken, to be congratulated. He led her back then to prepare her for the next race, dipped each foot, each forelock, in the pot of lukewarm water and gave her the crust of honeyed bread which Breege had put in the basket. He rubbed her whole body once again so that the liniment soaked into every pore, then covered her in her tartan blanket and crept with her alone into the back of the van until it was her turn to run the next race, and the next, to run four races in all. He spoke to her in there in a quiet and matter-of-fact tone. Win these four and she would qualify for the feature stakes, and from that to the Oaks, and then the Derby itself, distances away, but distances that had to be run. She was his life now, and Breege's too. Breege loved her, and though she never said so, she would have liked to have come to the courses, to be part of the fun, except that Daly forbade it. Daly trained her and was against women coming; women, he insisted, were a bloody nuisance and made the dogs skittish. Daly's own wife, Eileen, his queen, was not allowed, so why any other woman?

By twilight it was all over, rain coming on, a maze of swallows swirling and circling, dogs and their owners walking back to their cars, winners and losers, commands to meet down in the pub, vehicles lurching in the mucky field, and a pride for Joseph as passersby cross to admire her.

"She's more like a changeling than a dog."

"Spectacular."

"You hear that," he said, and he held her, and they waited for the crowd to fall away.

All of a sudden she started to yelp, and break loose of her leash. He saw what it was. On the far side of the track in the shrouding rain thirty or forty hares were being chased back towards a hut, and though not being able to see them she sensed them, the leaflike tongue moiling now, brain and muscles in an urgency to be let go, to be let free, to be let loose among them for slaughter.

"You witch, you," he said, clasping her tight, but she twisted and strove, no longer content with his touch, all nearness gone, all silkiness gone, far from him now, as rabid and estranged as a creature of the wild.

Down in the pub the winner of the big race carries the cup around, proud, insistent that everyone, even children, drink from it. He stands before Joseph, bulky and with an angry look until he smiles, then commandingly raises an arm. "Bets on who will be taking home this cup, this time next year."

Suddenly Joseph is being lifted up, lifted high on the shoulders of strangers and being made to drink the dark brew, a blend of whiskey, brandies, and God knows what else, stronger than any drink he has ever tasted but yet one that cannot make him drunk. His is a different drunkenness, fired with thoughts of the future, the pre-dawns up on the mountain, the meets, Daly, himself, and the Crock in the front of the van, great stories of great dogs, legendary dogs, Violet Hill among them, her name enshrined in the annals.

B UGLER WAS UNDER no illusion that the day he started to cut turf would lead to more strife and a last division. But he was callow then and certainly callow in that he did not know, did not want to know, the inward pernicious trickle of fear and ire that Joe Brennan was consumed with.

It would take Breege to show him that, and he would not be so callow then, and many things would have unfolded.

Moreover, he wanted to cut turf. It appealed to him, a new skill to be learned, to be mastered, a whole tract of it spread out to dry, then brought home and burned in his big new inglenook fireplace. He had only smelt turf once and that was in a big hotel where he had gone one evening for his dinner out of an unwarranted loneliness.

He had had to make searches to ensure his ownership, and in the various bits of correspondence he read the names of tenants, over fifty at one time, the acres and roods and perches that had been allotted to them, the rents they had paid, a place their sweat fell on, their hopes too, until eventually they had gone away from it. He hired an engineer to map out his own bit, and they marked it with blue twine which seemed gaudy in that universe of tawny grasses that reached up to their chests; pools of bogwater weirdly and pulsingly green, scummed with mosses, the occasional bird, the occasional aeroplane, a habitation gone back to nature, and the only remains of man was a rusted gas cooker and a pair of grey flannel trousers with holes in them.

"You could murder someone here and get away with it," the engineer said drolly.

"So you could."

And they laughed over it.

He had read the books on turf cutting and consulted Thady, an old man who had once been the fastest slanesman in the country. Earnestly he had listened, then watched as Thady brought in a rusted slane from an outhouse and, using the kitchen floor as a bog, enacted the stripping off of the top skin of grass, then marking out the bank, and with the slane having to dig and dig, doing it slantwise so as to cut the sods straight.

In the kitchen it had been an amusement, but out there in the heat and the dryness, insects crawling over him, his back breaking from having to bend and push in an unaccustomed way, he realised that he had never worked so hard or so gruellingly and yet so satisfyingly. Between himself and those wet strips of loamy bank there was as much a relationship, a tussle, as with an animal or a person, that give and take, the strength of him versus the strength of it, the yield of the sod under the slane, and for some reason as he pulled it up his mother's voice came from nowhere.

He worked all day, and it did not worry him that someone had come up at the gap beyond, a youngster crouching in the high grass to snoop on him. It did not worry him in the least. The aloneness of the place, the queer solemnity of it and the spread-out, wet gallumpen sods, like the hewn pieces of a priceless carpet, made him feel monarch of it all.

"It's mine . . . It's all mine," he said to anyone who cared to listen.

At the end of the day, with dusk coming on, he sat and smoked a cigarette and listened to all the gathering life, creatures coming out, big creatures and little creatures, birds, animals, wading in the brackenish water, the air sweeter now, not so scalding, and a curlew letting out its lonesome cry. Once again he spotted a figure coming in at the gap, taller than the one earlier, and he whistled to challenge it to make itself known to him.

It was on the Monday that O'Dea's letter came. He knew what would be in it even before he tore it open.

Dear Sir:

For the past week I am informed that you have been cutting turf in breach of your own rights and that of others.
From the information that I have received from my client
Mr. Joseph Brennan, you have been cutting turf into a bank
which projects thirty or forty feet into the Brennan portion of
the bog. You have also left several piles of turf to dry on the
Brennan area just north of the boundary line. Mr. Brennan
has claims of the turbary rights over fifty-two acres south of
the boundary line, some of which includes the area which you
suppose to be yours. All work on this must be suspended
until it is established clearly where you are situate. Should
you ignore this warning, we will, reluctantly, have to institute
proceedings.

T HE CALVES HAD been separated from their mothers that morning. It took three men to do it, and afterwards Joseph stayed outside. Outside he felt safer; his fields, his boundaries, his wall to sit on, to think things over. A vantage over the four surrounding counties; hills soft, undulating, misted at the rim, the sky with cavities of turquoise between the skimming cloud. Refuge and sanctuary, were it not for the tension in him. Ten brokenhearted sucky calves bawling, beating at the fence to get back to their mothers.

"Calm down, calm down," but he pitied them all the same. He pitied and recognised their predicament. The mothers from the lower field were answering back, but not at the same pitch and not with the same tenacity, the mothers maybe knowing within that there would be another season and more young, whereas the calves were banished for ever, their despairing choir more pitiful and heartfelt than any human. In a huddle they tried to storm the fence, kicked and pucked at the wooden posts so that the wires began to rasp, their big trusting eyes and the bouclé curls on the crown of their heads in direct contrast to their assault.

Gradually the cows saunter up from the lower field and stand around him, expressions of murderous stupidity in their blank and rheumy sockets. They converge around him, stomping, tossing their square heads as if intending to attack.

"Ye're cowards, blasted cowards," he said, disliking them because they did not match the tenderness of their young, who for months lived in the precincts of milk, milk smell, milk warmth, the soft bosomy udders to drink from, to pillow on, and overnight without warning were driven through a gap into a big wide world called nowhere. Were they not calves themselves once? Were they not once, a few years back, as disconsolate as that? Or had they forgotten? He expected answers. He didn't care if they butted him. Looking up then, he thought he must be imagining it as three calves came flying over the upper barb of wire, trapezewise, so fast they did not even touch it, two of them landing topsy-turvy into the field and the third falling back, then trying again as the wire bent, recovered, then slammed it back to make a gash on its pink underbelly, back to hard ground where it lay, its little thin legs scrambling in the air. The new arrivals leapt and romped as a host of mothers circled around them.

"What's going on?" Breege called as she hurried up, stumbling, because Goldie, excited by the pandemonium, kept walking between her legs, or in front of her, impeding her, in a lava of joy.

"I couldn't believe my eyes . . . Two of them leapt the fence . . . lurchers . . . The third cut herself."

"This came," and as she handed it to him, he scoffed.

"You read it," he said sullenly.

She had to shout to be heard. The two calves had nuzzled under their mothers, causing others to mutiny, to implore for the young that they had recently forgotten. Out there juxtaposed against all that bedlam the letter seemed uglier and more indicting. It had been forwarded by O'Dea, who had written at the top: "Where do we go from here?"

Attendance on Mr. Michael Bugler, who called by appointment. He denies that he has wrongfully cut turf on your client's lands as alleged or at all. He and his ancestors in title have for upwards of 200 years had a right to cut turf as part of a lease agreement between his ancestors and your client's in consideration of a certain sum.

I said that in default of documentary evidence that he should produce to us persons who were familiar with the bog and who lived in the locality and could swear they had seen him or his ancestors cut turf in the area under dispute for the last 70 or 80 years and that to their knowledge there was no objection.

I showed him the land registry map of his holding. I also showed him the map which was attached to the civil bill. I asked him to establish for us his right to cut turf within the area edged in green on the map attached to the civil bill. I pointed out that this was a basic question to be established.

Mr. Bugler took with him the map attached to the civil bill and also the land registry map of his folio 13037 and said he would consult an engineer and return to us.

We cannot understand the claim made by your client or why he should place barbed wire and other impediments across the exit gate by which Mr. Bugler could take out his turf.

We would suggest that in the interest of good neighbourliness that your client does not interfere with our client or his heirs or assigns in the quiet and peaceful enjoyments of the said turbary.

To summarise, my client denies that he has wrongfully cut turf on your client's lands as alleged or at all.

My client denies that he at any time sought or requested or received the consent of your client to cut turf as alleged or at all.

My client denies that he has at any time interfered with your client when they lawfully worked on their lands or boglands.

Yours faithfully,

"It'll break us . . . Joseph," she said pleadingly.

On the other side of the fence the calves passed up and down, with a furious and useless motion, the injured one berserk and bawling.

"You better get a poultice for her," Joseph said, and he began to pelt the cows with soft fistfuls of earth to drive them back to the lower field.

SLURRY DECOMPOSES in storage and produces a mixture of gases including methane, carbon dioxide, ammonia and hydrogen sulphide. All are unpleasant, some can be inflammable, and one in particular, hydrogen sulphide, is extremely poisonous to humans and animals alike and is the most likely one to be involved in fatal accidents. Hydrogen sulphide is a clear gas with the characteristic smell of rotten eggs and is slightly heavier than air. It burns in air, but its main danger is that it is poisonous. It affects the nervous system, causing symptoms which range from discomfort to sudden death. High concentrations over one thousand parts will cause breathing to cease, while low concentrations will, after a time, affect the nervous system, causing severe headache, dizziness, excitement, and a staggering gait.

"How about that . . . Discomfort to sudden death for the bastard," the Crock says. They are in his caravan, plotting. Rain against the curtainless windows and from a leak above the lintel drops the size of pennies plopping into a burnt saucepan. There is barely room enough for the two of them, squashed in between odd bits of scrap furniture, broken chairs, stacks of newspapers, and a television over which flecks of snow randomly scattered. A calendar pinned to the wall shows a young girl in a yellow cling vest, very suntanned, her nipples sprouting. At times, the caravan and the contents seem to tilt and the two men sway as if on board ship.

"Let's o'er to delicious murder," the Crock says as he lifts a used tea bag from the waste bucket, dips it into two mugs of boiling water, and ceremoniously hands one over. His "Maundy" money from the state, as he calls it, isn't due for two more days and his luck at the cards and the bingo, dire.

"We'll shambolical his entrances and his exits . . . How's that! We'll lock the outer gate for starters . . . the one near the little hut. We'll lock it and we'll put barbed wire all around it. Not one little loop. But loop after loop . . . Like you see on the gaol wall in Port Laoise. Picture it . . . He'll get there on the tractor in a big hurry. He'll jump down. He'll probably be able to break the lock with a pickaxe or a hammer, but by Jesus he will have cut his hands in numerous places from the barbed wire. Now, that takes him the best part of an hour and he's cross . . . He's bucking. He's effing and blinding and he's in a bigger hurry. Wasted a fecking hour . . . Back up on the tractor across to the second entrance, farther up where there's no gate at all. He's making up for lost time. Speeding . . . And lo and behold, there's this godawful lurch. The tractor starts to sink . . . Down . . . Down. He's sunk. Are you with me?"

"Not entirely."

"Well, there's a slatted wooden bridge in that second entrance. It's covered over with briars and gorse, but underneath it there's a big drop, a gorge, full of bogwater. So . . . if we remove the beams and put the briars back, Bugler is in a hole shouting for help and no help in sight. He'll get himself down, but he won't be able to pull the tractor. He has to go back home and ring Vinnie from the garage. Vinnie takes his time about coming . . . They eventually pull the machine out . . . But it's a sick Dino. It needs surgery. Net result: a whole day wasted, a broken tractor and a bill for several hundred pounds. In short, a warning, a foretaste of things to come. Stop cutting turf, boyo."

"Can we do it?"

"Treason, stratagems, and spoils," the Crock says, dragging

his toolbox from under the bed, picking out his hacksaw, then putting it across his knee, and with a delicacy that is new for him, he begins to sharpen each tooth with the long sharpening rod, all the while whistling, "If I were a blackbird I'd whistle and sing and follow the ship that my true love sails in."

THE LETTERS WENT back and forth, faithfully and in grinding succession, the dry words as distant from their daily lives as a thronged city street from the bronzed ghostliness of Yellow Dick's Bog. Sometimes there came two in a week, then a silence, as if by some miracle, some amelioration, it had resolved itself or Bugler had got fed up and was preparing to go back to Australia, as some said. He bought his groceries and his diesel now in a town twenty miles away and he was not seen at Mass. Just as once Breege had prayed for a glimpse of him, she now prayed that he would go away.

❖　❖　❖

Dear Sirs:

I act for Mr. Joseph Brennan of Cloontha, who has handed me a copy of a preliminary letter from Mr. Michael Bugler via his solicitor.

It is clear that you have not been correctly instructed in this matter. The true facts are as follows:

Your client and his predecessors in title did have a right to cut turf in a spot on my client's bog a few hundred yards distant from the place where he is now cutting turf.

This turf bank in respect of which he had bona fide right to cut turf became exhausted. It was in fact "cut away" for several years past.

Now, without any right or authority whatever, your client has moved over to another place, a few hundred yards away from the original turf bank, and has calmly proceeded to open a fresh bank.

In other words, having abandoned the original bank he has proceeded to move to a different spot and open a new bank.

About two months ago he asked Mr. Brennan for permission to cut turf in the present spot, but Mr. Brennan refused.

Now, Mr. Brennan has no intention whatever of tolerating an invasion of his rights in this fashion.

If your client enters into this part of my client's bog again, my client will at once issue proceedings in the Circuit Court for damages and an injunction.

Yours faithfully,

Bugler thought first to tear it up, then decided to make a scrapbook for Rosemary to let her see why he had to keep postponing to save her from this mess.

❖   ❖   ❖

Dear Sir:

Our client Mr. Bugler insists that he is entitled to cut turf on Yellow Dick's Bog, and he objects strongly to your client trying to cut off his mode of ingress and egress thereto. He cannot understand why your client should place barbed wire across the gate by which Mr. Bugler was endeavouring to enter.

We have bespoken Mr. Bugler's land registry map to see if it can be of assistance in solving this difficulty. In the meantime, you might kindly let us know if your client denies that Mr. Bugler and his predecessors have been cutting turf on this bog for many years as claimed.

Yours faithfully,

❖   ❖   ❖

Dear Sir:

We are not able to go ahead with our enquiries, and you will see from the enclosed file the difficulties with which we have had to contend. Mrs. Cleary of Messrs. Dowling & Co., architects, has visited the bog on a number of occasions but has met with great difficulty in drawing a map and instructing us as to whether or not Mr. Bugler is cutting turf in the area occupied by your client.

Your client has on occasion used improper if not to say foul language and once tried to frighten Mrs. Cleary. This is totally inappropriate and unacceptable. You must instruct your client to give Mrs. Cleary proper access with regard to the boundary under dispute, as otherwise your client runs the risk of losing his tenancy altogether if a map cannot be prepared and presented to both parties.

Yours faithfully,

❖   ❖   ❖

Dear Sir:

I acknowledge receipt of your letter dated 10th instant, the contents of which I have discussed with my client. My client has confirmed that he did attend his bog on the 6th instant accompanied by Guard Cosgrave, as they wished to request Mr. Bugler once again to leave his property, on which he was cutting turf and furthermore interfering with the drain which our client created at great expense. When Mr. Brennan, accompanied by his sister and Guard Cosgrave, arrived at the area in dispute, they were very much amazed to discover that Mr. Bugler and two persons unknown to them were walking on Mr. Brennan's property at a place not referred to in the proceedings. Mr. Brennan, in the presence of his sister and Guard Cosgrave, asked them to remove themselves from his property. You are wrongly instructed that the people concerned, i.e., Mr. Bugler and helpmates, proceeded onto the public road, because in fact they were in clear view the entire time it took them to cross from those lands to the dwelling house of Mr. Bugler. After Mr. Bugler had gone, Mr. Brennan and his sister discussed the situation with Guard Cosgrave, who then left the scene, as he said the Bugler crowd would probably not return to the bog. However, shortly after this time, Mr. Brennan and his sister saw Mr. Bugler returning to their property accompanied by one of the strangers, and Mr. Brennan requested Mr. Bugler not to go on his property. For the first time during the evening the person accompanying Mr. Bugler, now known to be Mrs. Cleary, the architect, approached Mr. Brennan to tell him he was not the registered owner of the lands in question, and when requested by Mr. Brennan to identify herself and the purpose for which she was standing on these lands Mrs. Cleary said nothing and did not engage in any further conversation. Mr. Brennan denies completely that he shouted at her or behaved in a most unreasonable manner. In fact, to be quite clear about the matter, it was Michael Bugler who removed his coat and used words to the effect that he would fight Mr. Brennan, something which caused such distress to Mr. Brennan's sister that he was obliged to take her home. Later in the day he had again gone for Guard Cosgrave, who returned to the scene and who spoke to Mr. Bugler, who in due course left the bog with Mrs. Cleary and went home.

Yours faithfully

VIOLET HILL, fluid, flowing, a brindled phantom upon the mountain in the early morning, a vision that streaked back and forth like a painted picture and then again in the dusk, becoming one with the dusk, except for her eyes, which glowed wildly. "You flyer," Joseph would say each time she broke out of her kennel. What he did not know was that she was digging the soft clay under the surround of the wire meshing. It was in wet and dusk that she ran to her delirious destination.

Bugler had been going slow on account of the poor light, and when he heard the cries and turned off the ignition, he knew that it was a wounded animal and hoped that it would not be Violet Hill. He found her at the side of the road, and kneeling, he picked her up and listened to her small strangled cries. Then he carried her, willing her not to be dead, carried her into their yard and down the three steep steps to the back door, which he knocked on with his foot, holding her with both hands lest she unmesh. Her hind leg was broken and bent backwards, and the long sleek trunk of her body was damp with blood, but she was still alive. The blood dripped harmlessly onto the outdoor mat as he waited for the door to be answered. Opening it, he saw Breege first with a smile and then drawing back shocked, unable to look at the crumpled heap in his arms.

"Oh no," she said.

"I found her out on the road."

"Oh my God," she said in a whisper, and looked in towards the kitchen.

"Where's Joseph?"

"He's sick . . . He's in bed."

"Can I go up to him?"

"I'll tell him . . . It's better that I tell him."

"She's still breathing," he said, and together they listened for the little splutters of breath, faint as a faltering watch. Between them they held her then as if somehow holding her they would keep her alive but letting her go would bode the end of everything.

"Who is it?" Joseph called twice.

"You'd better go," Breege said, and made a basket out of her apron as Bugler laid Violet Hill into it.

"I'm sorry . . . I'm very sorry," he said.

"I know that," she said, and pushed him back out.

"It was Bugler," Joseph said, seething. He was at the top of the stairs with a thin patchwork quilt around him.

"It was," she said, and turning to face him, she held up the apron. She did not know what he would do, what he would say. He did not roar, he did not speak, he closed his eyes for several seconds, then came down the stairs, took Violet Hill in his arms, and with his hand he gripped the stiffening face and held it and saw. He began then to help her to die, to allow her to die, telling her it was not dying at all, it was running faster and faster into the free and untrammelled emptiness, under the dew and the rain and the stars where none could wound or kill her because she had gone from flesh to spirit.

"I'll ring the vet," Breege said.

"No need," he said, and went back to cradling her, moving back and forth, his voice getting lower now as the life expired in her, and then he bent down and said some farewell thing.

They laid her on the towel on the table, and he bathed her and fixed her like the pieces of a jigsaw so that she was the perfect but unbreathing simulation of what she had been, forever consigned to memory, intact, the fawn delicacy that he had known, that the countryside had known, and with his thumb he closed the almond eyes that were trusting even in death.

"Get me her rug," he said.

"It's too dark to bury her now."

"She likes dark . . . She likes wild spaces . . . Don't you?" he said, gathering the four corners of the towel to make a litter before laying her into her tartan rug.

"Bugler didn't do it . . . It was someone else," she said gently.

"Someone else! No other car went up the road. I would have heard it."

"You want it to be Bugler," she cried mutely to herself, and then put a dab of holy water on the white oblong of Violet Hill's forehead. He did not ask her to go with him, and he did not tell her where he intended the burying to be.

JOSEPH WAS IN the shed when he saw the patrol car pull into the yard. He recognised it by the extra tall aerial. It was the fat guard, Garvey, whom he knew quite well.

"Hello, Joe . . . How's the form?" The voice apologising for itself as he got out and crossed the yard. A curtain of rain, a shibboleth hung over everything.

"Down for the day," Garvey said.

"Down for the year."

"My wife can't dry the baby's nappies, but it's worse for you farmers."

"What brings you to my mountain?"

"You won't believe this," Garvey says, and trying to delay his mission, he launches into a story about going to the High Court in Dublin only three days before, and guess what, there were crocuses on the dual carriageway.

"You've come about something other than crocuses."

"I have and I wish I hadn't, because I know you won't like it any more than I do."

"Then don't bother."

"I have to . . . I have to take your shotgun off you."

"You can't . . . It's like my walking stick."

"Come on now, it's a bit more serious than that."

"Who reported me?"

"No one, Joe . . . No one."

"Mick Bugler did."

"He did not, though he had plenty of reason to. You lay in wait for him in the bog . . . You tried to ambush him. There's nothing to be gained from that sort of behaviour."

"I went in to shoot snipe . . . I've done it all my life, so why can't I do it now?"

"We don't want you shooting people."

"Look, it's myself I do harm to and not that blackguard."

"All the more reason then why I should take the gun off you."

"He wants to retire me . . . Every day he's up to some other stunt. He's not satisfied just to cut turf. He covets Yellow Dick's Bog."

"Oh, a crackpot . . . The best thing is to ignore him."

"I can't and I won't."

"Look, Joe, we'll only keep the damn thing for a couple of months until the case is settled and the heat dies down . . ."

"The heat won't die down."

"Joe, for Christ's sake, just give me the gun. Stop making it hard for me."

"I need it . . . Soon it will be lambing time. There will be lambs."

"You have no sheep."

"Sheep stray over onto the mountain from Galway."

"I was sent up here to do a job, so let me do it."

"You're wasting your time, Garvey."

"If you don't give it, I'll get it from your sister. Out of the wardrobe where it's kept."

"So she's the informer."

"She isn't."

"How would you know where it's kept unless you were told. Holy Jesus, she actually went to the barracks and informed on me."

"It's for your own good."

"She places Mick Bugler above her own brother."

"If I go back without it, the superintendent will come up."

"Go in and get it from her . . . Tell her that when Oedipus blinded himself with the hooks of his mother's corset, her ladies in waiting split themselves laughing."

"For Christ's sake . . . Why would I tell her a cracked thing like that?"

"In case it hurts. In case it hurts, my good man."

❖   ❖   ❖

It was a divided house then. He took his meals out in the shed. He wrote notes to communicate the duties that were ascribed to her and those ascribed to himself. She wrote on the back of a brown envelope that had come from O'Dea; she said, "I am not on Bugler's side . . . Please believe that." He inked it out.

The morning the decisive letter came he sat at the kitchen table and read it and broke down. She read it over his shoulder.

> Dear Sir:
>
> I refer to your letter dated 12 instant and I wish to inform you that the holding at issue in Yellow Dick's Bog subject of receivable order no. 7/5/642 Folio 29596 was vested in D'Arby Bugler together with the right of turbary as formerly exercised on plot 6A, Yellow Dick's Bog, containing 52 acres 2 roods 8 perches in the occupation of Michael Bugler and his antecedents.
>
> Furthermore, I have to inform you that your registration in relation to Yellow Dick's Bog has a mistake. Contrary to your own assumption, you are not in fact the owner of 0.7 turf bank in question. As a result of inspection of the land registry maps our client is now assured of that portion and intends to make every use of his rights and to bring home the turf he has saved and which as you are aware is a back-breaking task. You will see from the enclosed map that it is blatantly clear, and should you object, our client has no compunction at all about going back to the courts to prove adverse possession of his rightful bank. He is sorry that there has been so much wrangling about this but wishes you to know that it was not of his own making.

For two weeks there had been a heat wave, the ground baked and dusty, the dogs drowsy, leaves on the trees motionless and spent, a haze of pollen and dust that sifted through the days and at night gorse fires breaking out on the mountain three in a row. The men from the local fire brigade had had to go up there and Bugler was foremost among them. He had insinuated himself into everything, and no one thought any the worse of him because of his vendetta with Joe Brennan. "More power to your elbow," the men said when they met him.

Farm work had to be put off until nighttime, and people worked under the stars up to midnight, the air so still and permeable that voices could be heard across the lengths of several fields and the barking of dogs for miles around. The turnips that they had already dug had lost their greenish neck frills and lay along the drills withered and prone. There was about two tons to be brought home and Joseph had calculated what he would get for them. He needed the money. Every solicitor's letter and every barrister's letter had a bill enclosed or a note that further costs were being drawn up.

They worked almost in silence, Joseph digging, the Crock forking them to Breege, who threw armfuls of them onto an upturned cart. Sometimes the men stopped to wipe the sweat from their faces or under their arms with a towel that they shared, wondering why it was that Breege didn't sweat.

Whisht, whisht. It was the Crock who heard it, heard it because he was wise to it.

A police siren like a high-pitched scream carried across into the field where two corncrakes had either been serenading or outwitting each other minutes before. It came from the direction of the mountain rather than the lake, and for a moment Joseph thought that it was another fire or else that weapons had been found up there, as there was a rumour about a cache of them. Hard upon it came the sound of the tractor, the two sounds, siren and tractor, in alternating and usurping peremptoriness, then a second of suspense and his absolute disbelief.

"It's Bugler bringing home the turf . . . with a guard escort," the Crock said.

"What? What?"

"The guards are escorting the load in case of any trouble."

"Oh, Holy Jesus . . . He's won, he's won," and thrusting the shovel into the dry ground, Joseph began rolling his sleeves down so as to go out and impede them.

"Don't," Breege said. "Don't go up there . . . it's too late."

"It's not too late . . . He can't do this . . . It's not settled."

"It is settled . . . it's settled now," she said.

"A ruthless man . . . a hobo . . . sans feeling . . . sans nature," the Crock began.

"Sans everything," Breege said, and by her saying it Joseph knew that she was restored to him, they would be inseparable once again.

They were one then, one in their commiseration and one in their humbledness. The months of letters, maps, drawings, folios, bills all made useless by Bugler's power and Bugler's effrontery; the two sounds now, siren and tractor receding but still scornful, defining their progress up the steep track to his house.

"You see what he's like," the Crock said.

"I see," she said, weary.

Many a time she had promised herself that she must put Bugler out of her thoughts completely, that she must go into the hidden house of herself like an orderly and rout him out. That time had come. She even saw the vulpine grimace that lurked behind his winning smile.

There was an interval then, with only the sound of the tractor, steady, putting, reiterative, as Bugler went over and back, over and back, obviously unloading the bales of the turf and stacking them in a shed.

"How would you describe that sound, Joe?" the Crock asked.

Joseph thought for a while, but made no answer. He was far away, like someone in a bitter trance from which he did not want to be disturbed.

"A wail . . . A banshee wail," the Crock said, and to prove his ire he kicked out at the turnips that lay like lopped infants' heads in a dreary and lumpen inertness.

THE SOUND OF the tractor ran on from that night under a reign of timid stars to starless nights and brilliantly burning ones, the sky a muscled and pulsing swell of bright nebulae. It ran on through the summer, through ripeness and stubble, to come ultimately to the mountain, that coveted wilderness that was a test for each of them, beginning and end, a place where pride and stubbornness and perpetuity would be put to the test, then and in time to come.

It was about a week later that a lorry with a digger attached was seen going up the road. The three workmen were all strangers. Soon as he heard it, Joseph ran with the binoculars, and when he climbed onto the barn roof, his worst fears were confirmed. Bugler was going to cut a road up to his own house. The lorry had a load of black slag that was tipped out, and soon the digger began to scoop up the stubborn earth. It took three days before he succeeded in stopping it. The periwinkle black slag and crushed stones lay to one side, and a quenched lamp attached to a pole said MEN WORKING.

He would pursue his cause now with the energies of a madman, divination in his words and in his will; his stock, his farm, Breege, everything sacrificed to it. It was well known how a Bugler ancestor, a D'Arby Bugler, a rake, had lost his right to that part of the mountain, lost it to Joseph's father's father over a winter of cards. It was written down and witnessed, and his own father had even repeated it on his deathbed, how D'Arby Bugler ceded that corridor of mountain and had only a bona fide right to go up and down it. The folly of D'Arby Bugler was often talked of and how in the end he lost everything, even his shirt. It was written and sealed and deposited somewhere, in some safe, the humbled and hurried and slightly drunken scrawl that would be Bugler's undoing. Finding it entailed more journeys, overnight stays in cheap rooms, overhearing doors banging and drunks coming in late. Even before he held it in his hand Joseph could picture it, a sheet of crude ruled paper and the ink, rusted almost to a powder and in whose dried traces lay the revelatory words.

A colleague of O'Dea's had hopes of finding it through his partner, but when various searches failed, he had to go to the city, to the Land Commission, where every moiety was registered. He parked his van a few miles out because he was nervous of traffic and walked through the streets until he came to the large leafy square where the doctors' and dentists' brass plates were now obsolete, as each building housed many offices. He stood in a massive hall with the clerk politely telling him that questions about land took months if not years, there being such a backlog of it, and that the English name of the mountain would have to be ascertained before the dispute could be settled.

"Slieve Clochan," he said accusatorily.

❖　　❖　　❖

He became so racked and thin that one night Breege went to him in the front room and stood behind his chair and said, "Can we talk?" He was deep in the law books, believing now that O'Dea had deserted him.

"What is it?" he said.

"Don't turn in on yourself . . . Please don't turn in on yourself."

It had happened once before, long ago when he had done something terrible to himself, though she did not know what as she was too young. It was something to do with a girl, a Catherine whose name could not be mentioned ever again. He had gone away for a while and her mother said it was to the seaside, but she knew that it wasn't. The thing he had done was a big secret, but she learned of it. He had taken some sheep dip to poison himself. When he turned round there were tears in his eyes, and she thought, He is listening to me at last. But he wasn't. He asked her if he could ask a favour. If he could have her savings book. The bank was refusing to loan him any more.

"It's only temporary," he said.

"SLOW ON THE puck, Joe. Joe. Joe. Watch the *sliotair*. Jaysus, Joe."

Bugler and himself were playing a game of hurley in a big field with no fences and no goalposts. He could hear the clatter of the hurley sticks, each boss slashing the other, as if they were animated, as if they were animals, a fleeting sight of the ball with wire instead of cord around the leather sphere, the ball slipping off his spatula of wood and Bugler getting it, then a free flow bursting through and up and away into the air, his jumping to grasp it and feeling the heavy oar of the wood smack on the back of his hand, and a crowd of lads screaming and the referee in old togs, pointing a finger at him: "You will meet him again at a venue to be decided."

He woke panting, his body drenched with shame and wet, and he knew that they were about to come, either through the door or in the window, the lads in the dream, cheering and jeering. He had been playing hurley with Bugler in a big field with no fences and no goalposts and they were in their pelts, his skull still rang with the tough sound of the hurley sticks, the leathered ball, and someone either out of pity or jest shouting, "Justice for the little man." Then the referee telling him that they were to meet again at a venue to be decided.

He opened the window to breathe. The air smelt of some over-sweet rotting flower, not normal, nothing was normal in those moments, pre-dawn a bilious green and "Justice for the little man," as the boys lifted him back for the replay; ten Josephs, nine Josephs, eight, seven, six, Mother of Jesus, down to the last little Joseph, little and belittled, alone in the strange field that was now sprouting great bunches of yellow ragwort and nowhere near home. It was only a nightmare and yet "We will meet again at the spot where hurlers bury their dead" struck him as being prophecy. His secret self laid bare, no longer safe and solitary in that crippled virginal baulk known only to himself and maybe to his sister, innocents both, pitted against a world that was too smart for them.

Soon as he stopped panting he flung open the bedroom door to make sure that there was no one out there, kicked it twice, and then crossed to where Breege slept. She did not hear her door open, and for an instant he stood and looked at the peaceful, almost seraphic calm of her face in contrast with her arms, which were flung out, and the heavy head of brown hair, which looked libertine on the white pillow, her chest rising and falling under the pleated nightgown. She sat up startled and pushed her hair back out of her face, saying nothing, only listening.

"This is what I've come to," he said as he stood there, lean and abashed, tying the cord of his pyjamas childishly.

"What is this is what you've come to?"

He was about to describe it, but then suddenly he shook his head repeatedly, like someone freeing himself of water, and said it was nothing, it was a load of nothing, just a bad dream he had had. Hearing not just what he said but hearing his heart's woe behind it, she knew that he was entering a zone in which dreaming and waking, wrongs and semi-wrongs, would be translated and magnified into an enormity to suit the dark mad mould of his thinking.

BUGLER WAS ON a ladder with his back to her, in his shirt-sleeves, the wind flapping the bright red patterns of his shirt, green and blue and yellow pouches breezing out. He was tapping various parts of the wall with a hammer, then listening intently. She watches, thinking, He does not realise I am here. It is the first time that she has ventured up there since she was a child and was sent up once with a letter. Though only half a mile from their house, it seems wilder and more mysterious, more native to the mountain, the sound of water everywhere and streams running down the sides of the house, rushing as if through a sluice gate, a different-coloured water to theirs, darker, blood-coloured. When she saw him there on the ladder, her heart went pit-a-pat and she realised that the feelings she had for him had not lessened, not lessened at all, if anything they were more. The yard itself was like a builder's yard — heaps of gravel, huge buff-coloured stones, lesser stones, a cement mixer, and slats of wood of a delicate pink like tinned salmon. She coughs to make her presence known.

"I suppose you think I'm mad," Bugler said, turning round to explain that he is tapping to find which of the render is hollow and which is sound, which he has to strip and which to merely make good. He comes down the ladder backwards, then raises his hand as if it were his hat and says, "Welcome."

"I'm afraid of what might happen to my brother." She blurted it out.

"What might happen?"

"That he might go to the reservoir."

"The reservoir!"

"People have . . . One man after he got out of gaol and a woman . . . a young woman . . . Drowned themselves."

"You better come in," he said.

"I won't."

"Come on."

The joists swayed a little as she tiptoed over them, and he pointed to the gutted room, the missing staircase, holes in the wall which one day would be long windows. All his energy has gone into planning it, it is his dream, his castle, can she understand that?

"I can . . . It's my brother," she says feebly.

"What would be the point of my building a house if I can't make a road up to it . . . If I have to go halfway around the mountain to drive to it . . . It makes no sense."

"I know," she says.

The kitchen with the mattress and duvet in one corner is obviously his makeshift bedroom, a razor on the table next to a cold chop bone, washing to be done, all the signs of a bachelor life.

"I better go."

"Let me show you my Rolls-Royce," he says, and leads her to the new stove of dark green enamel with metal hoods shiny as mirrors. As he lifts them and opens the oven doors, she has a memory of something childish, some lost moment, the opening of a cardboard door into a doll's house, into a realm of magic. He holds his hands out to be warmed, gestures her to do the same thing. The woodwork is warm and cheerful, a butcher's block and an old dresser with gold knots and beaded gum, the life of the trees still within them and his shirts drying on the backs of chairs.

"We have the same jugs," she hears herself say.

"They're very old, I believe," he says, and coming closer to meet her eyes, he says, "What has your brother got against me?"

"Everything."

"What do you feel?"

"I don't know."

He says that at least she can sit and have a cup of coffee with him and maybe go away not feeling so antagonistic.

"I'm not antagonistic . . . I'm worried."

Taking a new coffee machine out of a box, he asks her to read the instructions, then he fills it with water and they sit and wait as the boiling water bubbles up, then the coffee percolates quietly and the kitchen filled with the enticing smell makes them talkative. When he has poured their two mugs, he drags a second stool close to her and sits with his legs extended, saying she is his first visitor ever and perhaps she has brought him good luck. It is as if he has forgotten or has decided to forget why she came.

"I'll talk to my brother," she says then.

"Are you able?"

"Oh yes," she says rapidly, too rapidly, trying to banish the memory of him in his pyjamas in her bedroom in the middle of the night and her having to lead him back in a fluster.

"I'm willing to pay . . . I've said so more than once."

"I'll get O'Dea to talk to him," she says.

With the stealth of someone who has thought up a little surprise he opens the drawer of the kitchen table and takes out a worn leather case, its gold clasps slackened, and inside it in various cavities, a spoon, a knife and fork, their silver handles a fretwork as of lace, snug in their recesses, the purple of the velvet bleached and faded from time.

"It's beautiful," she says.

"It's yours," he says, thrusting it into her hands.

"I can't," she says.

"Yes, you can . . . There's still a debt to be paid."

EVERYTHING SEEMED THE SAME, the same chores, the same crows, rain, Goldie with her wet fawn back to the window feeling sorry for herself, then sudden shafts of sunlight yellowing the rained-on grass and around the roots of the beech tree a crop of weirdly orange-coloured mushrooms.

Then one night everything was overturned.

She had gone out to close the hens, and finding Bugler's dog, stretched, lying in wait for Goldie, she chased him off with bits of sticks. At the gate she came on Bugler calling and whistling.

They stood for a few minutes, saying what awful weather and how many trees had come down in the freak storm, and when they heard a car down at the crossroads, then hurtling up the mountain road, they guessed by the sound of the stalling engine that it was the sisters.

"Jesus," she said.

"Jesus," he answered. They ran together into the yard, stepping over puddles, on down towards the hayshed to hide as the car swerved into the drive and the headlights bounced off their retreating shadows. They had to jump over the platforms of baled hay and then wade through a corridor of it that had been forked loose, going farther and farther in, sliding through it, until they sank down with a muted double thud.

Soon the voices were within hearing. The sisters lavish in their praise of Joseph, saying how well he looked, how well he was bearing up, and he with the big court case looming and God's curse on that bastard Mick Bugler.

"We lost a cow with the red fluke," Rita says, her voice plaintive.

"I'm sorry to hear that."

"I think one of Bugler's animals infected her."

"It's a bad thing, that red fluke . . . I've had it in the past."

"To see her die would wring your heart, and we had to pay to have her taken away . . . Money, money, money."

It was from that to the fact that they had bought too much hay in the summer and now needed to sell it.

"Oh, I have hay to burn . . . As you can see," Joseph says anxiously.

"Buy a little bit. Enough to tide us over."

"I can't. I'm hoping I could sell some."

"You wouldn't call this hay, would you," Rita says, as obviously she put her fingers through it and then struck a match to pronounce that it was sawdust.

"Jesus, keep back, keep back," Joseph shouts.

Goldie, sniffing something within, comes scampering, finds the submerged pair, starts to yelp with delight, then runs her snout over each of their two faces. From the tweak Breege gives to her nose she knows not to bark, and after a silent investigation of things leaps off, bounding, high-shinned.

They lay there quite quiet; miscreants, suspended in time and place, close and barely breathing, not touching, but their eyes agog in the dark, the voices and the footsteps coming nearer, then receding, the parrying and the joking, an ugliness creeping in as the sisters now realise that they cannot persuade him. They made one last and desperate appeal to him, said that if he helped them they would go as character witnesses for him into the High Court.

"I'm nearly bankrupt," Joseph said.

"Shite," Rita said, and added vindictively that maybe his hay would burn after all.

With his hat Bugler brushed her down, and with his hand he removed wisps of hay from her hair, fingering each strand as if he were unbraiding it. Then he moved very close to her, the shape of his mouth searching out the shape of hers. The kiss withheld for so long, given, taken, and retaken. Their ripe lips. Unfolding once more. Once more. Silently wooing. Silently clasped. He held her then, and the constraint that was between them was gone.

"I didn't think anything as nice as this could happen to me," he said.

"Is it wrong?" she asked in a whisper, meaning Rosemary.

"Do you think it's wrong?"

"No."

"Then it's not wrong," he said.

A promise was struck although no words were said. They merely stood in that radius of astonishment until the rattle of the car died away, and then raising his hand in the air and making the sign of the cross he said, "We have to thank the sisters for this."

BUGLER KEPT BUSY, that was his way. Off at six on the tractor, up to the woods to saw bits of scrub and fallen trees. It was a new saw, a block-breaker, it was called, and it could be heard for miles around, rasping, sucking into the wood as it cut. It wakened people, it aggravated people, it made him more unpopular. Rosemary had grown suspicious. She had taken to phoning even though they both agreed that it was too expensive. His phone was ringing the night he came in the door after he had that kiss in the hayshed. She felt there was something wrong. Was he sick? Had he fallen into a ditch? Had he hurt himself? She was ringing at some godawful hour of night, talking low so as not to be overheard, repeating her hunch that she felt something was amiss. No. No. No. He tried to put her at her ease. She wanted reassuring, wanted the words that are expected at a time like that, ringing on an instinct, wanted to be told that she was the only one and that was It. He saw his own face guilty and enlarged in the back of a ladle that was on the kitchen table, near where he stood. He was shaking. Women could do that. Rosemary, who always referred to herself as a witch, and Breege, light as a leaf yet full of passion, passionate. He had promised her to go dancing. Jesus. A dance hall in which they would be noticed even if it was a hundred miles away, and her brother and himself bound for the courts.

He could taste her kiss, so fresh, so fearless, fresh as that river they had seen that day months before, from which he had cupped water for them to drink. He made himself a hot whiskey and walked around his house proud of his own handiwork, the more practical half of himself gauging how many more months until the rooms were completed, plastered, papered, beds put in them, rugs put down on the wooden floor, which he would lay himself. There was a load of teak advertised in the paper and he had put a bid in for it. It was somewhere in a lorry in Gambia, probably waiting for a middleman to give the permits for it to be let out. Someone's livelihood for a year or maybe two years packed into that lorry. It would be a beautiful floor, the colour of a ripe cornfield. Gypsy followed him around the house, his tread as light as if he had donned slippers. He was not supposed to be indoors. You are not supposed to be indoors. He was supposed to stay outside like the dogs on the station, obedient to a master. The important thing was not to go dancing. Maybe she would forget it. Maybe she never heard it. He thought of something then that he had not thought of in twenty-odd years — how he slept with his brother Charlie and they had feasts under the pillow, and when things were very happy between them he called his brother Tom and neither of them could ever say why he called him Tom, but they found it funny and laughed over it. He thought of how he looked up to Tom, adored him, and the same weak kind of emotion washed over him the night he proposed to Rosemary in a dark room watching television. He could still see her as she was, curled up on the sofa bed, her foot inside his pocket, not fucking him, but begging to, and she so quiet, so unusually quiet and vulnerable, because she had come back to the station unexpectedly and he had been curt with her; the two of them quite silent watching *Frankenstein,* and her toes curled and trying to rouse him and his sudden spontaneous certainty that she was the girl for him, that they were for each other, and his joy and yes his tears when he proposed to her and she said yes, yes, I will marry you, Mr. Moody Mick Bugler. Now Breege, soft as moss, mossy, quiet-spoken, one kiss, admittedly a very long kiss, and there were rainbows inside his head and danger signals. Women sapped his will. The love of a woman or the fear of a woman, and now the unthinkable, two women, having to fail one or the other, or both. A traitor whatever he did.

THE MORNING HE took down the suitcase from the top of the wardrobe Breege begged Joseph not to go. Word had come of the name of the solicitors who had merged with another firm of solicitors who had acted for his grandfather and where the document might just be. He was surprised at her asking him not to go, and turning to her said with something of the old tenderness, "Don't worry about me . . . I'll be all right." She could not say to him that which she wanted to say, which was that left alone she would find Bugler and Bugler would find her, because since the night in the hayshed it was pending.

When he got to the town it was late, but having thrown his bag down on the bed he went to search for the solicitors' office, just to know its whereabouts and to be there first thing in the morning and maybe home by evening, home on the evening bus.

But it did not work out like that at all.

Each day he went to the secluded street with its row of stone houses, stone steps up to the hall doors with their highly polished knockers, stiff from non-use because everyone rung the bell. In the downstairs windows on canvas blinds the faded but venerable names of solicitors, six firms in all, side by side and possibly rivals to each other, and each day he curses his luck at being at the mercy of an impostor, a chancer who refuses to see him. He has been three times in as many days, crawling out of the poky room at dawn, to walk, to inhale the fresh air, and to buy a roll when the bakery opens. Each day the same sight, a straggle of people going to convent Mass and a lorry with a double orange yard broom affixed to the back sweeping up the skins and rinds of the night before. Always the same, the chapel bells, pigeons in the convent trees, hooting lorries, and across the broad sweep of the river a view of the hooting courthouse where he once was and will be again, then down to the solicitors with the secretary calling out, "He's not here," before he has spoken at all. When he rings Breege at night he says nothing of these frustrations, of being humiliated so, he says that things are progressing slowly, asks if she has counted the cattle and if she has noticed if any of them might be sickly, then promises to ring at the same time the following evening.

Each day he has been made to sit in a waiting room, his eye on the half-opened doorway leading to the hall through which everyone including the impostor must pass. He cannot get to see the man and is not told why. Moira, the secretary, keeps him in the dark, offering no explanation except that her supremo is a law unto himself, can't be hustled, won't be hustled, doing one hundred and one things at once.

Moira sits behind the desk feigning surprise at each face, each arrival, people she has lied to or insulted or sent away disheartened.

On the fourth morning he decides to be tough with her, to give her an ultimatum. He decides to go in there and threaten her boss with the Law Society, and he imagines how she will look up with her fat eyes and will get up, go through a door, and presently the double doors leading to the inner sanctum will unfold and he will be brought face to face with Mr. O'Shaughnessy. After some polite exchanges he will tell his story, and before long he will be let rummage in files and boxes, and as certain as he has been in each day's disappointment he is equally certain that he will find it because it is there. Thinking thus as he walks down the quiet street, he feels buoyant, but then he thinks of the woman he will have to sit next to, steel-grey hair, steel-grey eyes, crocheting a long strip of white lace and counting the stitches to herself. For two days she ignored him, then the third evening just before closing time, with Moira bustling to get rid of them, the woman turned to him and said, "You're here because of your land," and before he could even answer she went on, "Go home and forget all about it or you'll end up like me in the asylum."

"Are you in the asylum?" he had asked her.

"For fifteen years. I come here days because it was here I came before I lost it all . . . And they won't help me. And they won't help you, my dear man." She did not say it out of sympathy, not out of pity either, but in a kind of ecstatic revenge.

When he arrives determined to tackle Moira, he says, "I'll wait," before she even uttered a word.

"Oh, you could be waiting all day."

"I'll wait," Joseph says, and goes towards his usual chair, astounded by the fact that a screen has been erected around it, an ugly oat-coloured raffia screen blocking his view of the open door and the hallway.

"This is new," he says, and hits it with his elbow, hoping it might topple.

"Good God, no . . . It's always there," she says, and as he sits he realises that he will have to crane his neck to communicate with her or else shout underneath it. He has a full view of her feet, one stockinged foot placed on top of the other, massaging and mashing it, a worn court shoe kicked to one side.

"It wasn't here yesterday," he says.

"It was away getting fixed," she says, no longer the smarmy friendliness of other mornings: "Oh, poor you . . . the bother he's putting you to . . . away from your farm. If only you had a car phone like him, I could phone you the minute he stepped inside that door and you could chase over here and the two of us could nail him . . . get the effing thing out of him and by now all would be roses."

"I'm not taking it anymore . . . Go in and tell him."

"Jesus," she says, and with a hysterical laugh asks how anyone could risk doing that, intruding on a man with six different personalities, leaving herself open to a load of abuse and maybe getting sacked.

"Is he that bad?" he says, realising that she is his one and only chance.

"A divil," she says, and puts her hand to her upper lip in case the crochet lady overhears.

"You're not yourself today, Moira," he says.

"I'm low in energy," she says, and kicks off the second shoe to show friendliness.

"And why is that?"

"I was out late. I went to listen to this band . . . Marvellous . . . Outstanding, I would say . . . You should go yourself. They're every Wednesday. They're two miles outside the town. There's a pound admission but they're well worth it; outstanding," and as she rambles on he hears footsteps, the door being banged, and almost at once she is summoned by telephone. He has to crane to hear what she is saying. He guesses that what she is saying is that the mountainy man is back again and what is she meant to do and what is she meant to say. Her voice gets even lower as she mutters sorry a few times, obviously in answer to a reprimand, and when she replaces the receiver she starts to write very studiously into her big black notebook, ignoring the question he has put to her.

"He's in there . . . He's on the other side of those double doors," Joseph says. He has risen. He is staring lividly into the huge grey fogged eyes.

"He's with a client," she says, slightly apprehensive because of his nearness and his fist.

"I'm a client," he says.

"God's sake, will you keep your voice down or he'll flip."

"That makes two of us . . . Because I'm about to flip."

"Look," she says, and it is whispering time again, "I wouldn't advise it . . . He's in a foul mood. Effing and blinding. He must have been on a bender . . . Wait till after the weekend and I'll have talked to him, and with the help of God and St. Anthony I'll have it for you . . . He's always sparky on Monday mornings after he's followed the hunt."

"How can I believe you."

"Joseph Brennan, that's a horrible thing to say," and as umbrage wells in her she reminds him of the four days when she allowed him to sit and wait, twice making him coffee and listening to rubbish about the countryside, the gold dome of the mountain, bog cotton, and the tasty way his sister poached trout in milk and scallions.

"All I want is my piece of paper with my rights. I don't care what I pay for it. I don't care if I have to break his neck in . . . I want it."

"Oh Jesus, I don't envy him," she says, tears of commiseration in her eyes now as he dares her to lift the telephone and announce him, and in the fracas which follows as they call each other names he hears a door, then the hall door being banged, and in an ecstasy of righteousness she jumps up and says, "Mr. O'Shaughnessy has gone a-hunting."

Later, she finds Joseph walking up and down the street, talking to himself.

"The town crier," she says, mocking.

"I'm sunk," he says, making one last and desperate appeal to her. She scolds him, says he should not have spoken to her in that insulting manner, but being a good sport she is prepared to forgive him. She has a brainwave, she had it a minute or two after he left, he is to go down to Daffy's, the drapers, get himself togged out with cavalry twills, find a horse somewhere, and next morning join the hunt, and out there Mr. O'Shaughnessy is a different man altogether, hot punches, lords and ladies, hills and dales; out there they would be equals and they could do business.

"Where would I get the money for cavalry twills?"

"You have lots of money . . . Farmers always have money. I know that from the boss . . . The money that's found once they're dead. In jugs. Under mattresses. Fortunes."

JOSEPH STANDS IN his new shoes, good blazer, and best white shirt already regretting his impudence for having come at all. It was a junior who found him out on the street looking after Moira as she drove off in her bubble car. He was aware of the trouble and said that if it were him he would go and see Mr. Barry, a very highly regarded man who ran the firm before Mr. O'Shaughnessy came and was a sort of father figure to him.

"You think he'd help?"

"I'm sure he would."

They are out in the grounds, Mr. Barry's grounds, with Mr. Barry pointing to the cedar tree, taller, more striking than all the other trees, and in the roomy spaces between the paw-like branches, pigeons are rustling and cooing. The house itself is of brick, softly mellowed, the steps up to it covered with mosses and blue flowers faint as drizzle. The setting sun has turned the long windows into panels of fire.

"Would you care to guess how old the cedar is," Mr. Barry says, and without hesitation goes on to describe how a city man, an arborist, found the precise age by standing next to the trunk, measuring the girth, dividing, multiplying, and by some wizard calculations coming up with the age of the tree, which coincided with the age of the house.

"Arborists!" he said, walking his guest around the grounds as Joseph follows on tiptoe, to smother the sound of the new leather rasping in the piling of gravel and marble chipping.

"I wouldn't have come to you only I'm desperate," he says.

"I'm very glad you did . . . I always say," and here Mr. Barry breaks into song, "if I can help somebody as I pass along, then my living shall not be in vain."

"You have a fine place," Joseph says awkwardly.

"Shall we repair to the drawing room?" Mr. Barry says.

"Whatever you say."

"Damn midges get you out here, it's why I smoke," he says, and laughs shallowly at his own mischievousness.

"Sixty fags a day and never felt better." He leads the way, boyishly, up the steps.

As they step into the drawing room Joseph's first thought rushes to Breege and how she would love it — the white ceiling, like wedding cake, crisscrosses of carvings the icing, thin branches running in all directions from a centre rosette, and from overturned flower pots heaps of flowers spilling out. On the walls trellises of plaster arbour in between the paintwork, which is a bright saffron colour. Sumptuousness. Leather-bound books, a piano, armchairs, sofas, fresh flowers in several bowls, and music coming from the four corners of the room as if it were coming out of the spheres.

"Beethoven," Mr. Barry says, and scoffs at the native balladeers with their goatskins and their unwashed locks beating out barbarian tunes. He pours a whiskey each and leads them across to the fire, which as he says burns winter and summer, a ritual of theirs. The fire is his job, the flowers Mrs. B.'s. Yes indeed, he does remember Joseph's grandparents, especially the mother in her little black bonnet with the chinstrap.

"You have a palace," Joseph says, staring up at a plaster maiden offering a basket of fruit to a knight.

"Francini Brothers . . . Swiss . . . Did all the great ceilings in the country," and Mr. Barry tries to recall the exact locality which the brothers came from, then smites his failing brain cells and laughs jubilantly as he swishes the whiskey over the knuckles of ice, then winks at it.

Either to put his guest at ease or because the memory of it has just surfaced, Mr. Barry thinks aloud of his childhood, his beautiful childhood, the young nurse in the nursery ladling the porridge, a Miss Delany with a marvellous crop of auburn hair, an incitement to every young man who clapped eyes on her. Wicked Miss Delany, stealing out at night to meet the game-keeper in the malt-house, all of which, as he said, was hunky-dory were it not for the peeping Tom. A man with a flash lamp, who felt it his business to keep up with the erotica of the day or the night, spied on their courting, then went to the padre, who could not tolerate this on two counts, the commission of a mortal sin and with a man who was married. The upshot was that the priest called to the house and poor Miss Delany was dismissed and went to Spain to work for a duke and duchess, letters written back about her little dark-eyed charges, then no communication at all as she was put up against a wall, along with the royal family, and machine-gunned, by the Reds. He paused for a moment, blinked to correct a tear, and said how he always had a great interest in people, people were his adrenaline, he soaked them up. With an easy smile and wagging a finger, he said his antennae told him that there was something bothering his visitor.

"I'm worried sick," Joseph said, blurted it out. Then, in as concise a way as possible, he described Bugler's arrival to a farm that had been unoccupied for a few years and in no time at all lording it, first a field, then a bog, then a mountain.

"A grabber."

"You said it."

"Without a yea or a nay," Mr. Barry says, taking the letter which Joseph wishes him to read. He resorts to a more formal voice, occasionally looking through the open door lest they be overheard.

> We are obliged to tell you that the area between the lands marked red and blue, in other words the area marked brown, is not yours and desire you to give up all rights to it and to pay arrears for your usage of it for the last five years, profit made by you yourself without paying any rent or making any apologies for same. Our client intends to finish the road which he began some two months ago. His reason is quite

logical, it is to make egress to his house more possible. All we desire to know is that you do not stop him in this endeavour. Our application to the Courts will be to establish the registration of the ownership of the brown section to our client and to warn you that servants or agents entering that disputed corridor or causing obstruction therein will lead to further proceedings, which would be strenuously pursued.

"And you are quite sure that the brown area is yours?"

"Certain . . . My great-grandfather got it from a grand-uncle of his who had no issue . . . He won it. It was signed and sealed above in their parlour. The uncle was a gambler. My father told it to me often and repeated it on his deathbed . . . The papers are missing. That's my problem."

"And we need that piece of paper to take action against the depredations of the fly boy."

"If he finishes the road, I'm finished . . . The mountain becomes his."

"You've tried mediation."

"I hit him."

"Good man . . . A bar-room brawl. He deserved it." Looking to the ceiling Mr. Barry wonders whither the next step and whispers aloud: *"Regain de vigueur."*

"Grimes and O'Shaughnessy are the firm of solicitors," Joseph says, and as Mr. Barry hears it, he is struck once again by a bolt from the past, the distant past, and his eyes water as he remembers a Mr. O'Shaughnessy senior, a grandfather or possibly a grand-uncle of the present incumbent, who walked around with half his office in his overcoat pockets, yes, his big frieze coat with the pockets stuffed with all the evidence he needed to go into court, kept to himself, and hence earning him the sobriquet of Foxy O'Shaughnessy.

"The present man won't give it to me. Won't even see me," Joseph says balefully.

"That's very unprofessional."

"I go in every day and the secretary says to come tomorrow."

"Does she pass on the information?"

"That's what I don't know."

"He is moody . . . He does go hot and cold. But he's an okay fellow, likes a drink and so forth."

"I was wondering . . . Since you know him . . . Since you were partners, if . . ." Joseph begins, but Mr. Barry has already guessed.

"Now, my dear Joseph, I will, if I may, interrupt you . . . If I ring Mr. O'Shaughnessy . . . And of course I could . . . Nothing simpler . . . It will seem presumptuous. Think on it. He'll feel cornered. One of his ilk pulling him over the coals . . . It wouldn't look good. It wouldn't help. Now, the real solution . . . The cat's pyjamas, you might say, is for you yourself to compose a letter . . . A nice letter. A human *cri-de-coeur*. In a twinkle you will have his sympathy and eventually your piece of paper."

"I tried that."

The fire has gone down, the burnt sods like bars of molten pink, a few sparks intermittently bursting. Out in the hall Joseph can hear people arriving, greetings being called out and answered back, some with foreign accents as Mr. Barry explained that they take paying guests to keep their beautiful Kincora from going to some fly boy. On impulse he threw a kiss of gratitude in the direction of the hall. There was a smell of roast at intervals as when a door swung open, and Mr. Barry tried to recall whether it was lamb or pork for dinner. Distantly, there came the sound of a bell, light, appealing. Joseph knew that he should be going, but sat there forlorn, hoping that he might be pressed to stay.

"You and I should keep in touch," Mr. Barry said, rising, then he bent down and removed a smear of cut grass from his velveteen slipper, saying he could not look ragamuffinish in front of paying guests.

Joseph thanked him, thanked him profusely for the advice, even while knowing that he was going away disappointed.

Out on the road, away from the talk, the painted ceiling, a hallstand with only one hat on it, and cars coming at a hectic speed, he is lost, frazzled, directionless.

He stops to let the night air fall on his face and his features, trembling with disappointment, as if he were just finding out that there is only him . . .

To help himself along, he starts to recite, bits of poems, poems that he learned at school and others when he was away in that place and a nurse brought him back to his senses, made him read poems and learn them by heart. A line, lines, comes into his head.

> We met
> At the Hawk's Well under the withered trees
> I killed him upon Baile's Strand.

A car has stopped, a driver with his head out to ask directions gets for answer Cuchulain's adage: "And drew my sword against the sea."

"Oh, a basket case," the driver shouts, and tears off.

A HARVEST MOON LIKE an orange gong appeared over the ridge of the mountain, and soon it seemed to sail down in stately pearliness to hang above the lake, slits of moonlight creeping into the bottom of the boathouse as Bugler unties the rope, then, lifting an oar, he steers a slow passage through a lattice of tall bamboo and gold-rusted rushes. Water birds start up in revolt, their cries strangled, signalling outrage that the nighttime solitude of the lake is interrupted. A windless night, the water a mirror in which piles of moving cloud make soft, expiring patterns.

They sit facing one another, Breege directing the route, steering him away from the rocks towards the island with its tall tower as grim and admonishing as some elongated monk. Their shadows tilt and dance in the water and moonlight spills over onto her lap. They rode in silence and in silence he tied the rope to the make-shift jetty and they picked their way over the wet grass where a herd of cattle, some with wheezing breaths, were guarded by a young bull who looked as if he might charge.

The graveyard beyond the stone wall was divided into two sections, one for the remains of saints and ecclesiastics and the other for a few local families, including her own. There were several churches and a roofless stone oratory naked to the moonlight.

The tombstones glittered and the rings of stone which circled their double crosses held haloes of silver light. The only sound came from the lake, water being sucked in, a slurp-slurp that became muted as it was drawn back out. On the tombs splotches of moony shadow in contrast to white medallions of lichen, black flowers and ashen flowers, both.

It was Breege now showing him her world as if it were her house, a place she moved about in as easily as in her own yard or her plantation, walking over the graves, calling out the names, old people and not so old, young people, infants, handwritten mildewed messages under the broken glass domes where obviously the cattle had broken in and trampled. Last of all, she read him her own family names and then pointed to a strip of ground next to theirs but bordered off with smooth round stones which she had painted white.

"Why do you want your own bit of grave?"

"A bit of peace."

"Do you not have peace?"

"Not much . . . There's always something," and by the way she said it he knew what she meant and said that he was sorry, he was really sorry, but that maybe one day her brother and he would be reconciled.

"We'll forget about it for this one night," she said, moving across under the shadow of the tower, then opening a little gate that creaked and beckoning him into the cold oratory that smelt of mortar and limestone. Alone, in pairs, in triads, were the carved faces, solemn, bulbous cheeks and hollowed cheeks, the stone eye sockets filled with a grainy nothingness, all around the spectres of death that were a spur to the living.

"This church is named after you . . . St. Michael's," she told him.

"What was he good for?"

"A dragon slayer," and as she said it they laughed.

"We could live here," he said, his hand touching the stones, saying that with a bit of heat the place would be half habitable.

"We could an' all," she said saucily. Her shyness had lessened and she even accepted a cigarette to keep her warm. It was better than any hotel or any dance. Her reward for months and months of looking out at wet grass, or a bit of wet path drying in the sun, and sometimes even thinking that a garment blowing on the line prefigured the arrival of a visitor that just might be him. The tractor near or far, music to her ears and a gall to her brother's.

"Sometimes up at home at night I'd think of you only half a mile down the road," he said.

"Ah, men!" she said, pretending to be wise.

"Except I didn't know what would happen if I knocked on your door . . . What you would feel . . . What you do feel."

He stood before her, the light of the moon full on the top half of his body, so that his white shirt and his chest underneath it was like a ladder of dark stripes and lighter ones.

"Is it all right if I take your hand?" he said softly.

"I suppose so," she said, but she did not let him hold it for long.

Outside, she led him once again over the graves, telling him stories of the different families, loving families and feuding ones, families who had fought and wrangled and died wrangling, wills that had been changed on deathbeds, a husband and wife, Jack Darling and Betty Love, as they were known, dying within a week of each other and exiles brought from across the sea to be buried at home.

"When you marry, will your husband have a share of your grave?"

"Who said I'll marry?"

"Of course you'll marry . . . A beautiful girl . . . A beautiful woman."

"Talk!"

"It's not talk, Breege."

"That's the first time you ever said my name."

"Well, there's always a first time," he said, as if rebuked.

When she told him to look away he did, and he waited for her to recall him, but after he had finished the second cigarette he decided that he must go and look for her. He called, then whistled, then repeated her name, and the echoes came close upon one another, eerily distinct in that lonely place. He would not want to be there without her, and maybe neither would she.

He searched behind the gravestones and felt his way around the base of the round tower, expecting at any moment that he would feel her hair or her thin hands stretched out to be held. In the end he decided that she had left and gone down to the boat. It was only as an afterthought and on his way out that he looked in the moon-drenched oratory.

He finds her in the far corner, prone against it, like someone flung there, shivering with fear and cold, excitement and terror, her body a vessel with a zip of fire running through it. He is kissing her now, kissing her face full of tears. Holding her, he can feel the agitation as she both rests in his arms and wrestles to get out. He smooths and resmooths her hair, sparks of electricity shoot out of it, zoom out of it, and her face, always pale, is blanched and votive in the moonlight. She is like one of the stone figures except for her eyes, which are mad and shiny. He speaks fond hushed words, the two clasped bodies like one, their shadows one, and what seems like only one heartbeat hammering out.

All of a sudden there is commotion beyond the low stone wall as the cows and bull race around frenziedly.

"Why do they keep a bull here?"

"It's the butcher . . . He rents the grazing. My brother says it's to stop people getting across to their own graves . . ."

"Your brother," he says, half apologetic and half annoyed, and then asks her if she too thinks that he is a scoundrel.

"I do."

"Then why are we here?"

"We're here because you're two people . . . Like everybody."

"Are you two people?"

"Yes. My brother always said I was. He used to give me parts to play out in the fields. He said that I was Persephone."

"Who's she?"

"She's in a fable."

"So why her?"

"Because I loved picking flowers, primroses and things . . . She picked flowers."

"And what happened to her?"

"She was half the year in Hades and half on earth."

"Oh, Breege," he said, and then adds quite contritely, "I was sorry about Violet Hill . . . Really sorry."

"I know you were . . . He's never mentioned her again. He's like that."

"You're very good to him."

"Why wouldn't I be?"

"If we stay here, you know what will happen," he says, solemn.

"I want to stay here."

"You're a dreamer."

"Would you rather I wasn't?"

"No . . . I would not. I wouldn't change a single second of this."

"Still, in the year you barely spoke to me."

"There was a reason for that and you know it."

And they would stand a little longer in that sphere of moonlight, among the stone likenesses of saints and martyrs, not doubting, not hesitating, looking into one another's carved face as if for the first time and for all time, saying nothing at all, full of happiness and dread, as though love and fatality were one and the same.

"You're trembling," he said.

"So are you," she said, and they held each other then in that ordained nearness in which self is lost, self and other becoming one, one against cold desperate death and cold ravenous life, in that nimbus of heat and light, that ravish of courtship, that covenant which would be theirs for ever and yet never theirs, like flowers that are hatched in the snows.

❖   ❖   ❖

They rode home before dawn, the swish of the oars, then the creak of the timbers in steady alternate regularity, the sky streaked pink and mirrored in the glassy water, low hills all around plunged in a lilac drizzle, the water birds busy, bossy, preening and grooming, perched on whatever matting of reeds they could find. She felt strangely detached. Going back to the same life and yet different. She did not think that she would miss him. She did not know. He dropped oars as they passed into the thicket of bamboo and he began to whistle. It was a low whistle, rapt, sustained, attenuated; it was for her, for the pink of the sky, for the pink shimmer on the water, and even when it hurt his windpipe and his lungs felt as if he were being punched, he went on whistling, the pain in exact and excruciating ratio to the happiness that he felt, a whistle with joy and exhilaration and suspense in it.

"AT LAST, at long last." Joseph is clasping his hands together in a celebration and praising himself for having persevered.

Very soon it will be in his hands and he will walk out of there down the street a free man, then later to the bus station with his suitcase and a shop cake in a white box. They are on the first floor, with Moira knocking on a door marked *Private,* a yellowed lace curtain over the panel of glass. She is beaming, nudging him with "Didn't I tell you."

It is a big gaunt room with a desk, a chair on either side, and a surprising lack of clutter. In the excitement of being allowed in, he is slow in starting to talk, taking in all the features of the room, surprised by how shabby it is, a carpet full of cigarette holes and lifelong dust settled over everything. The fire grate is empty, but on the slate mantelpiece is a statue of the Infant of Prague, the little boy with his plastered and curled orange locks, and on the opposite side a carved black figure that could be man or woman. A bare room, a cold room even in summer, but what does it matter, he is in. The man who has agreed to see him is not the Mr. O'Shaughnessy whom he has been seeking for days, as he is now abroad on business and with no knowledge of when he is coming back.

"It's good of you to see me," he says, feeling at home with this man, who is not in the least bit crusty, big darns on his old jacket and a sty in his left eye.

"I'll take down all the particulars," he says formally as he opens a diary on which there is not a single entry. He flicks the pages, and all of them are bare, unwritten in.

"I've given Moira the particulars, it's a document about my father's ownership of a dirt road on the mountain near Derry Goolin . . . Where I was born."

"I've never been out to that part. I believe it's very scenic," the man says.

"You ought to. It's as near to heaven nature-wise as you could get . . ."

"And you're in litigation over it?"

"Not yet. That's why I'm here, you see . . . It's an old track that belongs to me and he has a right of way."

"So how can I help?"

"The proof is here. The piece of paper is here somewhere in this building."

"How far back was it?"

"Eighty or ninety years."

"We've had the odd fire and things."

"Jesus Christ, it can't be burnt . . . Don't tell me it's burnt."

"I'm not saying it is. All I'm saying is that it wouldn't be easy to find."

"Can't we look . . . Even if you're a busy man. You could let me root around. I have plenty of time."

"I couldn't do that. I haven't the power. All I can do is make a note of your case and talk to Mr. O'Shaughnessy on his return . . ."

"He's no use. Just let me open the files and search."

"That would be a breach of the profession. Every solicitor takes an oath."

"Goddamn your oath . . . Can't you see that I'm desperate. And I'm stuck."

The man seems to melt for a moment, then clears his throat and says, somewhat haltingly, "Unfortunately, I'm not a solicitor myself."

"What are you?"

"I'm just helping out. I used to be their bookkeeper."

"This is crazy . . . Craziness."

"As I said, I will bring it to Mr. O'Shaughnessy's attention."

"Don't send me out empty-handed."

"I have no choice. It all hinges on Mr. O'Shaughnessy."

"On Mr. O'Shaughnessy," Joseph says bitterly, and asks the man in the name of God to recognise how big a thing it is to him, his mountain, his life, his all.

"I can appreciate that."

"No, you can't, because you're a crook like him and you cover for him."

"I have to ask you to retract that."

"Think . . . Just think how easy it would have been any day this week for him to have seen me . . . To have helped me. But he didn't. He slunk away, either because he was too lazy or too busy or too afraid. And what does it do to me . . . It sucks up every ounce of hope. It finishes a person."

"That's a bit extreme," the man says, puzzled, and looking into the face with stark intensity up to and into the tortured blue eyes, he says, "I can't promise, but I'll look around for you."

"You won't let me down?" Joseph says, leaning across now and wanting to grip the man's hand.

"Ring me tomorrow to remind me again."

"Don't let me down."

HE ARRIVED PANTING in O'Dea's office just before closing time bearing a ribboned box of chocolates for Miss P.

The document which he handed over was thin as parchment, so that O'Dea held it gingerly as if it might disintegrate. It had obviously been torn from a larger sheet and it was a very faint copy, the boundary lines a spotted and fading brown. It carried the name of the mountain. There were divided sections within it, but no names and no entitlement, no writing save that of a blind lake and an area liable to flooding. It was over a hundred years old and bore the signature of an English colonel. At the bottom were the three capitals UND, which meant Undefined.

"This is like the Turin Shroud," O'Dea said, holding it up to the light to make sure there was no faint likeness concealed in it.

"We're in mighty order," Joseph said, excited.

"It has neither appurtenance rights nor servient rights . . . In short, it's a bollocks."

"We have him."

"We can't go into court with this, we'd be laughed at."

"Whose side are you on . . ."

"Common sense, God help me."

"If you don't help me there are others who will."

"Of course they will. They'll take your money. Think on it. Eight hundred quid a day for counsel. Two firms of solicitors. Ourselves and the boys in Ennis . . . Tot it up," and then recalling

Breege's desperate visit to their house late one night he relented, leaned across, and said, "Play ball . . . Let him cut his road and give us x number of pounds. That'll cover some of the outstanding bills."

"I always pay my way."

"Look, Joe . . . Stand back from it. Take the moral high ground."

"I'd sooner die."

"Jesus . . . Why are you driving yourself nuts?"

"I hate him."

"Sad. For sure that's sad."

"What is that supposed to mean?"

"You need a doctor. You need to get yourself sorted out."

"I never felt saner."

"Okay, then. Hear it from the horse's mouth . . . This document can't deter him from building his road, and if you go into court the most you'll win is a partition suit. They'll make the road a yard or two narrower."

"He'll die doing it."

"Christ, you're warped."

"He's out to get me."

"What does that mean?"

"I met him late one night . . . I was out at our own gate and he asked me if I would care to come for a ghost ride on the mountain."

"That's bizarre. Why didn't you go to the guards?"

"They wouldn't believe me. They're on his side."

Looking at the frazzled eyes, hearing the rapid jerky breathing, O'Dea saw the first dangerous sign, but because he had seen it so often, had seen men and women in that very same chair shouting murder, he thought, He'll get tired . . . He'll give up . . . They always do.

"Forget Mick Bugler. Go home and stock your farm. Get back on your feet," he says with a fatherly touch.

Sensing some slight, some slur, Joseph rises and leans towards him in that pose of useless and aping belligerence.

"Just because your daughter's pony is allowed to graze on his lands."

"Listen, Rambo, I'm no whipping boy . . ."

"You're on his side. I could report you . . . I could have you struck off."

They are standing now about a foot apart, the one chalky, fanatical, the other with a ruddy expression and the eyes emptied of everything except the terror that he would be reported on once again to the Law Society and this time it would be curtains.

"I take it back," Joseph says, quashed, as O'Dea lunges at him with bruising punches.

"You can't take it back. But you can take your junk," O'Dea says, handing him a folder that is bulging open, and then he pushes him out onto the stairs.

He stumbled out into the street with the folder. He was alone and evicted. He bought himself a naggon of whiskey and drove straight to the mountain. He parked his car at the point where work on Bugler's road had been begun and then halted. Looking in at it was like looking in at a crater, a wet hole with a few tins and bottles dumped in it.

He went up the mountain shouting, roaring against Bugler, who had loosed such grief and harm upon it. With each swig of whiskey he got braver, the roars more bellicose, like the bulls of old across the provinces shouting the commands of their kings and their queens. He felt brave. He sat himself on a height of rock, drinking, and every so often roaring, to confirm his claim. The mountain became nearer and dearer to him, like it was a woman, like he could embrace it, like he could pick it up and put it down again, like he could defend it against all marauders.

It was Boscoe who found him squatting in the heather, sunk into it, singing a song that was both sad and warlike.

"Hello, Joe."

"What do you want?" The voice hoarse and strangled from all the use he had given it.

"Come on home . . . It's no night to be out."

"I'm staying put."

"You are not."

They fought then, up there in the grey solitude, like two figures in a windy tableau, cursing, shouting expletives at one another that could not be heard because of a sudden blinding rain; they stumbled and dragged one another down and got up again, and in the end they tired of it and linked one another for balance and came perilously down, as lavish now in their praise and solidarity with one another as earlier they had been in their denunciations.

"He'll never own the mountain, 'cos," Boscoe vowed.

" 'Cos?" Joseph challenged.

" 'Cos, he's not able to talk to it."

"Correct . . . And what's more, it will never talk to him."

When they arrived at the crater they stood and stared into it.

"How about deploying our personal artillery?" Boscoe said, and with telling vehemence their volleys drenched the slag stones and the debris.

Full of verve now, they asked and answered their own questions. Would they be beaten, would they be dispossessed; nay, nay, and never. The long campaign was on.

❖　　❖　　❖

After that Joseph became a recluse. He was to be found in the parlour each night poring over law books that he had spread out on the table, a light bulb suspended above his head, the very first grey hairs above his ears piteously silver. He read and reread with immense concentration and underlined passages that applied, finding in them crumbs of hope, and he filled his notebook with citations of cases similar to theirs, of which there were thousands. She glanced at one of the books, at a section concerning quarrels between neighbours, but it applied only to city people, to arguments about ball games or garden refuse. He ate his supper alone.

"You get no fresh air," she would say, standing there, waiting for him to talk, to at least tell her what he intended to do next.

With a cunning now akin to craziness, he never mentioned Bugler, and he stopped his surveillance of her, urging her to go down to the town and enjoy herself. He knew that he could trust her, knew that she would not deceive him. He told her of the fable from Aesop about the dog who grasped the shadow and lost the meat. That dog was meant to be Bugler.

On the way out from Mass, when asked how he was, he replied in the same quiet but convinced tone: "Oh, the finest . . . The finest."

THE OLD MAN has not had a visitor in years. The cottage shows all the signs of neglect, the path up to it choked with brambles. He jumps up as he hears the latch lift and his name shouted a few times, a voice saying, "Dan . . . Danno."

"Almighty God but it's you . . . My one and only friend," he says to Joseph as he grips the hands, mashes them, then repeats Joseph's name and his own shock at having a visitor. A nurse comes once a month, but never a visitor. Many's the time he has wished for this, and now at last it has come true. He's an old man, not wanted; his eyes bad, four operations in all, two for cataract and two for glaucoma, and another soon for the cornea if the drops don't work. Joseph is a blur to him, but the voice is familiar, the voice of old when he took him up the mountain as a youngster to teach him target shooting. He recalls the man's cap which Joseph wore, the makeshift rifle range that they set up, and his excitement when he fired his first shot and then the next and the next, and after an age shooting the bull. Years have passed, but the memory is bright, the broken post with the card taped to it, the scattering of the pellets a furore in the emptiness.

"I taught you first the rifle, then the shotgun."

"You did."

"You were mad for the shotgun because it made a bigger bang, and I used to say to you, 'Take care, we think we're alone up here, but there's always eyes watching us, there's spies everywhere.' "

"I hope I'm not bothering you," Joseph says.

"Bother! You bring sunshine into my life . . . You're the only visitor I would have wished for, and I'll tell you something strange, I've dreamed lately of the two of us on that mountain and your wearing the man's cap and your handing me the bullets to load the magazine . . . Yes, that tweed cap you wore, we left it behind . . . And now you're here, and if it isn't destiny I don't know what name to call it by."

"I should have come sooner . . ."

"Do you ever think of those times and the fun we had?"

"Often."

"Old Danno trying to get you to zero in on the bull's-eye, and you a kid . . . At first you pulled the trigger too fast. I had to learn you to squeeze it, just squeeze it, and eventually you did . . . Cripes, the day you got the cluster was the breakthrough . . . So you haven't forgotten."

Even before he asks, Joseph knows that he will not be refused. He knows the wardrobe upstairs where they are kept, wrapped in rags and old newspapers; he can see them as he saw them as a youngster: the shotgun, the rifle, the old leather holster, and a revolver case that belonged to an ancestor, the hoard of bullets and cartridges, and as he asks to be let see them again, the old man's clouded eyes light up as if the sun is beaming in or as if they are back on the mountain.

They are upstairs now, the wardrobe door creaking over and back, a smell of damp and must, old cartridges and a belt scummed with dust, all thrown onto the bed, as Danno laughs and cries by turn. He recalls the mountain carpeted with heather, the curlews, and the bullets that were able to put life and spark into an empty and desolate space. Then he remembers that strange dog that appeared one day out of nowhere and sprung on them and had to be hit with the butt of the rifle before it went away.

"I often think of it . . . And I'll tell you something, I don't think it was a dog at all."

"What was it?"

" 'Twas the supernatural . . . Some kind of a warning sign.

After that I wasn't welcome in your house anymore. They thought I was bad news."

"Ah, they did not."

"They did so . . . They were afraid for you," he says lamentingly, and then, "You never married."

"No . . . Someone has to stay sensible."

Danno laughs again and says what lovely girls there used to be all around, lovely girls with thick crops of hair.

"And little Breege, how is she?" he asked.

"She's a big Breege now. I'll bring you over one day."

"Wait till I have the operation . . . Till we see how I get on. I'd want good eyes to look on the old scenes."

Joseph braces himself to ask it. He takes the old man's hand, and it is like holding a reed, its life gone.

"I was wondering," he begins, but Danno guesses it and, with rapture in his voice says that there was no need to ask, that sure it is only an honour to give a good friend a weapon.

"Lock that door," he says, and then reaches into the back of the wardrobe and takes out the shotgun and a box of ammunition.

"It's yours," he says, taking a bandage off the long muzzle.

"It's only for a while."

"It's forever . . . You'll bring this home and hide it, and when Danno is dust you'll remember him."

"Don't talk like that."

"I'll be well butchered when they get me into hospital," he says, and he is crying now, but joyful too at being able to pass on the only valuables he has ever had, his little armoury, and pass them to one who will revere them and not throw them in a ditch or hand them over to the authorities. To make things less melancholy Joseph picks up the wooden whistle made to lure foxes to their end. As he whistles into it, the squealing cry of a wounded rabbit is mimicked back, and they nod to one another, recalling how once or twice it worked and Mr. Reynard himself from upwind walked into the firing line. The whistle too is to be taken as a memento.

"Thanks a million," Joseph says.

"Do your stuff . . . Do your stuff," Danno says, and they pile them into a bolster case.

Downstairs they each drink a mug of tea and eat damp biscuits, talking of the escapades they had, the fires they made on the mountain, the eggs boiled in the same water as they used for tea, then a smoke, night coming on, the stars like pieces of diamond on the cloth of the heavens.

"Did you know that the Aborigines think that stars are holes in the sky?" he said then.

"They could be right," Danno says, and talks of the evils of modern mankind with no longer any faith in God or the stars or Mother Nature.

"You could stay a few days with us," Joseph says, rising to go.

"I have a friend in you . . . I always had," Danno says. He is reluctant to let his visitor leave, repeats the goodbyes, utterly sorrowful, talks of the great things, the wild things, and the uncanny things that transpired on the mountain, like the crying they once heard and a gypsy woman saying afterwards that that crying could be traced to unborn children, the unborn children of sweethearts that were never allowed to marry. Something about it moves Joseph, moves him to thinking that he should kneel down and confess and say why he has wanted the gun at all. But then something stops him.

"You won't get me into trouble?" the old man says, half throttled.

OCTOBER. THE WINDS. Like the song about Dromore he once gave her. The winds ripping all before them. The small trees, the alders, stooped from it, the tall ones skeletons, their leaves gone. Leaves in the air tumbling about, thick piles of them, gold and apricot on the sides of the road where the winds have whooshed them together, winds so very determined, ripping and tattering. A few roses clung to a bow of a briar and she was glad of it.

In bed at night she listened to the wind, thinking, was he thinking of her up there. She had sighted him only once and he seemed not to see her. It was in the chapel and he was wearing a green tweed coat that she had never seen before.

She wrote their two names with a bit of white flour on the top of the stove — Breege and Bugler, Bugler and Breege. She wiped it with her sleeve as she heard Joseph coming down the stairs.

Self knows before all else and self is useless to prevent it. Hopes starting up and dying down and starting up again, like different lenses, rose-tinted lenses slipped in between her dark thinking and her fancies. Then it was not fancy. Very early one morning, coming in from the yard with four eggs — one too many — in the palm of her hand, she dropped them, and bending to wipe them up she felt sick and went to the outside tap, retching.

The following Friday down in the town she made a mistake, quite a big mistake. The butcher's had run out of sausages and Niall, the young assistant, told her that there were a few packets left in the freezer at Mac's but to be fast about it. She walked her bicycle up the towpath, the ten-pound note in her hand.

In the shop waiting to pay for them she had one of those sudden longings, and already she pictured the sausages cooked, sizzling, ready to eat. Then her turn came to pay and the note was not in her hand. Where had it gone? She couldn't remember who she met in the short journey up the street. Soon she was convinced that she must have given it to Mrs. Mac, unknownst to herself. They argued, with Mrs. Mac opening the till to prove it was not there and lifting out a little wad of notes with a paper clip around them.

"One of those must be mine," she said.

"It is not . . . I clipped those notes myself a short while ago."

Voices rising, tempers rising, other customers turning aside in dismay. She tried then to give back the sausages, but Mrs. Mac would not hear of it, she plonked them back in her hand and said, "Take them and take your business elsewhere."

Out on the street, she wheeled the bicycle down the towpath, all the while hoping that she would find it, knowing that she would not, and thinking, I have made an enemy of a woman whom I have known for many years.

Early the following morning, she bicycled to the Glebe, where the Dutch woman lived. She had heard of her, how she cured people with different ailments, using herbs. She waited in the yard for the first stir of life, for a blind to be raised. In the shed across the way a huge hairy dog, the size of a calf, looked out at her sullenly but could not muster the energy to bark. In the greenhouse nearby the few remaining panes of glass held the tracings of a white frost as beautiful and as intricate as the lace of a mantilla.

I DREAMED. *A gold bird. It landed on my pillow and lay there, not like an ordinary bird at all. The beak was soft. It dropped drops into my ear. In the morning it would be gone. I'd look for it under the pillow and under the covers, but it would be gone. Then one morning it was dead on the pillow.*

She looks up at the Dutch woman, relieved that after an hour of silence she has managed to tell her something, in lieu of telling her why she is there.

"What colour drops, Breege?"

"Goldish."

"Saying what?"

"I forget."

"And it died?"

"It did."

"Who killed it?"

"I don't know."

Unable to look at the woman, she stares at the pictures and drawings of flowers and plants, their Latin names and their healing properties written underneath them. There are yellow and blue flowers, thistles, balls of dandelion seed, flowers and plants she has seen all her life, walked over, driven animals over, not knowing that in them might be a cure. She looks from them to three marigolds in a jug, their spears on fire.

"Is it loneliness?" the woman asks. She cannot answer.

"Is it money?" Again she looks as if she has not heard.

"Is it depression, Breege . . . Are you depressed?"

She looks away at a shelf packed with tiny medicine bottles, the orange nozzles like the teats of babies' bottles. Everywhere there are reminders.

"It's a man," she said then, the sentence coming out suddenly, but the true sentence all the same.

"Is he someone you know well?"

"I did know him . . . He hates me now."

"Why would he hate you?"

"Because . . ." She is unable to go on.

"Maybe he's afraid," the woman says.

"Maybe he's afraid."

"Or maybe he's torn."

"Is there anything you could give me to steady me?"

"Let's try . . . Let's see if we can do that."

The woman has sat her in a deep rocking chair. A pink stone is being held in front of her chest, and from its oscillations the woman seems to derive a yes or a no to the questions she is asking the body. She writes down the names of the different medicines that she will prescribe. The curtains are closed, a nest of candles that have been stuck onto a dinner plate are all lit, flames shooting up, veering this way and that, licking one another, separating, faint music like the music she once heard when Lady Harkness put a seashell to her ear.

The medicine which the woman drops onto her lips reminds her of her first Holy Communion and rehearsing the receiving of the Host, with Joseph putting bits of blotting paper on her tongue, out in the fields. Her eyes are fixed on a white rose floating in a bulbous vase of water, each gold thread of calyx a wisp as the woman tells her to send thoughts to him, how a thought, if it is powerful enough, can carry across fields, across counties, across continents, across anywhere. She feels warm, relieved, the woman telling her that her fears need no longer be bottled up, that instead of anguish, instead of hard feelings and dead birds, she will melt and remember the candlelight and the purity of the white rose. It is all true. Except. She knows that when she has paid she will have to leave, she will have to go out and get on her bicycle and ride home, pushing the bicycle up the last bit of hill, the crows swooping down, black plastic bags of silage, a world she had come away to forget.

Then all of a sudden it is not like that. The woman has had an idea, a brainwave. In an excess of solicitude and not knowing the black heart whom it concerns, she hears the woman asking her if it is possible to get in touch with this man.

"He lives here."

"Then you must go and see him."

"Could I?"

"How do you know that he is not hoping for that? Women are always the stronger. It is the women who break the ice."

"What would I say to him?"

"Say what you feel."

Already she felt heartened; she remembered how he held her that night in the graveyard, held her against the night, against the cold, against all that threatened.

THERE WAS ACCUSATION in his eyes even as he hurried down the stairs. I had not gone to trap him. I might have gone to appeal to him in some roundabout way, but seeing his vexed eyes put a stop to that. The very early hour probably told him that something was not right. Not that I knew myself. I was still ignorant of it.

"It's six in the morning, there must be something wrong," he said. We might never have known each other, so abrupt was he. But it was not to trap him that I had stolen out of my own house and gone up there. He closed his shirt buttons as if my seeing his chest had some impropriety in it. His eyes were narrow, narrowing, like eyes through a visor. Half his face was flushed up to the sternness of those eyes where he had slept on something hard.

You learn lessons in a flash. Along with resenting my being there, he feared me as if I carried a plague. To have said anything, a soft word or a begging word, would have been useless.

"I meant to let you know . . . Rosemary is arriving in the next forty-eight hours," he said very pat, and immediately and with no alteration in his tone, "I shouldn't have gone to the island. Being engaged is the same as being married and I swore . . . I swore." To confirm it he held up a ring. It looked cheap and brassy in the dawn light, like a ring out of a plum cake which he had put on as a precaution. There was no mention of my being asked inside, and from the corner of my eye I saw that he had furnished the dining room with six mahogany chairs and a very long, lonely table, funereal-looking. There was a glass bell on it. An ugly black wrought-iron fender with stout knobs as thick as cannon balls stood before an empty fireplace. Then I saw a child's cot, painted white, and it was like there was a child already in it. He saw me gasp.

"The woman threw that in along with the furniture," he said.

One's feet get one away from a place of their very own accord. I was out of there. Yet out on the muck road they lurched as if on ploughed land, and my mind was racing, racing, at all that I felt and saw.

I could hear him following and he was breathless when he caught up with me.

"We will be friends," he said, his eyes looking into me through my raincoat as if he suspected something.

"No, we won't . . . We'll be enemies," I said calmly.

"That will never happen."

"Oh, it will . . . They'll all make sure it will," I said, glad that I too could be cutting.

"Emotions always get in the way," he said with vehemence, and the strangest thing was that I knew then that he loved me, I knew it by that rebuff.

Half an hour later we were still there on the road, morning things starting up, sounds, dogs, the mountain a cupola of gold, gold threads of light streaming down from the heavens and him trying to tell me what it was to be a shepherd, to be on a sheep station, to have felt a homesickness for something and then a woman coming along, Rosemary coming along, and now a homesickness for something else.

"It'll be all right when you see her," I said, because I knew that was what he wanted me to say, to let him go.

IT WAS HARRY DUGGAN who told of Rosemary's arrival. Boasted of it in Nelly's Bar. Described this fine lady singling him out at the airport where he had dropped off passengers and was on his way home. She was unmet because she wanted to surprise her fiancé by coming a day earlier. Her luggage, as he said, was something else — suitcases, bags, boxes, hatboxes, sheepskin rugs, and a gilded birdcage. A glamour girl in a long black leather coat and suede boots that went up to her fanny. He described the car journey, Rosemary laughing and smoking, asking him to pronounce the quaint place-names, then her good humour as three pieces of her luggage came tumbling off the bonnet. She sat, as he put it, on the ditch while he tied the pieces down with a rope that he had borrowed from a house nearby.

At dusk they headed up the mountain road, and arriving at the mud track that led to Bugler's house, she looked at it and said "Blimey," then put out her arms for him to carry her.

He spoke then of the lovers' reunion. Never seen anything like it, Rosemary so vivacious and Bugler walking into the yard flabbergasted, asking why she hadn't let him know. He described their eyes drinking each other in, something not easily discernible in the dusk, then Bugler taking her inside and himself having to bring the tractor down the dirt road to unload the luggage into it, ferry it up again, and lay it in the front hall. The most touching moment, as he put it, was when her ladyship took off Bugler's old hat and donned a new one, identical, and said, "Until the hat dies . . . Or until we die."

That, as he said, put the smile on Bugler's face.

He was questioned again and again about her height, her colouring, her age, what sort of accent she had, and his answer varied with the moment, but one thing he could assure them of was her magnetism, as they would soon see for themselves.

"They'll be tears in the crowded congregation," the Crock said.

"What does that mean?" Nelly said.

"Ivory Mary."

"I thought all that died down."

"It did, but it started up again."

"How do you know?"

"I have reason to know."

"Well . . . There's no woman in this neighbourhood that would hold a candle to Rosemary," Duggan said.

WHEN HE SAW the figure beyond the kitchen window Bugler thought for a moment that he was imagining it. A case of bad conscience. The old guilt thing. "Don't expect miracles" were his last words to her when she phoned the week before. Now she's in the kitchen, putting a hat on him, saying, "Mick, Mick."

"Surprised to see me?" Her voice so raucous, so full of vitality.

"Of course."

He takes her hand almost formally; her nails are painted bright red and long as beaks. He remembers that she used to bite her nails and put brown stain on them to break the habit.

"I can't believe it."

"You better believe it."

"You've got thinner."

"Not from shagging," she said, and from one of her bags she pulled out a sheepskin and held it to his chest for him to smell, to remind him of that smell of before.

"I can't believe you're here," he said, looking from her to the naked bulb on which the dead flies from the summer had scummed.

"That's because you don't expect miracles," she said, burying his face in the sheepskin, which brought it all back, the station, his favourite dog that lost a paw, the dark of the mornings, the weird lonely bleating of thousands of lambs, rain and drought, the old macrocarpa trees always creaking, full of magpies, thousands of magpies cawing and Rosemary coming one day into it to bail him out.

"How long was the journey?"

"I don't know, thirty hours or something."

"You must be exhausted."

"That's not a romantic thing to say."

"Oh, baby, baby," he said with her mouth everywhere on him, his face, his neck, his chest.

"Yes, I'm your baby, and you were beginning to forget her." She pulled him down on the sheepskin then and began to undress him with a remembered excitement for his body, his flanks, his knowing cock, the same sequence of words, half girlie, half whore, words that he was too shy to tell even his best mate Stuart of, when Stuart asked how they did it. Words that were triggers to some mad voltage in him and would be to any man, and he knew now that he would make love to her for days. She knew it too, she had come, his piece of pie.

❧   ❧   ❧

It was the same as before and yet not the same. In that other place with the mates, jealousy, her spunkiness, there was a thrill to it, a danger, but in this place it did not seem so right.

Not her fault that something had shifted inside him. Not his fault, either. Remembers the good times, that first day when she sallied into the sheep station in her woolly jacket, all businesslike, determined to keep her end up, not to be intimidated by so many blokes. "What's it like to be the only female around here?" the Swede asked, and Kitty, the wizened cook, called out from the kitchen, "Hey, cheeky, I'm a female in case you didn't know." All Rosemary did was shrug.

"Why do you all carry knives?" she had said, looking down the length of the mess table at the weathered faces, the totem knives, and the piled plates of greasy stew.

"In case we have to slit a sheep's throat," the Swede said. He didn't like the idea of women coming there, women took all the simplicity out of things and got the men into scrapes. He tried to frighten her then with tall tales about wild dogs and wild shearers having fighting bouts because there always had to be a winner and a loser. She ignored him.

"Ever see an eyeless sheep?" he said.

"Not that I recall," she said, and he insisted on describing how the gulls swooped down on the unfortunate sheep and took an eye out, then a second eye, for a snack.

"That's interesting," she said, and began to write it down for her report.

Out on the trail the mates were betting as to which of them would get a leg over her. That next Saturday night with the old roustabout, the guitar, and the beers, things got heady. Her sitting on the arms of different chairs in a short satin dress and the guitarist getting fresh with her and pulling her onto the sofa. Having to take him outside and give him what's what. That did it. They danced, and it was from that to his quarters, the mates on the veranda with their ear to the door, wondering how in hell's name he got her in there so fast. Academia no more. A little avatar. Like being with a bloke. Picked him, she said, because he had a good bum. Love didn't come into it. She didn't want love. Wouldn't allow for sleep either. Why sleep? Eskimos sleep. Not shepherds. Shepherds wouldn't miss the razz, would they?

Within a week things had changed. She had resorted to old-fashioned things like hand-holding, kissing, and on the last night admitted to be "absolutely melting inside." Got to like her more from her letters. Stories of her childhood on the beach, baked from the sun, boys and girls up to no good in the bamboo huts, and then at fourteen deciding she wanted a good education. Wanted it for him too. Their huge appetite for passion made it all the more essential. She would take him out of there. He was wasted on a sheep station. He was made for bigger things and a shepherd was not that. Promising him the trip of a lifetime, not just in the sack but in the workplace. He'd lie on the bed pulling at the florets of the candlewick bedspread and imagine her naked and wet under her jeans and sweatshirt, her nipples a dripping painted cocoa colour. He was homesick, Rosemary sick. He wrote poems and soppy letters. Very soon he was in the city working as an assistant in a shoe shop, which, as she said, was step one. Daddy would see to step two. Daddy a right pseud, flaunting his atheism.

❖ ❖ ❖

She wakens baffled, not sure where she is. He has been watching her while she slept. Watching the fire flames licking the brown-black nap of soot in the chimney stack and thinking what he would say. For a moment he was quiet. Looking at him she sensed that in the time since he left her he had altered.

"Are you okay?"

"I've come halfway across the world and you haven't even asked me why."

"Tell me why."

"I was starting to feel unsure, Mick."

"You needn't."

"I think the deep-down passion isn't changed . . . But your letters . . . Your letters made me quite angry. Don't expect miracles. Shit."

"That's me, Rosemary."

"No, it isn't . . . You're hiding something."

"You're just tired."

"I'm just tired," she says, and holds her engagement ring to the light of the fire, the blue stone itself a lit spark. He remembers with a qualm the Saturday he bought it, the second-cheapest one on the velvet-backed tray, the only one he could afford.

"Did you think this would keep me quiet?" she says, holding it up.

"You know I didn't."

"I don't know . . . Maybe you thought, I'll scoot back here to Ireland and leave her dangling . . . I wasn't in good shape, Mick."

"I know, I asked you to come with me."

"And I said, I'll come when we're married . . . Try to understand, Mick . . . My folks . . . They wanted the best for their daughter. The country is small, even if it's big, the society is small, they want a wedding."

"They'll have it."

"You don't understand how much I love you," she said.

"I do," he said.

For the first time he realised there were no curtains on the window and that anyone could have been looking in. Jumping up, he jerked and pulled on the buckled shutters that had not been dislodged in years and when he closed them there was a hollow clatter. Then a folded butterfly drifted out and opened up before his eyes into a tautened beige-and-orange fan of tortoiseshell.

"A visitor," he said as in his cupped hand drops of moisture leaked from its thin fidgety fibres.

"THIRTY! She'll never see thirty again, or thirty-one or thirty-two."

"And the skin — sallow."

"Excuse me, Josephine . . . It's yellow . . . It's jaundicy."

"And what about the accent?"

"Deadly, Miriam . . . Deadly."

How they chuckled, how they gloated in their demolishment of Rosemary. They were back from Mass, they had made their Holy Communions, and they pushed two tables into the corner of the bar, then sat on stools and window ledges, each bettering the other in their dissection of her. To Breege it was as though the words came down out of the air, disembodied, ugly words, about a woman who had no existence for her until a short while before when she saw her linked to Bugler in the chapel grounds and people congratulating them.

"Yous are very pass-remarkable," Derek said, bringing their tray of Irish coffees while the Crock predicted that they would outdo each other in their choice of wedding presents.

"June, I'd say."

"Sooner . . ."

"What do you say, Breege?"

She doesn't answer. She thinks, If they come in, I will have to go out, but I can't go out yet, I might bump into them, and so she sat there, half heeding, and then saw him put his head through the door and withdraw. He saw her at once and touched his hat, but the look he gave her was inscrutable, neither a liking nor a disliking, a blankness as if something had been erased in him.

Within minutes they had returned, and there was something almost rehearsed about it, the way Rosemary linked him as he introduced her to each one. The women were lavish now in their welcome, each offering her a place as she was being begged to hold out her hand for each one to admire the engagement ring. They marvelled at its blueness, one minute sapphire, the next minute amethyst, rating it much more original than the ordinary diamonds that you see in the jewellers' shop windows. It was Miss Carruthers who asked her if she missed home.

"I haven't had time," she said, and looked at Bugler and smiled knowingly.

She made a note of each of their names and said they would have to come up for the Christmas party and bring their hubbies.

"Christmas!" Josephine exclaimed.

"He's promised me snow," Rosemary said.

"You've never seen snow?"

"I've never seen it falling . . . I've never seen that bit of magic, have I, Mick?"

"We'll pray for a snowstorm," the dressmaker and her twin sister said.

Breege would always think that Rosemary had followed her into the ladies' room because she saw, she sensed. There were two Rosemarys in there, one in the mirror and one in the room itself, her high heels blatant on the tiled floor.

"And what do you do, Breege?"

"Nothing . . . I look after my brother."

"No boyfriend?"

"No," Breege said, very distant.

"If Mick gave me a good reason to shave my head, I'd shave it," she said, opening a tin packed with flat discs of lipstick that were like the paints in Aziz's paintbox, only cleaner. She blended the colours, brushed them on, pursed her lips, and smiled at herself. Then she held out the ring, and as if it had an enchanted power she said, "He'll always come back to me . . . Because I have this."

Breege stayed there, not looking in the mirror, feeling the cold truth of things run up and down her body, and then it happened. When she tried to say something to herself the words would not come out. It was as if a stone or an implement had been put down her throat, cutting her, cutting the words, and when she tried to say just one word, any word to reassure herself, it would not come out. She opened her mouth and looked in at her gums, which were moist and beaded, and she tried desperately to say the letters of the alphabet as she had first learned them at school, but she couldn't. They would not come. Holding on to one bit of ledge and then another and then to the glass door handle, she told herself to remember the things out there, normality, coffee, conversation, biscuits, Rosemary, Bugler.

"I'm getting a stroke," her mind said, though she did not know what a stroke was. Something awful had occurred and there was nothing else at all in her shattered world.

Derek, who saw her run out, said that she ran like someone called to judgement.

MRS. NOONAN, THE sacristan, about to lock up, hears noises in the rear of the church and runs to the sacristy calling "Help, help!" She lifts the intercom to the priest's house and waits, fearing there will be no answer. No one there, no one to come to her assistance, only the vestments laid out for next morning's Mass, white vestments, ghostly in the gloom. She had already turned off the lights and is now too afraid to walk out to the side of the altar and turn them back on again. Her heart is churning. She who used to be afraid of dead bodies in the coffins that were put there for one night is now more afraid of vandals. Half of her wants to escape through the sacristy door and out the garden, but her long years of service oblige her to stay. To leave now would be to allow the intruder, whoever it be, to rob the collection boxes and do unspeakable things in the sanctity of the chapel of which she is so proud — the scrubbed tiles, the polished pews, and the jugs of berries on the altar steps, there being no flowers in season. It is December. She thinks of this vandal as a him, out there, a sacrilege to the red glow of the sanctuary lamp, to the Host in the tabernacle, to the priceless stained-glass windows, those rivers of blue within blue, virgins and martyrs with infants being born not from lower down, but coming out of their chests in clean and undefiled incarnations, others holding the bruised and bleeding heart of Christ in an ecstasy.

She waits, listens, opens the door a fraction, and, hearing nothing, decides it must have been wind or leaves that blew in, and so she ventures out, carrying her set of keys on a metal hoop and a broomstick. Slowly she goes down the aisle, and in the dark she hears what might be prayer or might not. Torn between going back behind the altar to where the set of switches are or going on down, she continues on, gropes in the big brass metal sconce for the matches, and relights the candles, which are still smoking, having been quenched only moments before. They are thin candles, halved for economy's sake, and the pencils of wan light are barely enough to guide her towards the source of the murmuring. She is flabbergasted. A grown body has climbed into the crib, a woman's body, as she can tell by the shoes. Leaning in, she sees Breege Brennan lying in the straw alongside the donkey, the zebra, the infant Jesus, and the Holy Family. Before shouting out she blesses herself, knowing that something profane has happened in the House of God, and soon she is striking out with the metal keys and the handle of the broom which she brought to defend herself.

"Breege Brennan, if you don't come out I'll drag you out," then receiving no answer she pulls first an arm, a leg, tugs at them to no avail. The hussy burrows herself down in the straw so as to be invisible. Hearing someone outside, she runs shouting for assistance, and presently Miss Carruthers and herself are tackling their stubborn charge. They pull in vain, they slap her face, they tell her the reprisals that will be hers. She has slumped down and is looking through the straw with huge and terrified eyes.

"She's possessed."

"With what?"

"I can guess what," Miss Carruthers says peevishly. "We better get the priest."

"He's not there, he's out on his farm."

"If he farmed less and paid more attention to the faithful, we wouldn't have this catastrophe."

"Miss Carruthers, I won't hear a word against Father," Mrs. Noonan says, marching to the outer porch to ring the bell, to summon help from the town. The loud jerky peals ring out in a mighty consternation and Breege knows how everything is listening, outside and inside, the stations of the cross, the sanctuary wick in its bowl of oil, the purple half-curtain of the confessional door, and that soon the townspeople will come trooping in.

They are mostly women who have foregathered. They ask if she is drunk or drugged or out of her mind. They lean in, sniffing her, and then Josephine, wondering if she is *compos mentis,* puts some test questions to her: "Breege, what day is it? Breege, name the President of this country, name the President of the United States of America." She doesn't answer.

"She's doing it for attention."

"Bold is not strong enough a word for her."

"Flipped . . . flipped," Lydia, a younger girl, says, and liking the word so much and her importance in saying it, she repeats it several times, saying shouldn't a doctor be called. Reaching to lug her out, to end this nonsense, Miss Carruthers pulls Breege by the shoulders, but is sent skidding, her rimless spectacles falling ahead of her on the tiles. Mrs. Noonan, who had shuffled off, has returned with an ewer of cold water, and with a determination that could only be called vengeance she douches her, feet, stockings, coat, and last of all her face. They are laughing now, all of them laughing at how grotesque she is in there, wet stockings, wet hair, hunched up like a wet hedgehog. One remembers how she saw it coming, Breege Brennan going into Mrs. Mac and accusing the poor woman of stealing her ten pounds. They speculate on what she might next do, curse, scream, maybe even bite someone.

"Keep back, keep back" is muttered now, all averring that something deadly has occurred. Hearing them, Breege raises her hand and moves her fingers to speak.

"Sssh . . . sssh . . . She wants to say something."

"What is it, Breege?"

She tries, but the words won't come.

W HEN THEY LED me in here and showed me my bed with the little plywood chest of drawers for my odds and ends and for treats that I might get, such as chocolate biscuits or orangeade, I wanted to die. Twenty beds in the ward, nearly half of them vacant. The counterpane was of a pale flowered stuff that feels coarse to the touch. A woman came and stood by me and offered to be my friend — Millie. She showed me around.

"That's the dining room, that's the painting room, that's the television room, and that's the Quiet Room." When she said the Quiet Room she made faces and stuck her tongue out. If anyone roars or screams, or smashes windows, or hits out, or goes effing and blinding, they're for the Quiet Room. In there, alone, to scream their guts out. There's a mattress on the floor. A room waiting for roars. The lamentations it has heard. If I were put in there, and I might be, there is no knowing what would transpire. Would I scream or recant? At the end of it something would have been hauled out of me. I don't know. And they do not know either — the nurses, the doctors, the psychiatrists. They ask questions. Are our minds racing? Do we think other people are reading our thoughts? They write down what we say; then three times a day someone comes with a plastic eggcup of pills and stands over us to make sure that we swallow them, to make sure we don't grind them between our fingers and put them in the potted plants. There are male and female nurses. Other staff sit in offices by their electric fires with sheaves of notes on their desks, trying to unravel the pickle of our lives. Country people. City people. Young and old. Strays. A woman across the way has not once opened the flowered curtain around her bed. Her meals are brought to her. We are of all ages. Two of the girls have teddy bears, they are studying for their exams in the summer.

Millie, who showed me around the first day, took against me on account of my not speaking to her. I tried my vocal cords in the bathroom and a sound came, but no speech. In the mirror, I saw the terror jumping in my own eyes. Terror of what. Terror of everything. Millie thinks I hate her. She is in love with a doctor, paces up and down in her loud paisley trousers that are much too tight for her, and says that she will write to him for Christmas and he will come. She can wait until Christmas, but not a second longer. She'll burst then. She called me Loretta the day I arrived and asked me to hold her, said no one ever held her, not even this doctor of whom she dreams, to whom she sends her voices. Often she curses. Her nails are bitten and so are the stumps of her squat fingers. All bloody, all bloodied.

"I'm like that inside," she said, and held them up for me to kiss. Minutes later she erupted, said that I did not like her, that I told stories about her, dirty things.

I prefer being out in the grounds, at least I'm outside, I can breathe. Therese is in charge of us. One day she's all over me and the next day she's shouting. Commands, commands. She dug up the pansies that I put in. They lay on the ground, their little purple faces shrivelled, their clayey roots dead. Another of the gardening brigade is called Nancy. She's not a local. Her husband went up in flames in his own house, in his own wheelchair. She laughs, splits her sides telling it. Took the house with him. Fuck him, she says. Left her nothing. She tells it to everyone, even the young man who delivers the trays of cakes and bread and sausage rolls. She tells him and others how the phone call came to the office, how a nurse had to break the news to her, and soon after the two of them got into a posh car to go home for the funeral. Nothing to bury, only this small pile of ashes. She laughs. I don't know whether she's telling the truth or not. You never know.

Sometimes out in the grounds someone will whisper, "What did you do?" They like to exaggerate. The men are dying for a kiss, even the old men. They sit on the wood benches and make slobber sounds. They try to get us into conversation.

No one will tell me how long I am to be here, and I haven't asked. There are some who have lost the will to go home because they have company here, even if it's company they fight with. The meals all taste the same — the stews and the roasts and the bacon and cabbage, all identical. The sweet things have a bit more flavour. I am never hungry. The opposite.

My brother put me here. Dr. McCann and himself did it. When he saw me looking back at the house and my little plantation, he turned and said, "Don't hold it against me, Breege." He was in the front with the driver, Tom Liddy. They talked to one another the whole time, as if everything was tiptop. They said that it was different to the old days, people were no longer in strait-jackets. It's not that different, it's still locked up. We had an uncle here, but my brother did not mention it. He stayed in our house once. He chain-smoked and would laugh for no reason. Tom Liddy said that March was the month when most people went loopy, like the March hares.

It was after I got into the crib that Joseph put two and two together. A piece of paper that he found on the dashboard of the tractor. The rain had run onto it, but he guessed it, my secret, my rained-on plea. I asked Bugler to see me just once. I begged. I hate that I begged. My brother said it was a sickness. McCann and himself said that it was a child's crush inside a twenty-two-year-old woman, a daftness. Maybe it was, maybe it is, but how can you stop liking someone, even loving someone, how. I would have got into the tabernacle that day if I could have fitted. It was a loneliness to get closer to Jesus or the Holy Ghost. Or else to disappear, to vanish. Bugler opened up some vein in me, and it is not his fault no more than it is mine. I will know him again, I will be the one to hold him when dead, the one to bury him. I know that. Hard ground, ground as hard and knotted as people, including him. You can go years and years of normal life, all day, every day, milking, foddering, saying the given things, and then one day something opens in you, wild and marvellous, like the great rills that run down the mountain in the rain, rapid, jouncing, turning everything they touch into something living; a mossy log suddenly having the intent and slither of a crocodile.

Down in the surgery, Dr. McCann and my brother tried to pluck it out of me. They couldn't. I had gone silent. That was my way. It was not the first time. Years ago, a different doctor, a lady, operated on me in our kitchen, no anaesthetic, no nothing, men holding me down while she dug the knife. Weeks after, she called on us and I was asked to say her name. I wouldn't. I couldn't. They stood me on a chair so as to be level with her face and her velour hat, but I wouldn't. She was livid.

So were they, McCann and my brother. In between coaxing me they thumped me, and McCann put a tiny torch down my throat, then a spatula on my tongue, forcing me to say A's.

"Unreal . . . fecking unreal," he said, and got out another encyclopaedia. Joseph gave me a cough lozenge to suck, thinking it might do the trick.

Leaving the world you see it more clearly. It is like things lost, earrings or brooches, they loom up in the mind's eye. People too. The way I see Bugler in his many guises: on that dance stage in the red shirt with the dappled patterns, his throat soft but stretched, emotion in his eyes.

It was a beautiful winter day that I left home, the trees bare, their trunks so sleek and damp, the sky all pageant, clouds of every denomination, their pink-frilled edges overlapping, like the waves of the sea. Sunset like a monstrance, spokes of light forking out from it, white white gold. I thought how in summer all the trees are twined together by foliage but in winter they stand alone, stark, leafless. The same with people. In happiness they seem all one, but in misfortune they are apart. It would have been useless to defy them. And I had nowhere to go. Certainly not to him. I will not be listening for the sound of a tractor in the future.

As we were passing the big power station, the pylons glistened, wires taut with messages, messages of love and hate and pity and condolence. Goodbye, Bugler.

There were no entrance gates, just a wide gap where two gates would have fitted, and my brother turned to me and there were tears in his eyes: "I'd do anything to see you better."

"Fine place," Tom Liddy said. He could not have meant it. The stone and the plasterwork of the main building looked dilapidated, slates had fallen, the gable wall full of cracks, with ivy growing out of them. That was when I first saw Therese. We all saw her, going across to the single-storey chapel. She holds the keys to the chapel and keeps it locked as it suits her. When she saw us driving in she put her shovel down and came across and asked us for cigarettes and money. Liddy said we hadn't any and she told us to fuck off, fuck off. A stubby woman in black boots with a shovel. If you did a drawing of her it would be that.

They encourage drawing and painting. One of the young girls, Dolours, does it. She draws pop stars with a single eye. The third eye she calls it.

Always coal black and slanting. She signs her name in flowery lettering. Otherwise she is a fashion plate — jeans, tight bodices, and very high platform shoes. Tall as a flamingo. She carries her makeup kit with her wherever she goes: to the bathroom, to the painting room, to the dining room, wherever. Her eyeshadow is a pale lilac, which makes her look in mourning. She was due for release, but not now. She went into the bathroom a few evenings back and cut her wrist, at least grazed it. With a broken bottle. Her friend Chrissie had done it, so why not her. Chrissie had told her that seeing the blood and watching it drip was brilliant, gave her a fantastic sense of release. They are supposed to be studying, but boys are all they can think of. Chrissie says there's not nearly enough men in the world; she'd do anything for a snog.

McCann was furious with my brother for having allowed me to see the herbalist, the Dutch woman; he was against her because a lot of his patients defected to her. He said no one with an ounce of common sense would pay for dandelion coffee or thistle milk or a thong of yarrow root. They kept asking things. Why had I got into the crib. Had I my faculties when I did it. Where was my voice box. Why didn't I mix more. Why did I cut up a silk neck scarf in two and then sew it back together. All the time I knew they were weevilling their way around to Bugler, because they wanted him nailed. By now I had a pen and a jotter to answer things. My head was fuzzy like glass paperweights with the snow in them, not clean snow, more like shovelled snow. It was after midnight. The ashtrays were bulging with their half-smoked cigarettes. They asked me did I consort with Mick Bugler, and I shook my head. No one knows about the night on the island, only him and me and the waves. They said that there was nothing for it, only to ring the fecker. Let's ask him, they said. I was sent out to the waiting room. I prayed that he would be sound asleep, or off at a dance with Rosemary. The phone must have rung a lot of times, because I was able to pick up comics and magazines strewn on the floor. They called me back in. I do not know what he could have said, or even if they spoke to him. All they did was to pronounce my condition: *Hysteria ad absurdam.*

McCann got out the forms and began to write.

"Your mistake is that you believed," my brother said, dismayed. He wanted me to forgive him for what he was doing to me.

❖   ❖   ❖

Dolours is at the end of the bed in a black satin skirt, her thin body atilt, her eyes with the glitter of marcasite. She wants to know if I'd like a tattoo. Her new boyfriend does them, it's his trade; he warms the needle with a cigarette lighter, pierces the design, and then paints over it. She shows me hers. It is a little serpent. He needs the money. She is hoping to go out on the quiet at the duskies to give herself to him. She'll sweet-talk the male nurse. There is nothing she loves more than giving herself to a man. She's had oodles. She says every inch of her body is covered in love bites. She shaves because they like that. All of a sudden, she is clinging to me, breaking, sobbing. Why are we here, why are we here? She's howling it. Explain. Explain. No one can.

Is it the serpent. Is it that we love too much. Or is it that we don't love at all.

"Aagh!" The young baby calls loudly in the pushchair. Oh no, not again, I fed that baby an hour ago, says mother. "Aagh!" The young baby calls loudly in the pushchair. Poor baby, must be hungry, let's give it something to eat, says mother.

Two different reactions to the same call from a young baby in need. Two women, mothers. One exemplifying worldly selfishness and the other willing to sacrifice herself for her young.

It is the third Sunday of Advent and the chapel is crowded, the nave, the main aisle, the side aisles, the gallery, all packed; people arriving and trying to steer their children ahead of them, looking around to see where there might be empty seats. Other children already in an orgy of screaming, and Canon Daly, never a patient man, irked by this bedlam, is glaring out at the parents as if that could silence them. Undeterred, he rested his arms on the edge of the pulpit and settled in to that half-slunk stance which he always took before a long sermon.

"We know not the day nor the hour, says the Lord," he began, stating that his theme for the day would dwell on women, the great reconcilers, women made in the likeness of Mary, the mother of Jesus, her sister Mary of Cleophas, and Mary Magdalene, the reformed sinner. He went on to expound on how these women in their several ways knew sorrow and joy through their beloved sons, women of whom the words of the Gospel could be said — "their own souls a sword had pierced." He moved thus to penance, the penance that was preparatory to the season of Christmas, to the birth of the infant Saviour that would in turn end in his crucifixion as a grown man.

"And . . ." he said, his voice high-pitched now, as with infuriated glances he strove to tell these parents to slap their children to chastise them, to take them outside and give them a good shaking, which they deserved.

"And," he continued, "the season of Christmas is not only one of love and joy but one in which we should try to put a stop to the hatred and the resentment that is at the core of our society. Why do we hate our neighbour? Why are we jealous if our neighbour has a bigger car or a bigger digger, why all this begrudgement . . ."

O'Dea had kept watching the door, hoping that Bugler would come and remembering that he almost always came towards the end of the sermon. He saw him then, saw them, Rosemary all tarted up, marching up the aisle and looking back at Bugler to follow, which he did not. O'Dea had given him the wink.

They move across near the crib, which due to Breege's recent maraud has a stout girder of holly guarding it.

"I waited for you last night down at the pier," O'Dea said.

"What did you want?"

"You were seen out on the lake with her . . . Ye stayed all night." O'Dea spoke between his teeth, though not exactly in a whisper.

"It's none of your business."

"If the brother gets to know this, you're a goner."

"Just because I want to cut a road."

"It's not only a fecking road . . . And you know that. Did you kiss her?"

"I won't answer that."

"That means you did . . . Did you lift the lid?"

"Feck talk is this."

"That means you did. You pup . . . You blackguard."

"I did nothing to hurt her."

"Well, if you didn't, someone did. She's in one big mess . . . A young girl that stops talking . . . She doesn't want to be found out. She's on the run . . . My wife's contention is that she has a pod in her."

"That's absurd."

"Maybe you helped with the Immaculate Conception . . . I take it you got your way."

"Why are you so concerned? You're a solicitor."

"I like the girl. She has no one."

"What am I supposed to do?"

"Go see her. Talk to her. Listen to her."

The sermon had ended without their noticing. The collection is being taken. Boscoe and Miss Carruthers, going down either side, carrying the knitted purses into which coins and the odd note are being dropped. Canon Daly is sitting on a dais, his hands across his paunch, a satisfied smile now, indulgent of the children who are still crying.

"Who told you we were there?" Bugler asks.

"The usual . . . Gossips."

"It doesn't mean a thing."

"It does . . . If she fell in love with you."

THERE WERE ONLY six people left in the ward, some had gone home for good and others were allowed out for the Christmas holidays. T.J., a young man dressed as Santa Claus, comes running in, apologising for the soot on his cheeks, incurred from all the chimneys he has scaled.

"Do you accept presents from small men?" he asks. He is carrying tiny parcels wrapped in silver paper and tied with thin silver cording. In his other hand he is holding out a colander of warm mince pies, describing how he soaked the raisins, currants, candied peel, and angelica, first in porter, then in whiskey, then rum, and he reckons that everyone including himself will be well boozed.

For each he has a special word, a special joke. For Kevin, the little boy visiting his mother who is marching up and down in a cowboy outfit, he plays the dumb cop. He has been playing it on his rounds and is now an expert at it: "The kid rises, cop gives chase, the kid spins, comes up with a 12-gauge sawed-off, puts cop square in his sights, there is maybe fifteen feet separating them — the kid pulls the trigger. Wow. Bow-wow." T.J. falls in a fit of laughter to the floor, his running shoes in contrast with the red crepe of his overall and the straggly cotton beard. Kevin stamps on him, shouting, "I won . . . I won," while behind the curtain, his mother still weeping, still refusing to come out, is calling to him to behave himself, to be a good boy.

Next it is Millie's turn. "How's my girlfriend?" T.J. says, and leads her into a dance. She throws her arms around him and tries to follow the instructions, toe-heel, toe-heel, her hips swaying as she snuggles up to him and says that it is the best day of her life, the best fecking day of her life.

"How do you like my steps?" he asks, to which she answers with a kissing sound. Given it, she starts to cry. He tells her life is too short for tears. He cites only a few weeks back he went with a friend to the hurling finals, brilliant day, brilliant seats, brilliant match, super great, then on down to Kildare, stayed for a week, and guess what — your man Patrick got a heart attack loading cattle onto a lorry a couple of days later. Life is short. He wanted her to know.

"Not in this flipping nuthouse," she says, hitting out now, punching him and pulling off his glued-on beard. He humours her with the worst joke he knows: "How do you remember your wife's birthday? Forget it once," then tweaks her nose until she laughs. Soon she is changing into her high heels and putting odds and ends into a big handbag to go off with him.

With the older woman he does a peasant accent: "What ish my nation, Astoor." She looks up at him blank, staring, as he hugs her and tells her that he is one of them aul leprechauns from Tir-na-N-og. He unwraps her present then, a teeny miraculous medal, gold-coloured, which he puts to her lips. Kevin is pleading to play cops again, Millie dances by herself, and Chrissie, a young girl still waiting to be collected, turns the sound of her cassette player so loud that the whole ward is deafened by it, the walls seeming to inflate and deflate from the throbbing.

"Are you medium rare or am I medium rare?" T.J. asks of Breege, who is sitting at the end of her bed in a black dress with a white organza collar. Only then does he realise that she is a patient also, and bowing, he gives her one of the Christmas boxes. He watches her opening it. It is a pen, encrusted with mauve and silver filigree, and he tests the colour of the ink by making a small x on the back of her hand.

"I was thinking that if no one sang I'd have to sing myself . . . but now I have you."

She looks away, then looks to Chrissie to save her.

"She can't . . . she's not able," Chrissie says.

"Just for me . . . go on . . . make my Christmas . . . 'Jingle Bells' . . . 'White Christmas' . . . anything."

It was the song that Bugler had given her:

> October winds lament around the Castle of Dromore,
> Yet peace is in its lofty halls,
> My loving treasure stored.

Her voice carried, clear and pure and trilling, down the length of the ward, but because she had turned away from the faces and towards the window, Ger was not sure from whom the voice came and he followed it on tiptoe, up close to her, his mouth half open lest she should falter or break down.

> Bring no ill wind to hinder us, my helpless babe and me —
> Dread spirit of Blackwater banks, Clan Eoin's wild banshee,
> And Holy Mary pitying me, in Heaven for grace doth sue,
> Sing hush-a-bye, lul, lul, lo, lo, lau,
> Sing hush-a-bye, lul, lul, loo.

Kevin thought to shoot at her, but the others gathered nearer, and a nurse arriving with a tray of lemonade plonked it on a chair in shock.

"You're cured . . . Jesus, you're cured," Ger said, his own voice singsong, charged with excitement and disbelief.

"Well, I never," the nurse said, picking up the tray to pass the glasses around.

"That was super great," T.J. said.

"That was super shite," Millie said.

"Say something, Breege . . . say hello," Ger said.

"Hello," she said, looking around, and she smiled, as helpless to tell them why she could speak as she had been that day in the ladies' room of the hotel when she felt it coming on her, a kind of brainstorm with words tumbling around inside, like clothes in a washing machine, words that were either too loving or too hating or too telling to be said, and her struggling to say them but finding they would not come, like a stone, a plum stone that was stuck there. She ran her hand down her throat, but it felt exactly the same to her.

"It's a miracle," Ger said, and he went out to find the matron and tell her.

T.J. is kneeling by Breege, inviting her to his shop as soon as she is allowed out. It is called The Pantry. She will recognise it by the man's bicycle outside the door with leeks and provisions in a basket and in the window a big bronze bell hundreds of years old. Will she promise? Will she come? For Millie it is too much, she has been relegated; she sits on the floor, kicking her shoes off, then peels down her grey lisle stockings, raises her legs, and moves them scissors-like and lewd.

"Now now . . . no wrangling," T.J. says, and goes to her, holding out a packet of cigarettes, saying she can take two.

"Am I ugly?" She bawls it.

"You are not . . . you're beautiful."

"They said I was ugly."

"Who said?"

"Them . . . them shites." She is looking from Breege, to Chrissie, to Ger, to Kevin, then back again, scowling, her tongue stuck out, undecided as to who she hates most.

"Okay, okay, you're all welcome to The Pantry, all of you," T.J. says, scanning each face, and then, looking at his wristwatch, he darts towards the chimney, shouts some abracadabra into it, and then vanishes out through the open door.

OUT IN THE GROUNDS Bugler is hurrying from one person to another, from one building to another in search of the right ward. He is wearing a dark serge suit and a white collarless shirt and is carrying a bunch of heather which he is trying to conceal.

A porter directs him to the main building, and hurrying in, he finds a man just leaving and says, "I'm lost . . . I'm completely lost." The man tells him he sure is, because only staff occupy that building and very soon it is going to come tumbling down.

"The bulldozer is a-coming," he says with a certain gusto. Reluctantly, he goes behind the desk, opens a drawer, and takes out a tattered ledger, unties the twine, then runs his finger down the list of names to find Breege.

"Brennan . . . Mary Nonnie," he says, victorious.

"No . . . Breege."

"A widow?"

"She's a young girl."

"Ah now . . . She must be listed somewhere," he says, insisting that every patient is docked and filed, and then he laughs aloud and says that it is no wonder he is confused, because isn't he looking at the wrong year. He concludes by saying that the best thing for the visitor to do is to go to the east wing, where everything, all data, is bang up-to-date.

The east wing turns out to be a ruin, broken windows, a boarded-up door, empty birds' nests hanging from bits of trailing creeper. From there he crosses to a low corrugated building where at least there is a light. Inside, a radio is going full blast, but the office is unattended. He calls, waits, calls again, and hears footsteps coming from within. An excitable nurse in a paper hat comes out and says merrily, "Santa Claus, Elvis," adding that without her, the place would go haywire. In case he would like to know, she's Fiona, which to some means white swan. When he says Breege's name, she frowns and recalls the young ones, brats, spoilt rotten, nothing wrong with them, only airs.

"She came about ten days ago."

"I know. I know . . . The hair always over the face, so as not to look at you . . . A dummy."

"Would you let me see her?"

"I'd do more than that for you," she says skittish, but seeing that he is in no mood to flirt she agrees to go off and find a Sister in charge. As she disappears to an inner hall, she turns to ask if she can get him anything, tea, coffee, or something stronger.

Soon they are crossing a cinder path to yet another building and she is asking him to guess what most of these lunatics' problems are. She answers for him. Sex. Sex. Sex — forever taking their clothes off. She says he would not believe the things she has witnessed, striptease, morning, noon and night, women no better than the men, turning it into a nudist colony. In the office a young pimply porter wearing a baseball cap looks up, irked at being disturbed. He says Sister is on a call.

"Try her, Jimmy," Fiona says, and gives him a wink.

"She's off now," he says, holding the phone, then frowns and says, "Jesus, she's on it again . . . She's never off it."

Nothing for it but to wait. Fiona says if she doesn't get back to her ward there will be blue murder. She gives him a peck and says if ever he wants a good dance he knows who to call up.

The supervisor is a stout crusty woman whose patience is sorely tried because Nurse Egan who was to come to relieve her has not shown up. As she lays eyes on Bugler she stiffens. He is the sort of man she cannot bear, the iron warrior on horseback. She tells him flatly that she can't help. The doors to each of the wards are already locked and no one, only night staff, can enter.

"Always locked at the peal of the Angelus."

"I've been out there nearly an hour."

"That's not my fault," she says. Their eyes meet, hers hot and puffy from having had three sherries, his overcalm, his jawbone clenched under his trimmed beard. She sees determination in him and thinks that the little pearl button holding the collar is about to snap off.

"I'll only stay a minute."

"No way."

"It's Christmas Day."

"Must have rules," she says, putting on a false accent, the better to dismiss him, her breathing flurried.

"This isn't right," he says, looking around as if there were someone else he could appeal to.

"Do you want to leave the flowers or not?" she says tartly.

He thought for a moment, loath to hand them over to her, fearing that they might end up in the reception hall.

"I need to write a note," he said, turning his back on her.

"Please yourself," she said, and went off, telling Jimmy that no strays were to be allowed beyond that door.

He stood by a ledge, staring at the crumpled bill head, on which he had written the few words: *I picked this near where we saw the salmon leap.*

It was not enough. There was something more he wanted to say, and despite the reserve of his nature he asked the young man for a sheet of hospital paper, and then he sat down and wrote it.

THE OVERCOOKED BIRD lies abject in a pan of lumpy gravy, diced apple and chestnut spewing out of it. It is going cold. Rosemary has been interrogating for over an hour. Why did he not telephone her? Why is he dressed up? She had been asleep when he left, so togged out. In the end he admitted it, said he had gone to the hospital to see a friend.

"Oh, the loony lady down the road . . . her?"

"Yes, her."

"Why didn't you bring me along?"

"I didn't think it would be fair to her."

"Shit . . . I'm your fiancée and you don't think it would be fair to her."

"She's very shy."

"I had an unfailing trust in you and you've broken it."

"It's not like that, Rosemary."

"Oh, what is it like . . . describe it to me . . . She's a kindred spirit . . . Cathleen ni Houlihan."

"You've met her."

"Of course I met her . . . What do you do, Breege? Nothing was her answer . . . no self-esteem . . ."

"Look, she knows I'm committed to you."

"Her brother taking us for every penny we've got and you're sweet on her."

"She never wanted war between her brother and me . . . She begged of me."

"This has gone much further than I thought. Did you bring her flowers or chocolates, or both?"

"Look, she's sick . . . she's alone . . . she's frightened."

"I don't care if she dies."

"That's the ugliest thing I ever heard you say."

"I feel threatened, Mick. I don't want to believe that there is something between you and her."

"My mates were right when they said that the softest bit of you is your teeth. Your own brother said it."

"I took this . . . this bog on board with you . . . My parents took it on board with you. Without them you couldn't have made it."

He turned aside, begging her to let it rest, to dish out the dinner, to pour themselves a glass of wine, to say Happy Christmas, to let bygones be bygones. But as he began to lay the table, she had started again, unable now to contain herself, talking of the sacrifice she was making, the things she had given up, a fantastic life, a stunning career, a warm climate, to come to an asshole, a nowhere, no friends, no stimulus, only a big wet prick of a mountain. Then she picked up the present which he had brought and which she had not opened. She dropped it violently to the floor. They could hear pieces of glass shattering, the abrupt crazy shatter of broken glass, and then the little squeals that were almost animal-like as the broken pieces resettled.

"What was it?"

"Perfume."

"I didn't mean it about wanting her dead," she said, and held desperately to him, to have him know that there was a Rosemary underneath the Rosemary that bitched.

"You're all right, you're all right," he said, picking up the box.

"I'm prepared to forgive if you promise me one thing."

"What's that?"

"I want you to bring me there . . . I want to walk into that ward with you holding hands . . . I want that. I want her to see that."

"I can't. I won't."

"You kissed her, didn't you?"

"Once."

"You fucked her?"

"You're disgusting," he said, and leaned across to tear a piece of the skin off the turkey to show his hunger. She would not have it. She picked up the pan and moved with it, moving unsteadily as if she might throw it at him. Seeing him go out, she rushed to get in his way and said that she would not spend another night in that house unless he told her everything, everything.

"Please yourself," he said, hurrying into the yard and over the wall to the field beyond.

❖   ❖   ❖

It was pitch dark and it had begun to pour with rain. He walked the length and breadth of three fields, as if he was just trying to discover what he ought to do. Three new bullocks, not used to their new surroundings, were bawling, ill at ease with his own animals, who outnumbered them. It was too dark to see them. The only single light in the whole gloom was from Brennan's house. How easy if he could go down there and knock on the door and say what was on his mind. Or how easy to go back up and tell Rosemary that her jealousy had no foundation. But it was not possible, because it was not true.

She was sitting cross-legged on the kitchen floor with a blanket over her, like an invalid. She had been crying. She looked up at him pitifully, said it was the shock of everything, the unfamiliarity of everything, and no friend to turn to. He had to be lover and friend, something not easy for a man to take. She had had a brilliant idea. They would be married sooner. They would not wait for the big wedding with family and friends, things he loathed anyhow, they would marry in secret and then everything would be all right, because she would not feel so threatened. He remembered the superstition he had overheard as a child, that the groom should never be let see the bride's dress. It was there in the wardrobe, all twenty yards of it, cream and with a flounce. The clemency that he felt when walking back, the guilt that he felt for having brought her all this way, and the remorse for going to the graveyard were gone now, and he was terse again.

"We did love one another."

"We did."

"And now?"

"I honestly don't know what to call it."

"Don't worry . . . I have enough love for us both."

❖   ❖   ❖

It was in the bedroom in the dark that she broke down completely.

"Mick," she said, then waited. "I can't go back there . . . Please don't send me back."

"I won't," he said. He could feel his breath rapid and he could feel her whole body sobbing. The bed was too confining for them, the room was too small, there was not enough air for them both, he felt he was choking.

"I've felt funny for days . . . I might even be pregnant."

"What makes you say that?"

"My hormones."

"You're not pregnant," he said, and reminded her crudely how he knew.

"You've no intention of marrying me . . . You kept stringing me along. I see it now."

"You're mad."

"You left me to come here when I was pregnant. Remember . . . the egg stayed as an egg . . . It didn't turn into a little person. Have you wondered how I felt . . . I was gutted . . . I am gutted. I said just now I was pregnant because I wanted to test you."

"What's wrong with you . . . you're a pragmatic person. This isn't you."

"She's what's wrong."

"She's out of the picture."

"I'll believe you if you promise that you will never see her again." And to make sure, she turned on the bedside light and held the bulb so close to his face he could read the wattage in singed black lettering.

THEY ARE HAVING a picnic, Ger, Breege, and Mrs. Hegarty. The overhead lights have been quenched and in the windowsill there is a stout red Christmas candle in a coronet of holly. There is a happiness between them and they smile at the sounds of the snoring, monotonous, phlegmy, from two patients farther down. Mrs. Hegarty, little Kevin's mother, has ventured out at last, because of the light being so dim and nobody able to see that her hair has been falling out. Only herself has witnessed it, tufts of it each morning on her comb, alarming her.

"Eeny, meeny, miney, mo, catch a beggar by the toe, if he hollers let him go, eeny, meeny, miney, mo." As Ger says it he has already guessed that it will fall to Mrs. Hegarty to tell the first story.

"I will too," she says, as if she has waited for this moment from the very day she was admitted. She begins it sitting on the bed, but as her courage increases, she stands, gesticulates, moves about in keeping with the anger that she has felt and has had to bottle up.

"I had a house that my uncle left me . . . A nice house with a nice name. Moss House. The lane up to it is mossy and a person can slip. Sometimes I let it, sometimes when it was vacant I'd go over and sit in the sitting room and look at my own things, my treasures. Then one day my husband asked me if his sister Ida could go in there for a bit. She had no home . . . Her husband had thrown her out and she was in a caravan. It was to be temporary . . . That was a year ago and she's still in Moss House. She won't go. All my things are flung up in the attic, my pictures and my bawneen cushions, getting damp up there, mildewed. She comes up to me last Easter in the chapel, it was Holy Thursday, and in front of the blessed sacrament she whispers to me, she says, 'Eliza, we'll each have joint ownership of Moss House, it's only fair.' "

She stops then and turns to them, close to sobbing. "That's what they've done to me, my husband and his sister, that's why I'm here."

"You're all right . . . You're all right," Ger says, and pours her more lemonade.

"You're next," Breege says to Ger.

"Crikey, I don't have a story, but I have a funny dream . . . Well, it's not that funny . . . My wife and I are somewhere . . . Up home probably in Cappaderragh, and then we're not there at all . . . We're in the city and there's a baby on a step, crying, crying its heart out, and my wife says to me, 'Jesus, we're going to have to do something,' and we're in this terrible fix looking up and down the street for the mother to come and take this baby and no one comes and the baby keeps crying and screaming and my wife says to me, 'We're going to have to take it, you see it's an orphan,' " and looking first at Mrs. Hegarty and then at Breege he says, baffled, "I don't even have a wife or a child . . . I'm not married."

In the passage they see a figure advancing towards them with something bulky in its arms. It is Nuala, the stout nurse, fussing, scolding, and, seeing remains of the picnic, asks if it is a five-star hotel they think they are in.

"It's Christmas, Nuala."

"Christmas! I did a twelve-hour shift, two admissions and that Ryan woman broke windows again."

"Sit down, Nuala . . . We're telling stories."

"Stories!" she says, and hands Breege the large bunch of heather with some sort of sarcastic grunt.

It is a vast bunch of two colours of heather tied with twine.

Holding it is like holding an infant and she can smell the mountain off it, the misted, brooding mountain. She thinks that it must be Bugler, but equally she thinks that it couldn't be.

"Big swank of a fella . . . tried to get past me," the nurse said. When she heard him described and the hat he wore, she was certain that yes, it was him.

"Ah now, Nuala, you're jealous," Ger said.

"Of course I'm jealous . . . It's always the young ones that get the flowers . . . that get the diamonds. Who gave me flowers? Nobody."

"Here you are," he says, offering her one of the mince pies, which she refuses, saying pastry gives her indigestion.

"You're a hard woman, Nuala. You should have let him up."

"Rules are rules," she says, but she is no longer tetchy, she will be home having a footbath in an hour.

It was as the nurse snatched the flowers away from Breege, to put them in water, that the note fell out. Breege held it and looked at it. She did not want to read it in front of them, and sensing it, Ger and Mrs. Hegarty moved away. She thought, Suppose I don't open it, suppose I just invent what it says, and then she thought of the morning on the road, how cold he was and how locked-in, when all she had wanted was one word, one word not to harm his future but to make her own less shorn. She had wanted so little, she had asked so little, yet that little would have been a lot. She opened it suddenly and without thinking, and looking down at the words she read them many times:

> Dear Breege,
>   I picked this where we saw the salmon leap. Something will come to make things better. I'll think of you and I hope that you won't think too unkindly of me.
>
> > Fond love,
> > Mick

If she keeps staring at the candle flame, at the way it veers, she will not cry, she will be able to hold back her tears. Then she is unable. The tenderness of the words becomes harder to bear than all the cruelty. The tears, the trapped tears of shame and love come pouring out of her.

"They'll soon stop," she says, embarrassed, as Ger hands her a wet flannel to wipe her face.

"I'm all right now," she says, though she is still crying.

"This guy . . . Is he why you're here?"

"Yes."

"And the song you sang this morning . . . Is that your story?"

"That's my story, except that I can't tell it," she says.

"Good God . . . A love child," he says reverently, and raises his hands as if he is saying a prayer.

"My brother will kill me."

"No one's going to kill you . . . We'll mind you."

"How, Ger . . . How?"

"We'll tell him for you."

"Ah no. I'll tell him myself . . . I have to."

"Is he a free man . . . this fellow?"

She turned then to the window and looked out at the stars, the same stars as he had driven home under. What would she not have given for just one minute of his being allowed up, just one minute for something to be said to bind them. What would she not have given.

"If he was a free man, I wouldn't be in here," she said, in a breaking voice.

JUST AS IT fell to Duggan to bring Rosemary there, it fell to him to take her away. They stood, as he put it, like two pillars, next to the tractor, down at the end of the track, not speaking, Rosemary holding a suitcase and wearing a headscarf.

"Let me know where you are," Bugler said after she got into the car.

"Find me," she said, shouting it through the half-open window.

She shook then so that Duggan had to light her cigarettes for her; her moods changed by the minute, missing Bugler, then abusing him, calling him all the nasty names she could think of, then asking for them to stop by a pub to get her a brandy for her nerves. She drank it in the car. Afterwards she was subdued and then got a little maudlin and said life with Bugler would be hell but life without Bugler would be a worse hell. She asked him if he had ever been in love, but did not wait for the answer.

When they passed the green gates and the sloping lawns of the castle, she asked what it was and he told her.

"Let's drive in there," she said.

"It'll cost you an arm and a leg."

"I don't care . . . I don't bloody care . . . Let the bastard pay for it."

And going up the drive she got out a little mirror to make herself dishy before she went in there.

A SWIFT FALL OF snow was what met Bugler when he raised the blind. He had never seen snow before except in a paperweight in Rosemary's family drawing room. He stood by the window and watched it, the sheer zest of it, the flakes spinning, chasing each other through the air, a coat of it like ermine on the young conifers and along the top rung of the gate under which Gypsy lay, plaintive. New Year's Day. A day of resolutions.

Dear Brennan,
    This is Bugler writing, and what is more, writing on an auspicious day. I am giving up the fight over the mountain and with it I could say giving up a part of myself. I do it on account of your sister. Let's meet and talk things over.
                                                                    Mick

❖   ❖   ❖

Unshaven, in a tremor, Joseph began to walk back and forth, digesting the contents of the letter. Its brevity was galling. He saw treachery in it, something in it above and beyond what it said. Bugler intended wooing her, which is why Rosemary had been jilted. Walking around the kitchen he slopped the tea, and with each reading became more crazed; he saw red, as he put it. "I am seeing red," he said as before his eyes there came some forgotten picture of a gored bull, its entrails puddling out. There was still time. He could persuade her, and if she defied him, he could keep her in there for a long time, for ever.

He was kneeling now, imploring her, and it was as if she answered back and said to fear not, his fears were unfounded. In his frenziedness he saw her come through the kitchen door in the tweed coat with the little squirrel collar, and for a moment he would have sworn that he heard her. The kitchen without her was no kitchen, cold, vacant, everything out on the table — marmalade, sugar, mustard, spilt cornflakes, spoons, knives, forks, table mats with pictures of wild birds, all needing a wipe. Three milky roses, dried and with the pink dredged out of them, were in a jug where she had put them the morning she left. When he broke it to her, she did not answer, she did not remonstrate, still a mute, but the look she gave him he would never forget.

He made to throw Bugler's letter into the stove, changed his mind, withdrew it and put it in his breast pocket, then lifted the telephone and slammed it down, cursing whatever bureaucrat had cut it off. The bill had not been paid. Bills were not paid. Bugler's doing. His stock now reduced to seven, and he would have to sell two more — "What you have done to me, what you have done to me," he shouted out, invoking Bugler's name. Feeling suffocated, he opened the door to let the fresh air in, and he was still talking to himself, remonstrating, gesticulating, when the Crock arrived, a crust of icicles on his nose and a black pixie cap that made him look like a wood sprite.

"What kept you?"

"I had to get the grub," and with that he plonked down the sliced bread and the package of bacon and a bill with a red sticker.

"They're not back rashers . . . They're streaky," Joseph said, nettled about the bill, the shame of it.

"You still have the flu," the Crock said, walking to the stove to warm his mittened hands. Seeing the copybooks with their glazed orange covers in which Joseph had written his monthly pieces, he exclaimed, "Christ, man . . . You're not burning these . . . Your pensées."

"Pensées," Joseph said, opening each little book at the centre page so as to be able to clutch a fistful and consign them. The sight of them being sucked in and the ensuing ribbons of hot flame which danced on his face made him almost jovial.

"No one can say that I don't keep the home fires burning," he said bitterly.

"You're all dressed up."

The jacket of his good suit hung on a chair, but he wore the waistcoat, and in the buttonhole was a sprig of withered shamrock from the previous March. There was, as the Crock would later tell it, an irrationality to the man and a craziness in his eyes. He said conflicting things, such as he had corresponded with county councillors, senators, and the local TD and had had assurances from them that justice would be done concerning the mountain. Seconds later he spoke of setting the land and Breege and himself going on a cruise.

"How is she?"

"How do I know . . . No phone . . . No post . . . Nothing. I'll go see her later this evening. I'm thinking of staying in a hotel. To be close by."

"Who'll milk . . . Who'll fodder?" the Crock asked.

"I'm hiring you to do it."

"I've never worked a milking machine."

"Come on out, then."

As they crossed the yard the flakes of snow seemed thicker, more purposeful, and they scurried in out of it. The cows had been milked only a short time before, and Biddy, the first one, bridled, then kicked soon as she felt the nozzles being pulled up over her teats. The byre was suddenly a den of moaning and kicking, Biddy swinging her hindquarters as if it was a torture instrument that had been put over her. The others, taking their cue, set about struggling to come free of their rusted iron halters. Little dribbles of milk passing through the glass tube looked blue and watery. Outside, Goldie yelped to be let in.

"Jesus, 'tis a circus," the Crock said.

" 'Tis a bloody lunatic asylum," Joseph said, belting them on their clotted rumps until the stick broke in half, something which frustrated him even more.

Inside, they sat close to the fire as Joseph lit one cigarette off the other and had a vast muttering cogitation with himself. To distract him, the Crock wondered aloud if Breege would make it, cited another young lady with the same complaint: Eily O'Grady, who never came back, died in there at the age of ninety, had grown a beard. When he got no answer he deferred to the ash pan that was overflowing.

"You could bake great spuds in that ash."

"In Jesus' name will you shut up and go home . . . You're an eejit."

"One minute you're kowtowing to me, you're begging me to come up here, and the next minute I'm barred . . . I'm not a human football . . . I've had it. Kick someone else's arse," and as he rose to go, Joseph blocked the way and asked him in the name of God to stay, to have pity. Then, taking the letter from his pocket, he said, "That's why . . . That's why I am the way I am." The Crock read it slowly, first by the fire and then by the window, and shook his head solemnly.

"Oh . . . Helen of Troy. Blue seas . . . Blue seas and a romping woman," he said.

"No way . . . She wouldn't mix with a man that's wronged her brother."

"He went to see her in the place."

"Who told you?"

"A nurse that works there . . . A cousin. Sat by her bedside, Bugler did."

"Oh Jesus, My Father hath chastised you with whips but I will chastise you with scorpions." Joseph shouted it to the picture of the Sacred Heart, whose votive lamp had quenched for want of oil.

"Go up to him . . . Have it out. Man to man."

"I will not go up there."

"Are you afraid of him?"

"I'm afraid of no one," he said, grabbing the letter and hurrying up the stairs as if a brilliant strategy had occurred to him. Up there he could be heard opening and closing drawers and wardrobes, singing, stopping only to call down that he required a hot toddy.

"There is none. We drank it all."

"Get some."

"Where? There's no money."

"Anywhere."

"I'll tell you what . . . I could drive over to my godmother, she always has a drop."

"Don't be long. I'll need the van to go to Breege."

Coming down the stairs he seemed to the Crock to be revived, his hair plastered back with oil and his features sharper and more assertive because of it.

"Go up and tell Bugler to meet me here."

"Suppose he says no."

"Tell him . . ."

"It'll be some summit," the Crock said. Suddenly they both jumped as the door creaked and swung open. In the gust of cold air a robin flew in, its rust-brown feathers jewelled in ice so that it seemed not a real bird but an omen. It made three circuits around the kitchen as they leapt at it to kill it, then it flew towards their faces, then bashed itself repeatedly against the windowpane.

"Jesus, 'tis a weirdo," the Crock said, chasing it now with the parted legs of the tongs.

"Don't let it upstairs," Joseph shouted. Too late. The bird had already curled itself on the bottom step. The Crock hauled himself onto a chair and waited so as to be level with it when it got to where the stairs turned and there was a pocket of dark. It moved jerkily, dropping onto each successive step with a soundless thud, and in time his waiting hand came around it, soft, covert, murderous. There were two sounds then, a screech of pure delirium, almost joyous as his fingers squeezed its neck, then a stifled cry as he throttled it, the sound ending in a splutter. Bringing the hand back he displayed it proudly, the neck swerved to one side as if it had just been unscrewed, the beady eyes wide open.

"How much will you give me for it?"

"Get rid of it," Joseph said wildly. "Get rid of it now."

"Easy man . . . easy. It's only a feathered friend," and with that he consigned it to his pocket so that he could show it in the hotel that night, scare the ladies with it. There was a five-course dinner and with a stunt like this he might eat for free.

※　　※　　※

Joseph could hear him coming on foot. They met by the gate as he tried to put it back on its hinges.

"You haven't fixed it yet," Bugler said.

"Aren't you frozen?" Joseph said. Bugler was bareheaded, with snow on his hair and on his thick eyelashes.

"Warm heart," he said, and wished a neighbourly Happy New Year. They were at a loss, not knowing exactly how to begin and looking vacantly at the tumbling, thralling snowflakes.

"Do you want to come in?"

"I can't . . . I have a date," and there was something smug and insinuating about the way he said it.

"Good Christmas?" Joseph said then.

"I got drunk . . . I even think I felt sorry for myself."

Their laughter, if it had been laughter, ceased as Joseph waited, his eyes smarting from no sleep.

"You got the letter?" Bugler said.

"I did. You shouldn't have visited Breege in the hospital . . . Upsetting her."

"It didn't upset her."

"What's that supposed to mean?"

"I like her . . . A lot."

"She's sick . . . She doesn't need you."

"I've asked her to come up to the house."

"She won't."

"She said she will . . . She has something important to tell me."

"And what would that be?"

"I leave it to you as a man to guess."

"Don't touch her . . . Don't tamper with her . . . Don't go near her."

"I have touched her," Bugler answered back, the voice calm,

unhurried, but pitched with the certainty of a man who has found what he has been seeking. There was no more time and no more explaining; he turned and walked quickly away.

Joseph held on to the gate because he had to, his world was flushing out of him, if what he heard was true. With a cry then of intent and infantile need, he called out to the Crock to come, Jesus, at once so that they could drive there. The thought that she might have given herself, that Bugler's blood might be mixed in with theirs, drove him berserk, and he burst his hot heart's delirium and his hot heart's despair on the rungs of the gate.

He turned to go back into the house, but he couldn't.

For one minute he thought the shotgun was stolen so well had he disguised it. The muzzle felt like a poker of ice and his fingers stuck to it. He put the cartridges in different pockets so as not to look too bulky. He needed to walk, to walk and talk. He was talking all the time as he went up the back field and under fences to the next field and the next. Bugler's cattle were around a feeder; a bawling drove of them turned towards him, their moaning half supplication, half threat, the dark descending on them and on him.

In the next field there was something that unnerved him, because he was not sure but that he was dreaming it. A foal was being born. It was more than halfway out, shaking its moist head, tilting from left to right. The front legs were out, the chestnut face swivelling above them, breathing, looking about, the white lining of the placenta draped around its shoulders like a shawl and the mare pushing, pushing for the rear and the back legs to come out. It was Bugler's bay mare. Getting closer to it, he saw that at once she became agitated and tried to stand up, and even though he hated the man he did not hate the animal. She had gone in under those trees because like every mare she did not like to be watched when she foaled. In ten or fifteen minutes if he walked on, the foal would be out and up and suckling. So he walked on.

Rabbits were out in the farther field, a little apart from one another, nibbling at nothing, their underjaws a-quiver, fear in the eyes, as if they expected danger, and yet when they heard his step did nothing, only ran to one another and huddled. Safety in numbers, their tails like dirty off-white dusters and their rumps cleaved to one another in useless and abject camouflage.

Dark was coming fast and crows were convening in the cold sky. Tucking the cartridges in, he felt something of the old expertise, the way they snucked in, so nice, so neat. As he crooked his finger around the trigger, he heard them scattering, heard them tearing up into the sky, and then as he fired, the sound of the shots came strangely placid and unmenacing. One or two fell, but he did not cross to see if he had killed. How he had revered her. If she had spent one hour with Bugler, the best and sweetest and most trusting times between him and her would be ruined. He was still talking to himself when he ducked down into a drain, his shoes cracking on ice, like cracking a bread plate, and coming up he spotted O'Dea foddering from the open door of his van. The cattle were mounting it because he had never mastered how to keep animals back. They had not spoken since the day they quarrelled, but they each shouted now at the same moment and with the same high-pitched nervousness: "Happy New Year, Happy New Year."

He hurried on, pretending to be looking for a stray beast. He went down to the river to see whether it was brown or blue or bottle-green, as if that mattered. The swans, Aziz's mascots, glided by with a serenity as if it were a balmy summer's evening. The mountain was coated white, ridges of the rocks showing through with a mineral blackness. Each of the trees was weighed with snow, but inside their black branches were shroud lines like the mad thoughts running amok in his mind.

"Jump in," O'Dea said as he caught up with him.

"Ah no . . . I'll walk."

"I was going to call on you . . . We're having a sort of a party tonight. Why don't you come down?"

"Ah . . . You know me and the parties."

" 'Twill do you good . . . And Brunhilde would like it . . . You're about the only one she tolerates."

"I'll see."

They were level now, and spotting the rifle O'Dea said, "When did you get the rod back?"

"Weeks ago." He said it as casually as he could. As he watched O'Dea drive off, it occurred to him that he should go back to the river and hide the weapon. But something prevented him. He put it down for a moment and flapped his arms to warm himself. Flapping and hawing, he felt that strange exhilaration, that burning warmth in the limbs which follows upon biting cold. His spirits had picked up on account of O'Dea asking him down.

When he returned to the glade of trees, mare and foal had gone. He saw them walking in the distance towards a shed that was up there, their dark shapes carved out of the night, in a supple and miraculous conjunction. When he saw them so close together, his heart froze with a kind of agony at how outside everyone and everything he felt, an outcast in the world save for Breege, and he knew that by telling her that single grain of truth she would not desert him, and then in a headlong absence of reason he saw their lives return to normal, the pattern of the steady days as they had once been. At his feet there was the afterbirth, a big bunch of jellied mush glistening in the light of a risen moon, the bits of red like mincemeat where the mother had snapped it off with her teeth. She had done it right.

He walked with an urgency now, trampling on his own shadow, annoyance at the amount of time he had already wasted, recalling that insolent and vainglorious boast of Bugler's which would be null and void once he talked to her. The barn roof came into sight, a panel of sheer white, svelte as suede, with not a single bird track to mar it, and then a lurch in his breathing as he imagined that he had heard that detested sound, the rumble of the tractor breaking in on his newfound certainty.

Not knowing then that which he was about to do and yet with the repetition of that dreaded sound, knowing it, because it was always there, like a dream, waiting to be dreamed. It had thundered into the yard, music pouring out of it, the cabin decked with sprigs of holly to give a festive appearance. The bridal chariot come to carry her off. And then, the very worst thing. His own house lit up, illuminated, the upstairs and the downstairs windows, her way of saying "I have come home."

"Well, well, well," he said, putting the vicious pieces of the puzzle together. They had planned it.

The outside light, garish, fell with a carnival splash across a stretch of snow, crimsoning the cobbles. As Bugler stepped down from the tractor, Joseph raised the shotgun, his finger curling on the trigger as on a ring, and firing, he saw the brown hat soar away with a phantom-like easiness. It all felt like that now, easy and phantom-like and inevitable. There was nothing of craziness or frenzy in him, it was too lucid for that, the shells spinning out with unerring rapidity and Bugler turning, saying, "Don't . . . Don't"; then a louder cry as the last shell snucked away and the long bulk of his body fell forward onto the ruddied cobbles. It was like seeing someone fall onstage. The moon hazed, pearl-skinned.

Then silence followed, louder than any gunshot, the crows soundless, in a hush, hovering above the trees, and then a great bolt of terror as he put the gun down and walked, like one hallucinated, to his van, then drove off at such a speed that the broken gate swung violently from its hinges.

GUARDS SHEEHY AND FLYNN were swapping duty when Joseph came into the barracks like he was drunk, and blind too, one hand out with something in it as he blundered towards the table and just stopped before walking into it.

"I shot your man up in the yard," he said, throwing five cartridges down.

"Who?"

"Who else but Mick Bugler."

"Why did you shoot him, Joe?" Flynn asks, although he does not believe it, the man has not the belly to kill.

"I was afraid of him."

"How come?"

" 'Twas him or me."

"How far away were you when you shot him?" Sheehy, the senior guard, asks, giving Flynn the order to go out and telephone for a patrol car.

"About thirty yards, I'd say."

"Are you sure you shot him dead?"

"I don't know . . . I didn't go near him."

"Did he fall?"

"He fell."

"Did he say anything?"

"He shouted, but I couldn't hear."

"Why were you afraid of him, Joe?"

"From the day his tractor pulled into our yard everything went

bust . . . He broke us . . . All over Christmas I was demented . . .
My sister put away . . . Deadly . . . I wanted to kill myself."

"Can I get you anything?" Sheehy said then, watching the terror spread out from the skull and the petrified eyes down his
whole shaking body.

"I'd like some water."

When he was handed the water he was unable to hold the cup,
and his lips kept missing the rim.

"I hope I didn't kill him . . . Can someone go up and see?"

"The patrol car will be on the way up now."

"Why is it taking so long?"

"Calm down . . . Calm down. He mightn't be dead . . . Only
injured."

"My sister is up there by herself."

"Where's the gun, Joe?"

"The gun is there on the ground where I threw it," and suddenly terror turns to consternation and he runs from the door to
the window and back again like a caged animal.

"Don't get so excited, calm yourself."

"I'm afraid."

"Don't be. You're safe here."

"I'm safe no more," he says, and sits and stares out.

From the hallway as the phone rings they listen and wait in the
fraught suspendedness, knowing that they will know in a minute
or even less.

Sheehy goes into the hall where Flynn is standing shocked and
vehement.

"Dead as Lincoln," he says.

"How do you know?"

"Guard Tracy from Birdhill was shooting grouse up the mountain and he came on the body and the sister on top of it . . . A
blood bath."

"Jesus . . . Christ."

"We'll tell him together," Flynn says, and as they go into the
room Joseph knows what they are about to say. Then dropping
to his knees he groans and groans, and looking up at them says in

a broken voice, "Didn't I do a terrible thing, lads," and they are helpless to tell him that it was otherwise.

All of a sudden he began to take off his clothes, saying they were bloodied, they were contaminated, flinging them off as Guard Flynn rushed at him, outraged, saying he could not do that, he could not tamper with crucial evidence.

"Fecking evidence," he said, and flung his second shoe into a corner.

"Fecking monster," Flynn said, and went to hit him.

"Leave him alone," Sheehy said.

"He's an animal. He hasn't even shown one ounce of re-morse . . . Not one."

"Leave him alone."

And he stood before them naked, his arms dangling slightly, like a crucified shape of pity and desolation, staring into the space that was only a few footsteps away and into a long incar-ceration that he could not even yet imagine.

B REEGE HOLDS HIM, shivering. It took moments after the sound of the shots had reached her to run out, then turn off the insane music and kneel beside him.

There is breath in him. She puts her mouth to his and gives him more breath and still more. She listens. She breathes the life back into him.

"You're not dead, Mick . . . You're not dead," she says, and knows it to be true, because he is still breathing and he seems to see her there, seems to hear her and to be talking to her, though not able to say the words.

There are no gashes and no bloodshed, which she takes to be a hopeful sign. The fact that his face is going slightly blue is only because of snow, the reflection of snowy light from the stars. He is looking at her and he is still alive.

"Can you hear me," she says, and touches him down the length of his clothes to his high boots, which she drags off. As she feels her way back up along the other side of his body she finds a patch of damp, warm damp, becoming damper, like water oozing out from a ditch, except that it isn't water, it must be blood. She cries then and she prays, her cries and her prayers as one, all air, all heaven, all earth, all Cloontha rent with it. She will not allow him to die, he must live for his own sake and for hers. Then she sees the gaze going out of his eyes, that thing which a moment before had held him to her; and then he is gone, he is without breath, and she begins to drag him across the yard to the house, to bring the life back into him.

There are footsteps and Goldie racing out and snapping.

"In the name of Jesus, what's going on here?"

"Who are you?" she calls back, but without looking.

"I'm a guard," he says, and rushes and kneels by the body and starts to examine it with a chilling expertise. When he pronounces him dead, he looks at her as if she is the criminal and she cups Bugler's face in her hand, refusing to let it go.

"Let go of him . . . You're not to touch him."

"Why not?"

"You can't touch him."

"I can," she says, kissing the dead face, and he pulls her back then and pushes her like she is being sucked back into an immeasurable distance.

"He's mine," she says.

"He is not . . . He's not your property."

"Whose property is he?" she screams at him.

"The first rule is always the preservation of the scene," and putting his hands under the armpits, he drags the corpse slowly back to where a dark and uneven pattern, empanelled on the snow, shows him where it had fallen.

PRESENTLY THE MOUNTAIN road was alive with cars, cars arriving, cars leaving, the two dogs in separate outhouses howling ceaselessly. The doctor was the first to come, then more guards, then the curate, a white surplice over his overcoat, carrying his bowl with the sacred oil. Bending, he touched each of the orifices, then said the absolution and asked her if she wanted any spiritual help.

The superintendent, escorted by two guards, was the most curt. As he got out of the car and looked around at the bleak landscape and the untidy yard, he seemed to recoil. He stood formal and scrutinising, a red muffler around his neck, and asked if anybody had touched the corpse since the tragedy occurred.

"The young woman was trying to bring it into the house," the guard said.

"I have to ask you to go inside," the superintendent said coldly.

"I can't . . . I won't."

"Take her inside," he said then to one of them.

"Please . . . Please . . . Let me stay. I won't go near him . . . All I want to do is to be here . . ."

"She's not well, sir . . . She's in shock . . . She knew the man," Guard Sheehy said, and pushed her back gently as the other guards began to seal off the area with bright yellow tape.

It was a space the size of a room and she would sit beyond it, cut off from him in death as she had been in life.

A young strange guard was ordered to stay with the remains,

given strict instructions not to let anyone near it, which of course meant her.

Not long after they had gone, she went inside and brought him some tea in a flask, then went in again and came back with two kitchen chairs and two blankets. He drank the tea and ate the slice of cake, but sat with his back to her.

Some time after, he half turned and said, "I'm glad you're here . . . I'd hate to be by myself. It's kinda spooky."

"What's your name?"

"Fergus . . . Fergus Flynn."

"How long will we be here before they come?"

"Hours."

"What will they do to him?"

"Cut him up."

"Butchers," she said under her breath.

"Look," he said, "I'm fifty percent guard and fifty percent human. I'll walk over to that gate . . . I'll give you two minutes to say your goodbye."

But when she looked in on the face it was already remote, a mask of pallor without sadness or anger or anything; a blank stiffening bulk under the cold sheet and the cold stars.

They stayed through the night, getting up to walk around from time to time, to warm their feet, gradually pulling their chairs that bit closer.

"What do you think happens when people die, Fergus?"

"I don't know . . . I wouldn't like to say."

"Have you never thought about it?"

"Not really . . . Maybe I'm too young."

"I'm young as well."

"Was he your sweetheart?"

"Yes."

"And were you his?"

"I think so."

"That's tough . . . That's very tough."

The cold weary night gave way to the sullen light before dawn and the pale stars began to go back into the heavens as people gathered, quietly, solemnly, on the far side of the fallen gate which a guard had removed; too afraid to enter, they stood aghast, saying little, redeemed for a brief while by untimely death, which brought them to their compassionate selves but which could not bring Bugler back. Prayers were muttered for what had happened, for what had had to happen, for the slaughter to become an instrument of peace. Hatred and bloodshed. A hawthorn tree and a corpse. Atonement. Forgive us our trespasses as we forgive those who trespass against us.

Cloontha Garda Station

I am a member of the Garda stationed in Birdhill. I was up the mountain shooting grouse and on the way back a howling dog refused to get off the road. I tried lifting it, then I heard a woman crying nearby. On entering the yard I saw the body of a man lying on its back next to a tractor. It was a well-developed muscular adult with dark hair, a beard, and sideburns. I saw a wristwatch lying on the ground with the clasp open. It appears the clasp had broken off when he hit the ground. His pupils were dilated and fixed; he had absent heart and respiratory sounds and his pulses were absent. The face showed some purple suffusion in the cheeks and the hands were grease-stained and calloused. The genitalia appeared normal. Blood was oozing from his pullover at the back. Present at the scene was a very distraught woman who refused to move despite repeated entreaties. I pushed her away from the body, explaining that it must not be touched, but she seemed not to understand a word. I immediately summoned assistance from the nearest Garda station and asked for spiritual and medical aid to be sent to the scene.

LIFE AT THE CASTLE was ordered, ordained, a place renowned for an atmosphere that combines grandeur with freedom, guests coming and going with their children and their dogs and their fishing tackle, throwing their coats down in the great hall as if it is home, because the very essence of the castle is to make guests feel at home. They wander down the hall and glance at the paintings of ancestors, in browns and vermilion, some jowly, some overthin; they warm themselves by either of the two fires, remark on the nice peat smell, and maybe help themselves to a drink from the small impromptu bar, where there is a pencil and notebook to jot down what they have taken. The clock chimes quarters of an hour, the thick brass weights an intriguement to children, who are allowed to run up and down the hall in the half-hour just before dinner.

Rosemary likes her new surroundings. It was, after all, how she imagined her homecoming, a honeymoon of sorts. She has passed four days without breaking down and even rationing the number of times that she rung him. Her hunch tells her that by Sunday he will search her out. He will ask Duggan where she was dropped off. When she phoned there had been no answer. She has been successful too in persuading the manager that her fiancé is joining her at the weekend, coming expressly to discuss wedding plans. She believes it to be true. She has written several letters, nice letters, ugly letters, haughty letters, begging letters, and prides herself on the fact that each day as the postman came to deliver and collect the mail she has not been tempted to run down and hand them to him. She has reread them in the order in which they were written, the hour of day or night at the top of each one — how he conned her, conned her parents, broke her trust, how she was a person who worked for the couple, how disillusioned those recent days had been, how foolish she had been to allow for months of separation knowing that men lust for a woman, any woman that is there. Having voiced such sentiments she apologised for them and said she could not express herself in any other way and had she not done so it would chew away at her and make their future intolerable. By writing, it was all behind them. She let him know that since she came she had felt something was amiss, but now that it was out in the open she was able to forgive him his bit of wanderlust, and what is more, that they were the most important thing in life to each other.

For those few days she has decided to pamper herself; she has ordered the best wines, has had massages in her bedroom and purchased a few elegant garments from the showcase down in the hall. In her bedroom, looking out at a small lake on which there is invariably one boat or two, with men fishing, she is stoical. Fishing and fish are very much part of the place, fish large or small in glass cases with wisps of grass and greenery around them and the date each one was caught, the fly it was caught with, and the name of the proud fisherman. Yes, her letters have been harsh, she has said things which needed saying, galling things, cutting things, but she has also left him in no doubt as to her love. Bugler's nightly, juggernauty ride is worth everything else. It is evening when she has had a few gins and then some wine that she has dialled his number, and getting no answer, she thinks of him on his way to find her, as hungry, as yielding, as she herself. If he did not appear by Sunday she would be driven out there and she would wear the red tailored jacket bought from the showcase in the lobby.

When the receptionist dialled her room and asked her to come down, she was certain that it was about the bill and the various extravagances. Coming down a long carpeted staircase, moving with studied hauteur, she saw the two uniformed guards, a man and a woman, standing by the desk and she was certain that it must be her father who had been taken ill. She said so as she crossed towards them.

"It's Michael Bugler . . . He had an accident," the woman guard said.

"What kind of accident?"

"A serious one."

"Take me to him," she said, looking at each of the faces.

"Look . . . We might as well tell you . . . Joe Brennan shot him. Dead."

It took almost a minute to sink in, and then she began to hit out with words, with fists, with righteous anger. Why had they not found her sooner. Did they not realise that she was his fiancée, next best thing to a wife. Where was the body. She wished to be taken there at once.

"Nobody knew where you were," the guard said flatly.

"Get me out of here . . . I have to arrange a funeral."

"It's been taken care of . . . Breege Brennan is burying him. His body is coming down from Dublin later on today. They had to do an autopsy."

"She's not burying him . . . They're killers. Those Brennan people."

"Well, he's in their grave or he's going to be."

She went behind the bar counter then, and picking up a bottle of brandy, she poured herself a tumbler, drank a mouthful, and putting the glass down said decisively, "I'll have him dug up out of there."

"The state gave her permission," the woman guard said.

"Fuck the state . . . This is unnatural. This is bizarre," she said, screaming now as the woman guard held her arm, saying she knew that it must be terrible.

"I loved him . . . I adored him . . . Go up and read my letters. They're on my bed. He was my soulmate . . . My shepherd."

"I know . . . I know," the other woman said.

"You don't know . . . And you won't know," she said, and then she did something that made them sorry for her. She crossed to where the grandfather clock was, opened the glass-fronted door, and grasped the weights with a savagery to still them, and then put her hand up to move the thick black spidery hands back by half an hour, and for an instant the clock made a stutter as if to strike the noon, but was stopped and did not beat, and pointing to its yellow worn face, she said, "Half an hour ago I did not know it, half an hour ago he was in the fields, his hat, my hat, pushed forward to keep the light out of his eyes," and she picked up her glass and raised it to the man she had loved, truly loved.

Quite suddenly she looked about as if embarrassed and asked the woman guard if she could ask her something alone. It was with a child's face and a child's need that she asked it: "Can you come upstairs and help me pack . . . I'm going out of my mind right now."

A RAINBOW BRANCHED ACROSS the sky and lingered, inside it a second rainbow, a fledgling, the band of colours miraculously reversed. Earlier there had been a fall of sleet, pellets of it dropped onto the coffin like little eggs, then the first sods of earth were thrown in according to custom. There were not many mourners; the canon, pleading arthritis, had sent a visiting curate who did not know the locals and was hesitant as he began the prayers. It was a small funeral, partly because Bugler did not mix and also because there were only two boats at the quayside to bring people across. Lady Harkness wore a black hat with a cockade of black feathers and the sisters prayed fulsomely.

Breege was the one people shook hands with, because it was her family grave, and she thought, They think I am a fallen woman and soon they will think it even more.

It was at the second decade of the Rosary that they heard footsteps and a voice ringing through the cold winter air: "Wait . . . Wait for me." It was Rosemary in a bright red jacket carrying a red rose and an envelope. Hurrying past the gravediggers as they shovelled, she kissed the rose, then the envelope, then threw them in and looked around as if to defend herself, but was silenced by the intoning of the prayers, the repetition of Hail Mary, Holy Mary, Pray for us sinners, Now and at the hour of our death, Amen.

Afterwards, as they moved slowly away, she called to Breege,

"I want to talk to you." They stood stiffly and as if something drastic were about to occur.

"I'm not going away . . . I am not giving him up . . . I loved him and he loved me. Can you understand that?" The voice calm, overcalm, each word enunciated.

"Yes," Breege said, quiet, numb.

"Is that all you can say?"

"He would not want us to say more."

They stared at each other then, fearing each other because each held a secret that would never be disclosed.

The rain was coming on heavier, the rainbow at its most exquisite, just before extinguishment, the greens and blues and violets fading to a breathtaking gentleness, almost transparent now as the water seeped into the colours. People looked up and remarked on it. O'Dea, fearing that there might be an outburst, crossed to the two women and said, "Let's adjourn, ladies . . . Let's go and drink the good man's health."

While they waited their turn to get into the boat, he pulled Breege aside and whispered it: "The double rainbow, that was something else . . . Mind yourself and mind that child."

She thanked him without having to say a word.

Mountjoy Prison

Dear Breege,

They moved me here four days ago. It's worse than the previous place, rougher. At six o'clock we go down in the yard
for exercises. A fellow shouts at us to fall in and fall out, so
you fall in and you fall out. Then it's back to the cell, an entire day ahead of you. They're all townies in here. Trying to
make out that I'm insane. A fella was thrown in yesterday, on
the booze for days, his shirt hanging out. Tried to kill me.
One screw has it in for me. Makes me empty chamber pots on
our wing. I will not empty chamber pots. I told him so. He
has me down to see the psychiatrist. Oh, sweet Jesus! The
fields and the fresh air, I'd give anything for one minute of
them. I'll be old before I come home. Gone old. I thought of a
poem that I learned in the fourth class. Maybe you learned it
too: "To a child dancing in the wind." I'm glad you wrote to
me . . . I can't tell you what it meant. I thought maybe that
you'd hate me for ever. Now I know you don't. I have that to
live for. One mad minute stretches into a lifetime.

Your loving brother,
Joseph

IT IS BREEGE now that is holding it together. The same fields, fallow in the depth of winter, a few store cattle, the odd fall of snow, black frost and white frost both, raw mornings, and yet the purplish sap of spring bubbling inside the slender branches. Everything so very quiet and unfeuding, Yellow Dick's Bog a still-life of tranquil grasses and the pink stakes driven in to the mountain road weathering in the wet.

Rosemary is up there. Breege knows it by the lights in the windows each evening, and sometimes she looks up towards them and wonders if the old wars are brewing again and will they, as women, be called on to fight the insatiate fight in the name of honour and land and kindred and blood. Will their hearts too turn to treason.

Shaped by that place and that loneliness, she thinks that the longing which ran in her listening and ran in her veins was answered so, and holding her belly, she reaches back, back to those nameless and spectral forces of which she is made, and reaches to him too in the hope that there is communion between living and dead, between those who even in their most stranded selves are on the side of life and harbingers of love.

ACKNOWLEDGEMENTS

So many people in Ireland helped me when researching the trilogy. For *Wild Decembers* I must single out Billy Loughnane, Francis Neilan, Michael and Mary Blake, Jack Keane, Rory Smith, Karl Smith, Michael Hayes, T.J. and Brenda McGuinness, Carole Guyett, Gerry Allen, Dermot and Rosemary Gleeson, Albert Kelly, Sean Corcoran, and, from the other side of the world, the inimitable Pete Barry. To each of them and to any others who have slipped my memory, immeasurable thanks.

Lastly, I could not have completed it without the insights of my son Sasha Gebler, a master builder.